The Accident

ALSO BY GAIL SCHIMMEL

The Park (2017)

'A gripping story. Schimmel has the rare gift of having great material for a story, but also being able to craft it into a story that feels real. Expect a lot ... you won't be disappointed.' – *Pretoria News*

'Gail Schimmel has the knack of Liane Moriarty ... a cracking plot ... perfect bookclub read.' – Bookish blog

'It is real, it is wise and witty ... there is stomach-knotting unease.' – *without prejudice*

Whatever Happened to the Cowley Twins? (2013)

'It's been a while since I could not put a book down. Nothing beats the feeling you get when you really want to know what happens next ... This was my experience with this book.' – Lali van Zuydam, *Pretoria News*

Marriage Vows (2008)

'*Marriage Vows* ... is as nuanced and layered as, well, yes a 10-tier wedding cake ... This is an important debut by a local writer of real power, and I look forward to reading her next novel.' – Arja Salafranca, *Independent*

The Accident

A NOVEL

GAIL SCHIMMEL

MACMILLAN

First published in 2019
by Pan Macmillan South Africa
Private Bag X19
Northlands
Johannesburg
2116

www.panmacmillan.co.za

ISBN: 978-1-77010-627-7
e-ISBN 978-1-77010-628-4

Editing by Nicola Rijsdijk
Proofreading by Jane Bowman
Design and typesetting by Electric Book Works
Cover design by Hybrid Creative
Author photo by Nicolise Harding

Printed and bound by **novus print**, a Novus Holdings company

To Thomas and Megan, my children, my world.

PART 1

February

MONDAY

Julia

My mother isn't curious about my news.

She's not like other mothers. When I phone and tell her I have big news, she doesn't nag me, or beg me to tell her, or insist I come around immediately. I wasn't exactly expecting her to. But I always have a small hope.

My therapist thinks I subconsciously remember a time when she was different, and that this is the source of my hope. Everybody (including Jane, my therapist) insists that my mother is like she is because of The Accident. Everybody says it like that, like it has capital letters, even my mother. My life has been defined by something that happened to my parents when I was two, something I wasn't even involved in.

Maybe my mother *was* different before. When I was a child, I came up with the theory that she was a zombie. That she'd actually died in that stupid accident, but for some reason kept walking around like an alive person. 'My mom's actually a zombie,' I told some of the girls at school. They didn't believe me, so I invited them around to play. After that they still didn't believe me, but they also didn't *not* believe me. That's how much like a zombie my mother was. And still is. Luckily, I was friends with the sort of girls who were very kind and who wouldn't tease you even if your mother *was* a zombie. The sort of girls who went home and told their mothers how worried they were about me, with a zombie mother. Pippa Lee's mom took me aside one day and gently told me that my mother was definitely not a zombie, just a bit sad. I nodded and said yes, I understood. And I allowed her to pull me to her large soft breasts and stroke my head, because it's true that children of zombies are starved of physical affection.

When I told Jane my childhood zombie theory, she thought it was psychologically very astute. Jane's theory is that the reason I'm not more screwed-up is because I was a particularly astute little girl. My theory is that therapists have to say that to make you feel better. Making you feel better is a big part of their job description. As far as I'm concerned, I'm okay because I had an okay childhood. Yes, my mother is distant and cold – even her hands are cold to the touch – but she provided for me, and she was always around, and she came to all my school events, and she never hit me or even lost her temper with me. Even when I tried to make her. Even in my teens when I went out with unsuitable boys and came home late and drunk, and fought with her. She just stayed calm and told me she trusted me. People have much worse childhoods, I tell Jane. I have a lot to be grateful for. Jane says this is a very mature attitude, and I feel better about myself, and as I leave the waiting room I wonder if she has different compliments for all her patients, or if she just recycles the same ones. I don't really care – children of zombies take their compliments where they can find them.

So I'm disappointed but not surprised when my mother's reaction to my announcement that I have news is to calmly arrange a visit two days from now.

I phone Daniel.

'I told my mom I have something to tell her.'

'Was she excited for us?'

'I didn't tell her about *us*. I just told her I have something to tell her. I'll see her in two days and tell her then.' I can almost feel Daniel's confusion through the phone. 'I've explained to you, Daniel,' I say. 'She's not like other moms. If I announced that I'd decided to turn myself into a rhinoceros, she'd just nod and say, "That's nice, dear."'

'Maybe it would help if I met her?' says Daniel.

Daniel wants to meet my mom, and I don't want him to – this has been an ongoing theme for the last two months. Ever since Daniel left his wife.

'If she's so calm, she's not going to freak out about me,' he goes on.

'No, she won't. I'm not worried about *her*. I'm worried about *you*. You might not feel the same way about me after you've met her. She's very ... indifferent.'

He sighs. 'I love you. I don't care if your mother's an ice statue.'

'Well,' I say, 'you'll meet her in due course. Just let me tell her first.'

The problem, of course, is that Daniel isn't thinking ahead. He's just left his wife of ten years and their child. He isn't thinking about having a child with me, even though he knows that's what I want. He isn't thinking about what sort of mother I'll be, or even what sort of stepmother. But if he meets my mom, he's going to think about it. He's going to wonder if I'll become like her. He's going to wonder if he's done the wrong thing.

Jane says I won't become like my mother. She says she can absolutely guarantee it. She says I will screw up my children in entirely different ways.

'Maybe I just won't have children,' I told Jane once. 'Maybe that'll be better.'

'Don't be ridiculous,' she answered. 'You're always talking about how you want kids.'

Sometimes I wish I had the sort of therapist who just nods and says, 'How does that make you feel?'

Jane has a lot to say about my relationship with Daniel, of course. She says I was attracted to him because he was unavailable, because that's all I've ever known. She's very worried that I won't want him now that he's left Claire. She's especially worried because Daniel's a very warm and effusive man. He's always telling me how much he loves me and how excited he is about our lives together. Jane says I must be careful not to feel stifled. I tell her that's not going to happen: I'm very pleased Daniel left Claire and is with me. I just don't tell Jane how I creep out of his heavy arms at night because I'm worried I'll suffocate.

And I don't tell anyone that in a strange way, my mother's phlegmatic reactions – while constantly disappointing – are also strangely comforting because they are all I know.

My mother is a zombie and my world is on its axis.

Catherine

When I get off the phone, I can hardly breathe I am so excited. Julia says she has some news, and she sounds happy. Her news can only be one of two things, either of which could be the beginning of my plan to kill myself.

I have spent twenty-six years waiting. Feeling nothing. Going through the motions. Waiting and waiting for the day Julia no longer needs me so I can end my pain. That day is finally coming.

After The Accident, people told me time would heal everything, that eventually it would just be a painful memory. For years I felt nothing except a longing to die – but I couldn't because of Julia. Then I started feeling small flickers of life. When they started, I was hopeful. Everybody said all it takes is time, so I thought the flickers were the beginning of something – that I might be like everybody else and be healed by time. But they never took flight.

This is more than a small flicker of life, which is the most I have come to expect as I have navigated the years since The Accident. My body is fizzing with life, spilling over with it. I am so excited I can't sit down, I can't concentrate, I can't do anything. I want to tell someone. But the only person I want to speak to is Mike.

The only person I ever want to speak to is Mike.

Julia

Now that I have an arrangement to see my mother, I need to think about what I'm actually going to say to her. In most situations, the mother would know about the boyfriend *before* there's an announcement of them having moved in together. Never mind the rest.

But with Daniel it's complicated, so my mother knows nothing. In fact, as far as she knows, we're still at the stage where I'm great friends with Claire.

I met Claire at a pottery class about a year ago. I started pottery because my day job was boring, and I needed to do something fun and artistic.

People often find it hard to reconcile my personality with my job. I have untameable hair, wear loud colours, and every now and again I go off to Iggy Pop in my apartment. At home I am chronically disorganised, and I have a history of dead-end relationships. People expect me to be artistic, I think, or else they expect me to be a low achiever. There was a time I didn't expect much from myself either, to be honest.

But I'm an accountant. And a really good one. And I think it's because so much of my childhood had no answers, but accounts always have answers. From the moment I took my first high-school accountancy lesson, and the teacher said, 'If it doesn't balance, you know the answer is wrong,' I knew this was the career for me. With my mom, I never know if my answers are wrong. With my work, I know. Accounting makes life seem fair. Jane says she's heard of worse reasons to choose a career.

I don't work in a smart firm where I get to wear power suits, though. I work in an old-fashioned business where my boss wears a cardigan, is freaked out by my wrist tattoo and regards computers with utmost suspicion. My colleagues are all older than me. Good people, durable people – but cut from the same dull tweed cloth. Our offices are in one of those converted old-Joburg blocks of flats. The other tenants have knocked out walls and put in fancy flooring and cool lighting, and generally made the place quite trendy. But our suite still has faded carpets and that rough plastering that accumulates little wells of dust. You can imagine the sad lives that were conducted in these rooms before it became an office block. Sometimes it feels like the whole place is covered in dandruff.

I really need to get out, to find a more stimulating position. But I don't seem to be able to move. So last year I decided to do pottery.

Work probably wasn't the only thing that led me to pottery. I was also lonely. I've always had loads of friends; nights out and laughs and get-togethers. But something's happened in the last year or two. My closest group of friends has just kind of dissolved. My best friend, Heleen, who's the most talented dressmaker and fashion designer, and was always up for a party … She had a baby. Her husband is all my fault, because she met him through me. He's also an accountant – only he's the stereotypical type. I never for one moment thought they'd get together.

I listened to all Heleen's god-awful pregnancy tales, but it didn't end when the baby actually arrived. Then it was all breastfeeding and sleep habits and baby nutrition and the relentless trivia of his life. I tried to understand, but it bored me to tears. So I don't see Heleen much any more, and I don't know if she's noticed. And Agnes immigrated to Jamaica of all places, and now just posts enviable selfies on Facebook, and Mary-Anne kind of drifted off after she got married on a beach in Zanzibar and didn't invite anyone, which made things a bit awkward, and Flora decided to study medicine at the age of twenty-seven and is now never available, night or day.

I found out about the pottery class from a notice in a shop.

It wasn't my usual shopping area, and it wasn't my usual sort of shop. It was an art-supply shop, and I'd only gone there to get the particular brand of pencil my boss favours. But I saw this notice about a studio nearby, and I felt like a person in a movie, tearing off the telephone number and stuffing it into my pocket. It took me a few weeks to actually phone, but eventually I did it, and the teacher had a new group just about to start, so it was like it was meant to be. And it was great.

The class was made up of five women, and the teacher had crazy curly grey hair that came to her waist. Amongst her neighbours' carefully manicured suburban lawns and electric fences, her house was like Sleeping Beauty's castle – high hedges covered in creepers, and a wooden gate that you simply pushed open. God knows how she wasn't burgled daily.

It was just as well I wasn't doing the class to meet men, I remember thinking. Of the five students, only Claire and I were under fifty, so naturally we gravitated towards each other. In normal circumstances, she's not a person I would have chosen across a room – she's one of those tall, thin, aristocratic blondes who looks like she's either away with the fairies or thinking she's a cut above everyone else. But we were the 'young ones', so we found ourselves sitting together at the introduction when we had to go around the circle saying why we wanted to do pottery and what we hoped to get out of it. The old ladies were a group of widows who all lived at the same retirement village down the road, and they basically said a different version of what I said – new hobby, something to do, artistic outlet. But Claire announced that she was probably going to be shocking at pottery – she just needed something to get her away from her husband and child once a week, and pottery had been the first thing she'd seen that was reasonably close by. I was a bit shocked, but the old ladies nodded and one laughed and said, 'Been *there*.'

Claire wasn't shocking at pottery – she was the best in the class. I didn't know it then, but Claire is always best in the class, no matter what class it is. That first day, we learnt how to make snake bowls – those bowls where you roll the clay into a long snake and then coil it into a bowl. My snake looked like it had swallowed a series of small mammals – and my resulting bowl looked like a child had made it.

When I said that to Claire – who'd rolled her snake so thin, her bowl looked like some sort of perfect and magical air creation – she assured me I was wrong. 'I *have* a child,' she said. 'Hers would be much, *much* worse.'

'If she's anything like you,' I said, 'I doubt that.'

'Oh no, she's like her dad,' said Claire. 'Totally without any imagination.' Then she laughed. 'Oh, I don't really mean that. Nina has lots of imagination. But two left hands.'

I don't have lots of married friends or friends with children – other than Heleen, who makes it sound idyllic. I didn't know you were allowed to say bad things about your children, or say that you wanted to get away from them. I also didn't know you could slag off your husband. I figured her husband must be awful and her child particularly disappointing. The old ladies weren't shocked though – they thought Claire was very funny. When she told us, at the second class, about how her husband, Daniel, was floored by the idea that he had to cook himself dinner on pottery night, the old ladies cackled and agreed that men were hopeless.

When the widows laughed, I didn't like how it felt as if Claire had more in common with them than with me. She's a person you find yourself wanting to impress. Like the most popular girl at high school – the one who doesn't do anything special to be popular, and is nice and kind and interesting but never quite accessible. After the second class, I asked Claire if she wanted to come for a drink afterwards, though I was sure she would say no.

'A drink? *Now?*' She looked at me as if it was the most scandalous proposal. Then she smiled. 'You know what, I think I will! What a divine idea. How *mad!*'

Then she turned and asked the widows if they wanted to join us, and I plastered a smile on my face and said, 'Yes, please do.'

But they chuckled and said it was past their bedtime, and us young things must go and have some fun, and Claire laughed and said she wasn't as young as me, and I was corrupting her completely.

When we got to the bar – which was more of a restaurant that served drinks – Claire looked around like she was in a foreign country. 'Look at all these people out so late in the week,' she said, though it was just after nine. 'I forget that life goes on for other people.'

'Life's hardly stopped for you,' I said. 'You have a husband and a daughter. That's amazing.'

Claire smiled. 'Yes, I'm sure it is,' she said, as if we were talking about an entirely hypothetical scenario that had nothing to do with her. 'Oh fuck,' she added, 'I'd better tell Danny I'm going to be late.' She fished her phone out of her bag and sent a text. 'He's going to be so put out.'

'Is he terribly possessive?' I asked.

Claire looked confused. 'God, no.'

I couldn't figure out why else her husband would be put out by her having a drink after class, so I started to paint a mental picture of a selfish monster, a towering giant, who kept Claire a virtual captive in their house. Because Claire is so tall and aristocratic looking, I pictured him as very good-looking, to have captured her heart. And even *that* seemed glamorous – if Claire was being kept captive in a tower by an evil prince, then that was obviously this season's trend.

And Claire seemed fascinated by my life. She made me talk about going out and clubbing and dating, which I hardly even did any more, and she laughed at my stories like I was hilarious.

And I was fascinated by her. Her, and her perfect pottery, and her unseen family.

Claire

I drop Nina at school ten minutes late.

Nina's been at the same school since Grade 00, but now she's in Grade 1, so they have to wear a uniform. While most of the girls were excited about it, Nina was appalled. She's what my mother calls an 'idiosyncratic dresser', and what I call a 'great, big mess'. Either way, after two years of expressing her individuality, she doesn't like the conformity of a school uniform. So now she's transferred all her originality onto her hairstyles. She has fly-away blonde hair like mine, and it's difficult to execute her ambitions. This morning she wanted a French plait. I was quite proud of my effort, but she burst into tears because of the lack of a ribbon. Apparently 'everyone' knows a 'real' French plait has a ribbon threaded through the length of it. So, while she sobbed, I had to search for a ribbon in regulation school colours before undoing the plait and starting again.

She was still sobbing by the end, at which point I took ten deep breaths, told myself to find my Zen, and then screamed at her to get in the car. Which she did, muttering about how much she hated me, her hair and, above all, the ribbon.

And now we are late, and Mrs Wood has to pause her morning greetings to the class as we walk in. Nina hugs and kisses me effusively, as if nothing has gone wrong with our morning. Mrs Wood walks me to the door, apparently keeping the whole class silent with one glare. I wonder if she could teach me that skill.

'Late arrivals are very disruptive for all the girls,' she says to me at the door, and because I can't bear being in trouble, I spend the next three minutes charming her while the class silently waits, and by the time I leave, I've volunteered to help with the cake sale next week. Nina winks at me as I go, so I wink back and feel good for a moment.

In the car, I pull my Moleskine diary out of my bag. I know I should be all digital by now, but I love beautiful stationery. My diary is where it belongs, between my Lou Harvey make-up bag, which I keep for emergencies, and my pencil bag, because having something beautiful to write with always helps me think. I examine my pens, and choose my favourite black fineliner, which I bought from the shop Julia told me about down the road. But when I flip to the date of the cake sale, I see I've already committed to a meeting at the hotel I do PR and events for, to talk about their autumn functions.

I send a quick email to the hotel from my phone, asking if we can move the meeting an hour later, and then check my diary for what's next today. I realise I am now running seventeen minutes late for a meeting with another client – a wedding venue in Muldersdrift that has twenty-five weddings scheduled for the next three months, all of which they're convinced they can't do without me.

I send a WhatsApp to the woman I'm meeting, claiming my electricity has gone off and I'm stuck in my driveway, and promising I'll be there as soon as I can manage. It's Joburg, so electricity is no guarantee. She responds almost immediately with 'No problem.' She's always needed me more than I've needed her, but I don't know what's going to happen with money so maybe that's not true any more.

I look back at my diary. If I leave for the wedding place right now, I'll get there about half an hour late. That's okay, but then I'll have to be really charming and relaxed to make up for it, which will probably make me late for the charity lunch I've committed to with Janice, Nina's best friend's mother. I need to keep Janice sweet, because I need her to help me with lifts. Which reminds me that I need to check that Daniel will fetch Nina from school today. I try to avoid asking if it's not one of his days, but both Janice and I will be at the lunch today, so he's my best bet. I take a deep breath and send him a WhatsApp: 'Good to fetch Nina today?'

He responds almost immediately: 'Cool. If I can't, I'll get Julia to.'

I can feel tears gathering. I don't want Julia fetching Nina. I should have asked my mother, even if it means a forty-five-minute drive each way. She would have done it. I don't want Julia anywhere *near* Nina. I don't want Julia breathing the same *air* as Nina. I really, really wish Julia would die – that is my favourite fantasy. I close my eyes, holding back the tears, and take another deep breath. I breathe so deeply these days I'm probably going to sprain a lung.

There's a knock at my window, and I open my eyes slowly. A car-jack would just be the cherry on top. But it's the mother of a child in Nina's class. I roll down my window and glue a smile onto my face, scrambling to think of her name.

'Chrissie,' I remember just in time, 'how lovely to see you.'

After a few minutes of excruciating small talk she asks if I could meet her for coffee to help with an event she has to plan for her older child's class. She says she's the class mom, but she doesn't have my skills, and she just needs half an hour to pick my brain. I smile and open my diary again, making a time two days from now.

'Thank you, Claire,' she says, and I can hear that she's really grateful. 'You're just so amazing.'

I smile. 'So are you. We'll put together a kick-ass plan between us.'

She smiles, and waves.

Another satisfied customer, says Daniel's wry voice in my head.

I send my mom a message, telling her I hate everyone.

She immediately answers: 'Of course you do, sweetie. That's totally normal.' My mom's speciality is making me feel better, no matter how appalling I'm being.

As I drive to the wedding venue, I think of seventeen different ways Julia could die. I'm in a much better mood when I get there.

Catherine

I met Mike when I was twenty-three, and after that there was nobody else for me.

We met on what was basically a blind date. Neither of us had ever been on a blind date before and neither of us *wanted* to go on a blind date. It wasn't like it is now, where people happily meet up with complete strangers they find on an app. Back then, there was something a bit embarrassing about going on a blind date. But my friend Kerry was going out with Mike's friend James, and Kerry had decided that I needed to be fixed up with someone. James mentioned that his friend Mike had just got back from a two-year stint in London and had broken up with his long-time girlfriend, and Kerry seemed to think that because we were both only children – the only two she knew – we would be a good match, and next thing we knew, they'd set up a double date.

I didn't want to go. I told Kerry that my job (as a nurse) was time consuming and the last thing I needed was a boyfriend. All my previous relationships had ended because of my strange hours and almost constant exhaustion. We nurses knew the only way it could work was to marry a doctor, because they are the only other people who understand the stress. So I had sworn off men until a suitable doctor appeared – and so far, one hadn't.

Mike was not a doctor. Mike was an engineer. I had dated an engineering student a few years before. I did not want to meet Mike.

But Kerry told me she would look a fool if I didn't pitch, so in the end I said yes. Kerry had always been a good friend to me, and she really wanted it to work with James. Also, I presumed the men would pay, and I was always hungry in those days.

Mike told me later that he'd begged James to let him off. He'd come out of a relationship with his high-school girlfriend, who'd chosen to stay in London. And he wanted to be single for a while and play the field. James eventually convinced him that meeting me *was* playing the field.

But then, half an hour before the date, Kerry and James broke up. And this was the eighties – you couldn't get hold of people on the spur of the moment. So Mike and I rocked up at the restaurant, and found the table booked for four under Kerry's name, and introduced ourselves. At first, we joked about whether Kerry and James were actually late, or slyly giving us a few minutes alone. But after an hour – during which we drank a bottle of wine between us and told the waiter about fifteen times we were 'just waiting for our friends' – we got worried. I used the restaurant's phone to call Kerry, who sobbed something about a blonde and a sports car and a receipt that shouldn't have existed.

'All men are shits, Cathy – you should stay away from them,' she informed me before hanging up.

I walked slowly back to the table and told Mike what had happened, insofar as I understood it, and then politely said that I quite understood if he wanted to call it a night, although by then I already knew he was the funniest, nicest man I had ever met and I wanted the night to last forever.

Mike shrugged and said, 'Well, we're here now, aren't we? Seems a pity to leave.'

So we ordered some food and carried on talking, and before we knew it, the restaurant was empty and the chairs were all upside-down on the tables and staff were mopping the floor, and still we didn't want to go.

Finally, after the last waiter told us we had to leave or we'd be locked in, we stood up.

'I don't want tonight to end,' I said, and then cringed because maybe

Mike didn't feel that way at all. I could not believe I'd said something so stupid.

'Tonight is never going to end,' said Mike, reaching for my hand and pulling me towards him. 'Tonight is forever.'

Well, I wasn't sure if he was just trying to get me into bed, but I didn't care. I knew I would take every minute I could get with this man, because as far as I was concerned, he was the best one.

We had the words 'Tonight is forever' engraved on our wedding rings the following year. But nobody could have foreseen what our 'forever' would mean.

Julia

Late morning, Daniel phones and asks me to fetch Nina because Claire has asked him, and he has a lunch meeting. I can't say no because that'd be another point against me.

'Where do I go?' I ask.

'To the school,' he says, like I'm a moron.

'Yes, but where *in* the school?'

'To her class, obviously.'

'Daniel, I've never picked Nina up before. Where's the classroom? What do I say to the teacher? Do I have to sign her out? Where must I take her afterwards? Will she have bags?' I can feel my voice rising so I pause and let my voice adjust. 'I just need some detail, love,' I say in what I secretly think of as my best Claire voice.

'You must take her back to the house – I mean, Claire's house. You'll figure out the rest. I don't have time now.' He hangs up.

I look at my phone like I'm dreaming, and consider sending him a message to go fuck himself. But it's quite a big deal to trust me to pick up Nina, and Claire will find out if I say no. So I do what I used to do when I first met Claire – I ask myself what she would do.

My first hurdle is explaining to my boss that I might be late back from lunch.

'I'm not saying I *will* be, just that I *might* be,' I say. I don't know why I'm even telling him – he probably wouldn't have noticed. I realise that

Claire would've just gone and done what she needed to do. But I'm Julia, and I know about people not being available, and I don't just disappear from work in the middle of the day.

'What about the Madison deadline?' says my boss, looking hurt and confused, like I've just resigned.

'I sent it to you this morning,' I say.

'Where?' He looks around his desk and even picks up a beige folder, as if I might have hidden the report underneath just to confuse him.

'By email,' I say. 'It's attached to an email I sent you.'

Gerald looks at his computer like it has personally affronted him. I leave him to it, thinking that I really need to find a job in an accountancy firm that has moved into this century.

It's lucky that I warned Gerald, because things start going wrong almost immediately.

First, I can't find Nina's school. It's a well-known, exclusive girls' school, and I think I know where it is. As it turns out, I don't. So I have to put on my GPS, but a whole lot of roads are boomed off that my GPS knows nothing about, and I keep almost going through stop signs hidden behind ridiculously leafy vegetation. I'm ten minutes late when I arrive, and of course the security guard needs to stop me to ask what I'm doing there. When I say I've come to fetch Nina, he looks me up and down and tells me that I'm not Nina's mother. Like I didn't already know that. So I hiss that I am Nina's father's girlfriend, and he gives me a completely different look – not a very nice one. I had no idea school security guards were so judgemental. On a positive note, he lets me in.

Then I have no idea where to go, so I start popping my head into all the classrooms – most of which are still full of older girls. The teachers glare at me, and finally one steps outside and asks if she can help me.

'I'm here to fetch Nina Marshall,' I say. 'She's in Grade 1.'

'Which Grade 1 class?' asks the teacher, but I don't know.

She sighs, and gives me a list of instructions like 'go up the stairs and turn right at the statue', which seem to make perfect sense except that the school is brimming with both stairs and statues. I finally make my way to a classroom where Nina is the only child left waiting and the teacher looks stony-faced.

Nina takes one look at me and bursts into tears and says she's not getting into a car with me. Which leads the teacher to phone Claire, who is not available, and then Daniel, who is not available, and then we have to sit there because she refuses to let Nina leave with me until one of the parents has confirmed.

'It's not like she even seems to know who you are.' The teacher indicates Nina, who is sitting on the floor with her back to me.

'She knows who I am,' I hiss, trying to sound calm.

The teacher raises her eyebrows. I know that I shouldn't be, but I'm fed up, and the whole thing should be out in the open by now, and I've already told the security guard, who's probably sent out some sort of all-points school-security bulletin, and anyway what did Daniel think sending me here. 'I'm her father's girlfriend,' I say.

The teacher raises her eyebrows again, and this time she looks faintly amused by my claim, but then her phone rings and it's Claire so she takes it, and moves outside where I can just hear her saying, 'There's a woman here claiming ...' before she's out of earshot. And I know Claire's going to be furious, and so is Daniel, and I want to cry, and then Nina looks up at me and smiles like she's planned the whole thing.

At last the teacher comes back in, and she won't make eye contact. She gives her phone to Nina, and apparently Claire persuades her to go with me, because Nina gets up but also won't make eye contact with me, and we leave. I try to chat with Nina in the car, but she sits in total silence. Which takes quite an act of will, because usually Nina talks a lot. Utter nonsense, to be honest, but right now I'd take her inane chatter.

When I drop her off at Claire's place, Thandi, the domestic helper and childminder, holds out her hand as if I'm supposed to give her something.

'What?' I say.

'School bag.'

Thandi knows who I am. She used to greet me like I was the most welcome person in her universe. These days it's clear what she thinks about me.

I sigh. 'I'll go back and get it.'

I drive back to the school, where Nina's bag is parked outside the classroom door like an accusation.

By the time I get back to work, there are three urgent messages for me. None from Daniel.

Daniel

After my lunch meeting, I find a message from Nina's teacher sounding hysterical because a strange woman has come to fetch Nina.

Then Julia calls and yells at me, and as soon as that's over, Claire phones and says in an icy voice that maybe in future I shouldn't send Julia to the school.

I just asked Julia to fetch a child. It's not brain surgery.

I don't understand when everything got so complicated.

Catherine

From when we met, Mike and I became Mike-and-Cathy. We both had two types of friends: those who wanted to be friends with Mike-and-Cathy, and those who didn't. Before I met Mike, I didn't think I would be one of *those* couples. I thought I'd be able to have friendships separate from my husband. I thought he'd have friendships separate from me – maybe he'd play golf with his friends, or poker, or go and watch sport in bars. And I would meet friends for a drink or coffee or lunch, and have a bookclub and maybe a sewing circle or something. That's the sort of married person I thought I would be. But it didn't turn out that way.

We *liked* each other. We liked doing things together. Mike *did* play golf – but I took lessons and we made up a fourball with another couple. I *did* join a bookclub – but it was one that couples belonged to, and Mike sat next to me. We did all the things we both wanted to do, but we did them together. And so we lost friends. Because there were people who didn't really understand us, and Mike had friends who didn't like me and thought that Mike was 'whipped', and I had friends who didn't like Mike and thought he was controlling. Kerry, who was responsible for us meeting, she was one of them, even though she was a bridesmaid at our wedding. She told me eventually she didn't like that she never saw me alone any more. I tried to meet her for coffee occasionally, but it just felt stupid being there when I could be with Mike, and our arrangements fizzled out.

We didn't really care about the friends we lost. We told each other they couldn't have been such good friends in the first place if they were so happy to end the friendship. And the truth was that we were entirely happy just in each other's company. It was enough. The friends we did keep were a bonus.

People said it would change when we had a baby. But they were wrong. When our baby came, we realised we really *were* different. We still loved being together – and we loved our little family. We were the real deal. The ones who would actually live happily ever after.

The Accident changed everything.

The thing is, by then we were friends only with people who wanted to be friends with Mike-and-Cathy, the loved-up couple. After The Accident, I needed friends who wanted to be friends with Just Catherine.

I'm not saying people didn't try, that people weren't good to me. They all visited in hospital and told me to be strong and that they were there for me, and they did things like offer to look after Julia and bring meals and all the things you are supposed to do. And when I first came home, and later when Julia and I started our new lives, just the two of us, they visited. They invited us. They tried.

But we weren't Mike-and-Cathy any more, and I was barely even Cathy. I was the shadow of a person who had once been alive, and Julia was a traumatised two year old. Slowly but surely, most of our friends dropped away. I suppose I should have made new friends, people at the school, parents of Julia's friends. But I just didn't have the energy.

I had one real friend for a while after The Accident. The most unlikely friend. But I lost her too.

I don't really mind – I don't like being with people much. It's very tiring. You have to pretend to be interested, and you have to act like someone who is okay. When Julia was that age when I had to go along to the parties, I found it exhausting. I'd have to sleep for hours afterwards. Julia was probably the first girl in her class whose mom just dropped her at the house. I don't think either of us minded. I felt like the other moms judged me a bit. 'Sure you won't stay?' they'd ask. And, 'Wow, she's so brave to let you leave at this age.' But to be honest, it's not like Julia was missing much. And I was always willing to take her and fetch her. But I didn't make friends with the other moms. They were nice enough; I have only myself to blame.

Now, sometimes, I wish I had a friend. Someone I could phone and tell how excited I am about Julia's news. And we could speculate about what it is, if it's what I'm hoping for. And this friend of mine would come up with some ideas, and we'd enjoy the excitement together.

Except that if I had a real friend, she would want to know why I am so uncharacteristically excited. And if she was a real friend, she would be upset to learn that I'm hoping Julia's news brings me closer to suicide.

No, a real friend might prove an impediment. So it is probably better that I don't have friends.

TUESDAY

Claire

Nina's teacher's face today is all sympathy and understanding, and again I want to kill Daniel for sending Julia to school yesterday, and Julia for telling Mrs Wood who she is. I could not believe it when I got the call: 'There's a woman here claiming to be Daniel's girlfriend …?' And I had to swallow my pride and say, 'Yes, she can take Nina.'

'Oh.' Mrs Wood's voice was so heavy with questions my phone almost fell out of my hand, but I bit my cheeks and I refused to say more. 'All good then.'

And Nina was made to go home with Julia.

Today all those questions are jostling for a place on Mrs Wood's face and I want to punch her, but instead I smile and say, 'Lovely weather we're having.'

Mrs Wood puts her hand on my arm and pulls me to the side. 'Claire,' she says, 'it's none of my business what's going on at home, but it *is* important for us to know when there's a major change or disruption to a child's life, so that we can manage it from school.'

I close my eyes for a moment, because I know she's actually right.

'You're right,' I say, but I don't offer any more. She waits a few beats for me to carry on, to spill out my heart. But I just stand there smiling.

'Okay then,' she says. And I can see that not only have I failed to tell her what is going on, but I've also offended her. She wanted to be the one who got it first-hand. She wanted to be the one to tell them in the staff room, and cluck to the other mothers in muted tones. I know her type. I also know they make dangerous enemies.

'It's hard for me to talk about,' I say, touching her arm. 'I'll send you a mail with all the important information that affects Nina. I'm sure I can count on your discretion.' I squeeze her arm so she feels she's important.

And now she's glowing and I add a mental note to the medley in my head to send the bloody email.

I walk to my car and Janice intercepts me. 'Thanks for coming to the lunch yesterday,' she says, kissing my cheek.

'It was fabulous,' I lie. 'So much fun. Well done.'

Janice laughs. 'Oh, I had very little to do with it. But I'm so glad you enjoyed it. And thank you for the generous donation.'

'Such a good cause,' I say, although I can't remember what it actually was, because Janice has many causes and the speeches were very boring. Rhinos? Cerebral palsy? Syrians? No, it was definitely a disease – there were medical diagrams on the Powerpoint. Autism maybe. I'd arrived late after the mess of my morning, and after the call from the school, I couldn't focus on anything.

'So important,' I say to Janice, hoping that will cover anything.

'Not everyone sees it that way,' says Janice darkly, which doesn't seem to fit with autism. Gay rights? Persecuted Muslims? Persecuted Christians? Palestine? Israel – surely I would have remembered if it was *that* controversial? But then what were the medical diagrams about? I have another moment of insight: everything was pink. A woman's disease. Cervical or breast cancer, or maybe osteoarthritis. But who would have anything against fundraising for that?

I nod, looking serious. 'It's a challenge.'

'And it's people like you who help the cause.' Janice gives me another hug. 'Lots of love!'

'Lots of love,' I echo as she walks off. I really must check what her cause is.

I finally get into my car. I have back-to-back meetings this morning with the bands I plan to use at the wedding venue. I've drawn up a careful schedule of which weddings have overlapping guests, and have realised that I basically need to design three prototype weddings, and then let each bride tweak a few details, so no guest will attend the same basic wedding twice.

Before I meet the bands, I need to send out a press release for the hotel, and set up a series of scheduled tweets on their account. Time is tight, and I start the car, determined to leave before anyone else interrupts me.

My phone beeps with an incoming WhatsApp. It's Daniel.

'Please fetch my suits from the dry cleaners.'

My brain is already making the calculations – if I swing past the dry cleaners now, then I might not manage the press release but I'll still manage the tweets, but if I wait till I fetch Nina from school, then I can do the dry cleaner between her ballet lesson and the tea date we have with her friend. Or I can ask my mom to help, because since everything happened, she wants to help all the time …

And then I stop. And I remember. Daniel's suits are not my problem.

I look back at my phone and I type: 'Go fuck yourself.'

I'm still laughing as I drive away from the school.

Julia

I'm still exhausted from the fight I had with Daniel yesterday after the school fiasco. He just can't understand why it didn't all go smoothly, and why Claire'd become involved, and why I'd felt the need to tell the teacher about my relationship with him, and why I was so upset. His face had become very still and he'd muttered that he 'doesn't like scenes' and that he 'isn't used to this sort of thing', and he walked out.

And then of course I knew he was comparing me to Claire and everything he has given up to be with me, and I was sure he was regretting it. The thing about Claire is that she manages everything, and she manages it perfectly, and she does it all with a smile.

Oh God. At the beginning of our friendship, Claire used to make me laugh so much – she always had a funny observation. And even though she's so nice, she'd say mad bitchy things about people, but the way she did it, it was just funny, so when you saw her talking to them later it wasn't like she was being two-faced.

Like the widows in our pottery class – she could make me cry with laughter about the widows. She'd do these whole skits where she pretended to be one widow talking to another widow about replacing their dead husbands with pottery husbands, and it would be hilarious – especially the bits about sex with the pottery husbands (and the obvious advantages of the pottery husbands) and it was so surprising that for such a proper-looking person, Claire could be so outrageous about sex.

And we would weep with laughter; but then Claire would be lovely to the widows and knew which was which, a feat I couldn't manage. And before I even knew their names, she was doing little chores for them and popping in to have tea, and bringing little gifts, like a particular sort of jam that Grace (or Liz or Ivy) had mentioned that she loved. And it wasn't like she was a person desperate for company, because she has millions of friends and always has spectacular arrangements – coffee with this one and lunch with that one, and weekends away at someone's game farm. And she runs a successful business and looks after Nina. Because Claire can manage everything and then some more. And Daniel had asked me to do *one thing* and I had completely fucked it up and he couldn't grasp it because he thinks all women are like Claire.

So he walked out and I wept and then I phoned him and I begged him to come back. He made me wait. His voice was tight and he said that he needed to think. I was convinced he'd gone straight back to Claire and that she was listening to the call, with sad eyes because he was in this terrible situation with a crazy bitch like me. I couldn't think where else Daniel could have gone because he hates his parents, who fought throughout his childhood both with each other and with him, and in the times in-between basically forgot they had a child, and just paid other people to look after him. That's why Daniel hates chaos and conflict. And the truth is that Daniel doesn't seem to have many friends of his own.

So the only place he could have gone, I thought, was back to Claire and Nina.

But then after about two hours he came home and he smelt of alcohol, and I was so relieved because it meant he'd just gone to a bar. And as soon as he walked in, we were all over each other and ended up having sex up against the wall in the passage, and he yelled, 'I love you,' again and again as he fucked me. Which was very reassuring, and I'm trying very hard to ignore that I found it a bit of a turn-off, because that is just perverse of me – all I've wanted for so long is for Daniel to love me. And now I have that.

And then it was late, but I still couldn't sleep because Daniel had his arms and legs wrapped around me and he smelt of whiskey and was snoring, but every time I pushed him off, he found me again and clung on tighter. Eventually I must have fallen asleep because when the alarm went off I felt like I was climbing out of a deep hole, but I had to get up and go to work. Daniel just went on sleeping and barely even moved when I kissed him goodbye and whispered, 'Love ya.' He's the boss and in advertising, so getting to work on time isn't a big deal for him.

And then work today is crazy, with Gerald having various technical breakdowns trying to submit online tax returns and blaming all of us for it, so I eventually told him just to give me all his files and I would do it. Which he's done. And there are hundreds of them – great bundles of paper in no particular order and I want to cry.

In the middle of all this, Daniel messages me.

'Please can you fetch my suits from the dry cleaner near my office. Thanks, babes. Xx'

I glance around like maybe someone is playing a joke on me. I message back: 'I'm at work. Sorry. Xxx'

I put my phone down and it beeps almost immediately.

'I asked Claire and she was really very rude about it. Please, babes. X'

I type before I can think: 'You asked CLAIRE to pick up your dry cleaning?' I mean, what the actual? On what planet does a person ask his estranged wife to collect his dry cleaning? My phone beeps.

'She always does it. She's never been funny about it before. And someone needs to.'

I can't even believe we are having this conversation.

'She did it before because you were married. You can't ask her to do things for you any more.'

I send the message and then wait. I take a deep breath because I know I shouldn't do this, but I'm going to. I fucked up yesterday with the school, is it really so hard for me to pick up the bloody suits?

'Fine. I'll get them. But I'll be a bit late home then. Xxx'

I expect a response, a thank you, but I get nothing. And suddenly I want to phone Claire so badly. 'Can you believe the cheek of him?' I want to say to her. And we'd have a good bitch, and we'd laugh and I'd feel better. But that's not an option any more. I put down my phone and start inputting online tax returns, trying to ignore the headache building behind my eyes.

Daniel

I get home late because Julia said she would be late, and she's furious because she's cooked a special meal for me and now it's cold.

For a start, calling Julia's place 'home' doesn't feel natural. It's not a bad place, as flats go. It has the decent proportions of older flats, and the building is attractive and well maintained. I like the parquet floors and the high ceilings. And it's close enough to my old house for me to fetch Nina when it's my weekend, because Claire is very odd about driving Nina here. And there's a good mall nearby, which is nice when I need Julia to pop out for something, or when I want to have a quiet coffee or browse the bookshop. But even though there are two bedrooms, it's definitely not big enough for two of us. I have to keep my stuff in the spare room cupboard. And the few times Nina has come to stay, it's a squash.

When I first moved in, I told Julia we should get a bigger place and she looked really excited and started talking about good areas and swimming pools and how she'd love a garden. But she's done nothing about it and it's been almost a month, so I guess she's gone off the idea.

While she's slamming plates around in the small kitchen, I try to reassure her that the microwave also works, but she doesn't like that and starts saying things like, 'I don't know why I bothered.' I should point out that it's her fault because she specifically told me she would be late.

Then I stumble over the box of my books that Julia *still* hasn't unpacked, and go into our bedroom, which I always think of as Julia's bedroom, and I see she's flung my clean suits across the bed so they'll be all creased and unwearable. She's going to have to get them dry-cleaned again. I don't understand it – Claire always used to put them away in my cupboard with no fuss. And Claire used to calmly reheat my food if I was later than I said I would be. It was never a big deal. It's hard to believe Julia loves me as much as she says she does, but then I go back to the kitchen and see that she's crying. She's really upset so she must love me, and she clings to me and it's nice because Claire never needed me like this. This is what it's all about.

I put my arms around her and feel her sink against my body. 'It's okay about the suits,' I whisper. 'You can just take them back tomorrow.'

She pulls away from me and looks confused. And then all hell breaks loose.

When we fought yesterday, I promised I wouldn't walk out again, so this time I stay. But that doesn't mean I'm prepared to take this hysteria. So I sit down on the couch while Julia screams at me, and I allow my brain to drift away like I did when I was a child.

Eventually, she seems to run out of steam, so she stops and is almost panting slightly. It's a little bit gross and a little bit sexy, and for a moment I consider scooping her up and just taking her to bed. But first, I'd better say something that makes it sound like I've been listening, even though I'm only really aware of the keywords she's been repeating: 'dry cleaning', 'selfish', 'school' and 'Claire'.

'You're very irrational,' I eventually say in a calm voice. 'If this is what you're like now, I'd hate to see you pregnant.'

And Julia is completely silent and then our eyes meet, and even though I'm sitting down, it feels like I am falling into a deep hole, and suddenly I know.

Julia

It's not like I was deliberately keeping it from him. I'm barely sure myself. My period is late but it's not the first time, and I googled pregnancy symptoms and none of them applied, and with all the drama in the last two months of Daniel leaving Claire and us settling into living together and planning how to talk to my mother, I just kind of forgot about it. I haven't even done a test, so I might *not* be pregnant.

But when Daniel blurts out that he wonders what I'll be like when I'm pregnant, I know. Of course I'm pregnant. My period is more than just late, and I'm moody and tired and I feel a bit sick all the time. I thought it was because of all the other stuff, but I've been lying to myself.

Daniel sinks back in the couch and puts his hands on his head, and I sink down into the armchair facing him.

'I think I might be pregnant,' I say in a small voice, like I haven't just been screaming and this is all normal. I don't mean to, but I start crying again. Before it was tears of anger, but now I don't know what it is. I read somewhere that different tears have a different structure, and I think maybe these tears I'm crying are new to science.

'You aren't sure?' I don't know if the catch in Daniel's voice is hope or exasperation.

'I've been trying not to think about it,' I say.

Daniel looks confused and I suppose from his point of view it is confusing. Claire probably had a pregnancy plan that she followed from the moment of conception.

Daniel drops onto the floor and shuffles over to me so that he's kneeling in front of my chair, looking up at me. He wipes away one of my tears.

'Are you sad about being pregnant?' he says. 'With my baby.'

'I don't know if I *am* pregnant.'

'But if you are,' he pushes, 'are you happy or sad?'

'I'm confused,' I say. 'It wasn't supposed to happen like this. Nothing was supposed to happen like this. One day I was just me, and I had a nice life that didn't involve stealing people's husbands and having unplanned babies. And then I met you, and now nothing's how I planned.'

Daniel looks at me from under those hooded eyelids that enchanted me the first time I saw him. 'I didn't plan it like this either,' he says.

And then our arms are around each other and we're *both* crying, and I guess we're crying for all the things that have happened and for this baby we may or may not have made, and for how our love has caused so much trouble. And it feels good to be held and to cry together, although a small part of me is thinking that when I met Daniel, I would never have guessed how much the man could cry.

He seemed such a happy sort of guy.

I met Daniel because I had a date. I would have met him anyway, I'm sure, given my friendship with Claire, but this is how it happened. At pottery, I'd told Claire about my date. It was with a guy I'd met through work – a client – and at the time it was the biggest thing going on in my life because I thought he was so gorgeous and funny. His name was Steve. I even thought that Steve was the perfect name for a boyfriend. 'Julia and Steve' had, I thought, a certain ring to it. We'd worked together on an audit for weeks and it had started with me just thinking he was hot, but then I'd realised he was also funny and clever. I'd become more and more obsessed with him, but he hadn't seemed to look twice at me. Then, just as I'd resigned myself to a life of spinsterhood with seven cats, he'd turned around as he left my office one day and said, 'So, about that date we need to have?'

I blustered and blushed and stuttered, and he said, 'Send me your address. I'll pick you up at seven on Saturday. I'd tell you to dress up because I'm taking you somewhere special, but you always look great.'

So, after a statement like that – a statement that in a parallel universe could have been the beginning of the rest of my life – I was completely beside myself about what to wear. I had to look better than great; I had to take it to a whole new level.

I told Claire my dilemma, and she said she had some outfits that would fit me – 'From back when I had a social life,' she said, pulling a bitter face. Which was patently ridiculous because Claire always had far more of a social life than me, despite all her hot air about never going anywhere and always being in bed by nine. But her social life didn't include hot dates, I reckoned, so maybe that's what she meant. I even felt slightly smug.

'Come over tomorrow after work,' she said. 'We can have a dig around and see what I've got. You can stay for supper, but it'll be with Nina, so very low key.'

I left work a bit early the next day to get to Claire's house. It was magnificent, in a suburb I'd only ever dreamt of living in, with treed streets and deep pavements, and everything is quiet and green and even the gardens on the verges look like something out of a magazine. Security guards lounged in small wooden huts, calling out greetings to the domestic staff taking dogs for their evening walks.

Claire's house is set back on the property, with a long driveway that actually circles at the top, like some sort of English manor house. The garden is so pretty – I arrived early enough to see it full of flowers I don't know the names of, tall Jacaranda trees, what seemed like a field of agapanthus and a play area with a jungle gym for Nina. The lawn was green and perfectly mown like a hotel. It was a world that belonged to adults – not someone I thought of as a friend of *mine*. When you walked inside, the house looked like it was off Instagram – the perfect home. I looked around and thought, *This is what I want one day.*

'This is beautiful,' I said to Claire, after she'd led me through the entrance hall, which was a room that basically just contained a table holding a huge vase of flowers, and into one of what turned out to be several lounges. 'Did you do it yourself?'

Claire looked around. 'Thanks. Yes, I dabble with interior decorating but I'm sure a professional could've done a better job.' She tweaked a perfectly positioned scatter cushion as if to illustrate the complete hopelessness of the place.

'When I grow up, I want to be you,' I said smiling.

She put her arm around my shoulders and gave me a squeeze. 'I think you should stay you. You're pretty fab.'

We walked through that lounge into a room where Nina was enveloped in a deep couch, watching TV. Claire introduced us and then told Nina we were going upstairs for a bit to look at clothes.

'Please can I come?' said Nina, already clambering up and wrapping her arms around her mom.

Claire rolled her eyes at me, but said, 'Sure, sweetie – that'll be fun.'

The three of us traipsed up the (gorgeous) stairs, and about halfway up, Nina took my hand and said, 'Who *are* you?'

She was so pretty and so smart, with her blonde hair in an elaborate bun and her blue eyes like curious beacons. Maybe she wasn't the most unusual-looking child, but you could see how perfectly she fit here, a little Claire growing into this world. She chatted and told me about her day at school as we walked through Claire's (perfect) bedroom into a dressing room that is basically the size of half my apartment.

'Wow,' I said, standing still.

Nina tugged at my hand. 'My mommy has wa-a-ay too many clothes,' she confided. 'One day Daddy's going to take them all and give them to the homeless, and Mommy will have to live in a mangy old tracksuit and only one pair of shoes.'

Nina was clearly echoing something her father had said, and I added a detail to the mental image I had of Claire's Nordic-looking tyrant of a husband. But before I could say anything, Claire laughed.

'And tell Julia what Daddy thinks about your toys.'

'Daddy says my toys are appalling and disgraceful,' Nina said cheerfully. 'He says he's going to give them to the poor and I'll have to play with a cardboard box like he did when he was a child.' She paused. 'They didn't have toys back then. Or cars. Or phones. And everybody was poor. Daddy had to walk to school in the snow, you know.'

Claire laughed again as she began pulling out clothes from the cupboard, discarding them into two piles. 'Daddy likes to think he is a minimalist, doesn't he, sweetie?'

'I like boxes,' Nina said, sitting down next to a clothes pile and stroking the fabric as if it was a pet.

'I'll remember that at Christmas,' said Claire, gathering up the clothes and taking them back to the bedroom.

'Christmas is Father Christmas, Mommy,' said Nina, as the two of us trailed behind Claire. 'You can remember whatever you want but *Santa* won't bring me cardboard boxes.'

Claire and I both laughed, and then we started the very pleasing task of looking at her clothes. I tried on a few dresses, and so did Nina, and despite the fact that Claire is tall and thin and has small boobs, and I am shorter and fatter and bigger boobed, I still looked great in some of them. I suspect that's the magic of expensive clothes – my middle-class wardrobe doesn't make the same miracles.

Eventually we settled on a low-cut black dress – dressy without being over the top, and such a soft material it didn't feel like wearing anything at all, because we didn't know where Steve was taking me. Claire said the dress had never looked great on her – it made her boobs look 'stupid' – but I didn't believe her.

'Keep it,' said Claire. 'It looks much better on you.'

'Oh, I couldn't.' I held it close to me, feeling the soft fabric. Then I caught a glimpse of the designer label. The dress probably cost half my monthly salary. 'I'll give it back to you next week.'

Claire shrugged. 'Whatever. But really, if you decide you like it, keep it.'

I wondered what it must be like, to be able to give away such an expensive dress without a thought. To be able to move through life unworried. I almost wanted to hate Claire, but I couldn't.

Downstairs, Nina went back to watching TV and chatting unself-consciously with the screen, and I had a glass of wine while Claire put the finishing touches to a salad.

'We'll eat as soon as Danny gets home,' she said, and I found I was quite nervous to meet this 'Danny'. I wasn't sure what I'd say to a bossy, hulking Viking who routinely threatened to dispossess his wife and daughter of their clothes and toys, and who came from a place where they tramped to school in the snow.

'Maybe I shouldn't stay,' I said. 'It's family time. I'm intruding.'

'Nonsense,' Claire looked at me like I was speaking a foreign language. 'I've told Danny so much about you. He'd be furious if you left.'

That didn't make me feel any better about Claire's beast of a husband, and I took a great slug of wine, hoping I'd be inoffensive enough to him that he wouldn't forbid Claire from seeing me.

Then I heard a door slam and Nina's feet running down the hall.

'Daddy!' she yelled. 'Daddy's home. Daddy's home.' She sounded relieved. Maybe he routinely threatened to leave.

I put down my glass and eyed the door warily. Claire, on the other hand, bent over the oven to poke at a chicken pie.

But what came through the door made no sense at all. A dishevelled man wearing jeans and an untucked collared shirt was carrying Nina as well as a briefcase with papers and what seemed to be a giant lollipop sticking out of it, and a bunch of flowers that was almost the size of Nina's head. He had dark hair and a nose that was much too large for his face. This couldn't possibly be Claire's tyrannical husband.

He stopped when he saw me, and gave Nina a resounding kiss on the head before putting her down.

'And who is this?' he said, indicating me but speaking to Nina.

Nina looked at me, and shrugged. 'She's stealing Mom's clothes.'

'Ah,' said the man who was apparently Danny, 'then you are Julia. What a delight to meet you. Claire's told me that you and she have a marvellous time potting.' He somehow disentangled himself from his briefcase, and plonked down the flowers on the counter. Taking my hand in both of his, he shook it firmly.

'I'm Daniel,' he said. 'Claire's husband and Nina's father. And I'm sure I'll be your friend.' He looked at me from under hooded eyelids with freckled green eyes that were only slightly higher than my own. I felt like I was stepping into a forest.

Then suddenly his beam of light was diverted off me and he picked up the flowers. 'These are for you, Claire-my-sweet,' he said. When he walked over to her, I saw my initial impression was correct – he was slightly shorter than her, only slightly taller than me. I would never have expected that.

Claire took the flowers and thrust them into the sink with some water. I noticed she didn't kiss him.

'Idiot,' she said. 'Bringing flowers to show off to Julia. She's going to think you're so silly.'

Daniel laughed and it was a sound that danced along my nerves straight to my bones. I wanted to hear it again and again. He turned to me.

'I *am* silly, Julia,' he said seriously. 'I am very silly. If silly's not your game, then I will have to change. Should I change?' He looked at me, and then at Claire.

Claire sighed, but I was enchanted. 'Silly is fine,' I said. 'Silly is magnificent.' I giggled, partly from enjoyment, partly from relief. 'You're not at all what I expected.'

'I hope I'm better.' Daniel put an arm around Claire, who pulled away and bent to get the pie out of the oven.

I didn't answer. I couldn't.

WEDNESDAY

Claire

My day starts early. I get up before Nina and make three lasagnes: one for me and Nina to eat over the next two days because I know I'll be too busy to cook; one for Liandri, who has a child in Nina's class and has just had a baby; and one for poor Mrs James down the road, who had her appendix out last week. Mrs James has no family and I try to visit her often. Today I'll take her some new novels with the lasagne – because I think she'll like them, and I'll feel better if she has something to do.

I wake Nina up and we go through the usual drama of breakfast and getting dressed, which is a fraught business when you are six. Today Nina wants a ponytail, but apparently not the ponytail I'm doing.

'A different one,' she says, but she can't explain what she means and starts crying.

I know from experience that I have to stay calm, and today I actually manage it, and eventually we find a hairstyle Nina considers acceptable. She sprays almost a whole bottle of hairspray on it while I bite my tongue, and happiness is restored.

I get Nina to school on time, but Mrs Wood looks at me like a storm cloud and I remember I haven't sent her the email. I touch her arm and say, 'Such a comfort to me, knowing Nina has a teacher who cares.' Mrs Wood swells up with pride, and I promise to send her an email during the day.

As I leave the class, I bump into Trish, another mom, and we take a few minutes for small talk and air kissing.

'We must do drinks soon,' says Trish as we part.

'Totally,' I agree. 'Message me. Divine.'

On the way to the car, Janice runs after me, wanting to talk about a rumour she's heard that the school is going to make sport compulsory from Grade 1. I'm unclear if Janice thinks this is a good idea or a terrible one. I'm just worried it might disrupt my schedule and mean that Nina can't do horse riding any more, which she loves. Which reminds me that she has horse riding this afternoon.

As soon as I can get away from Janice, I pull out my phone to see that I haven't scheduled anything in conflict with the horse riding, and find that I have a hair appointment. I need to change that to this morning, and then I can work on the Pinterest boards for the three wedding plans while I am at the hairdresser. I'm about to call the hairdresser when my phone rings, and it's my old school friend Tatum, wanting to meet so that we can start planning our school reunion.

'It's sixteen years,' I say. 'Shouldn't we wait till twenty to have a big one?' But Tatum is determined, and I suspect a bit bored, so we schedule a coffee for next week and I ring off. Which reminds me that I'm meeting Chrissie for coffee now to talk about the event for her child's class.

I walk a bit faster to the car, dialling the hairdresser as I go. They fit me in for later that morning, which just gives me time for the coffee with Chrissie. If I'm quick, I can stop at Liandri on the way and drop off her lasagne. Hopefully the baby will be asleep and I can simply glance and run – if it's awake I'll have to stay for ages, reassuring her that it's the most beautiful baby ever born. And I can't even remember if it's a boy or a girl.

Then, after the hairdresser, I can drop off the lasagne at Mrs James and do some grocery shopping before I fetch Nina. Nina needs to go home, change clothes and have lunch before horse riding. I can work on setting up the meetings with the brides while she has her lesson, and then drop her at my mom, who's babysitting, on the way to a charity dinner at the hotel tonight.

I sigh and lean my head on the headrest for a moment – but I don't have time to stop. Chrissie will be waiting.

As I pull off, Daniel phones. I think about not answering, and I wonder why he always seems to contact me at the worst time in my day. But my mom always says that a problem delayed is a problem doubled, and I kind of live by that.

'Can we meet?' says Daniel. 'We need to talk.'

I think through the schedule I've just created, instinctively trying to make time for him. And then I remember I don't have to.

'Friday,' I say, two days from now. 'I can meet you at exactly eight thirty after I drop Nina, but only for half an hour.'

Daniel is silent, and I switch the phone to Bluetooth so I can negotiate the traffic.

'When did it become so hard for us to find time for each other?' he eventually says.

I suck the air through my teeth.

'When you fucked my best friend,' I say, keeping my tone conversational. 'I would say it dates back to that.' I turn the corner and pull into the parking outside the coffee shop where I'm meeting Chrissie. 'See you on Friday, Daniel.'

I have to breathe deeply before I can think of getting out of the car. Because I've just admitted a truth I haven't voiced until now. Julia isn't an old friend and she isn't a person I saw daily. But she never wanted anything from me except my company, and she made me laugh, and in a short time I'd come to think of her as my best friend.

It goes without saying that I was wrong about that, but when I lost Daniel, I lost my friend too. Julia probably has lots of people like that in her life, but I don't. And it makes me sad.

I straighten my clothes and get out of the car. Chrissie is sitting at a table inside and she brightens when she sees me, and gives a little wave. I plaster a smile to my face, and get on with it.

Catherine

I wake up excited. I can't remember the last time I woke up excited. Probably on the morning of The Accident, picturing a perfect family outing ahead of us, not knowing that my life as I knew it was about to end. But not even that thought takes away my excitement. This evening Julia is coming to tell me something. And it's either going to be that she's getting married or that she's pregnant. And I have always promised myself that as soon as Julia has a baby, I can die – it's the deal I made with myself all those years ago.

Because I, of all people, know that loving a child is bigger than anything. If she has a baby, she won't need me. I'll have done my job. I'll be free.

Today is different. Today, I'm excited. But I still have hours to go before Julia comes. And it's my half day and that usually means one thing. But first, work.

I had to stop nursing after The Accident. When it happened, Julia was two, and I had just gone back to work. I had a few shifts a week in the emergency room and emergency theatre, because that was my favourite area of nursing, and I had a postgraduate diploma in emergency medicine as well as my nursing degree. I loved the adrenaline rush and the feeling of being really important, making a difference, making choices that could save a person. For some reason, I could cope with the fact that I also made choices that could kill a person. I knew that in the big picture, my work was important.

Mike used to admire me for it. He used to say I had more balls than any man he knew. He used to say that the sight of me would give anyone the will to live.

I tried to go back after The Accident. We needed money, despite the insurance, and I knew my only hope of salvation was to keep busy. On my first shift back, everyone was gentle with me, and patient. When I spent ten minutes dithering about whether a victim of food poisoning should be put on a drip or sent for a stomach pump, another nurse quietly took over, pretending that she needed me to look over her notes. And when I froze when a child had a fit in the waiting room, my colleagues seamlessly managed the crisis. We all thought I would adjust. Nobody was worried, not even me.

And then there was a bus accident, and our hospital was the closest. There were twenty-two people on that bus – mostly mothers and children. Seven died on the scene, fifteen were brought in. It was the sort of situation where I used to be at my best – 'Queen of the Crisis', they even used to call me. But when I saw the first child being wheeled through, I froze. I was back reliving the night of The Accident, and all I could think of was that if I made one wrong decision, somebody's life would be as bad as mine.

I backed away from the trolleys being wheeled past me until I was against a wall. When the trolleys had passed, I heard someone calling me: 'Sister Catherine!'

I opened my mouth to answer, but nothing came out. Keeping my back to the wall, and my hands on it for support, I crab-walked my way to the staff room, where we kept our bags. I sat down on a hard chair for a moment, hands on my knees, trying to will myself back into the woman I had been, for Julia's sake.

But that woman was gone, and so was her career.

I packed up my stuff and walked out. Yet another chapter closed.

But I needed to work – both emotionally and financially – and I eventually found a job as a receptionist in a busy doctors' practice. There are six doctors and when I'm on duty, I'm the only receptionist. My duties involve answering the phones, making appointments, phoning various suppliers and reps, and doing mild medical tasks like taking blood pressure and testing urine. When I started, I was a bit worried the medical bit would throw me – but it's benign enough that I can handle it. Nobody is going to die if I get the urine test wrong. But it is lots of different things to juggle, so it keeps me very busy. That's what I needed then, and now. To be so busy I can't think.

When Julia was little, I only worked mornings. It took two people to do the same job in the afternoon, and the doctors were always amazed by that. 'Are you sure you don't need some help, Catherine?' they'd ask, and I would shake my head.

'It's easy,' I would answer, and compared to the life-or-death stuff I was dealing with, it was.

With Julia all grown up, I work all day – but I do have Wednesday afternoons off, and it still takes two people to relieve me.

When I get to work, Dr Marigold is already there, which is unusual – I'm normally the first in and the last to leave.

'Morning, Catherine,' says Dr Marigold, a young man fresh out of training who expects me to call him Ewan. I'm not usually a formal woman but old habits die hard, and I struggle with this business of calling doctors by their first names. So I just call them all 'doc'.

'Morning, Doc,' I say. 'You're in early.'

Dr Marigold looks at me. 'I am,' he says. 'I'm worried about a patient I saw yesterday. I feel like I missed something. I want to go over the file, maybe chat to one of the others, or phone a specialist.'

I like this about Ewan Marigold. Sometimes when young doctors start in private practice, they're arrogant. They think they know everything and they don't ask anyone for help. And then something bad happens, and they learn humility. I don't know if Ewan Marigold is just a humble person, or if he's learnt the hard way during his internship or community service. Either way, he's careful, and that's why I feel confident recommending him to patients.

Since The Accident, I haven't had the energy to actively like many people, but I do like young Ewan Marigold. I like Ewan Marigold, who is the colour of a rich cappuccino and just as warm, and I'm really excited about my day, and I find myself humming as I start my work.

Dr Marigold looks at me for a moment and then he smiles. 'I don't think I've ever heard you humming before, Catherine.'

I smile. 'It's not something I normally do,' I admit.

'You're obviously having a good day,' he says. 'I hope it stays that way.'

'Thanks.' I wonder what he would think if I told him I'm just very excited that I might be able to commit suicide soon. I picture him scurrying around, checking his textbooks, trying to find the right solution. 'You have a good day too,' I tell him.

Daniel

I'm at work but I'm just staring into space. I can't do anything or think about anything because it's all got so messed up. Julia is complicated. Claire is complicated. Even my baby-girl Nina is complicated, with arrangements every second weekend and every third holiday and every Wednesday night and phone calls only at particular times, and a whole lot of other rules that Claire's father's lawyer sent me before my slippers were even parked under Julia's bed. I can't keep track of all the rules, and Claire never tells me in advance what to expect. She's always making some demand and then referring to the goddamn letter like I'm supposed to have learnt it off by heart or something.

I put my head down on my desk.

'How did I get here?' I ask myself, but I'm not really asking myself. I'm asking Claire. But Claire is gone.

Julia

I'm nervous about seeing my mom. And I'm pretty sure Daniel is angry with me – about the baby, about telling Nina's teacher about us, about his stupid dry cleaning, about his life. Daniel seems angry a lot of the time, and when I met him, he was always happy.

After that first dinner, it was like Claire and Daniel adopted me. They invited me over for braais on the weekend and for dinners when they needed a 'spare girl' and just for a drink. And I could always make it, because of course my great blossoming romance – the one I'd needed the dress for – came to nothing.

It wasn't Steve's fault. It was basically the perfect first date. He took me for drinks at a bar in Newtown with a view across the whole city, and then we moved on to a restaurant in Dunkeld where you have to wait three weeks to get a table. He was attentive and polite and interested in what I had to say. He didn't order for me, or insist I paid, or ogle the waitress, or tip badly. He smelt good and looked nice. He was interested in a number of different topics, and he didn't pretend to know about things he didn't know about. Believe me – I've got a long list of things a man can do wrong on a first date. Steve didn't break any of the rules.

But I was bored.

Suddenly his model-like good looks that I'd been obsessed with the week before seemed a bit dull. He seemed a bit too tall and too muscly, and his eyes were too blue. I found myself thinking that such blue eyes could only result from inbreeding. And though he laughed and joked, his jokes were ordinary. He didn't have a sense of the ridiculous. He wasn't at all silly.

At the end of the date, when he leant forward to kiss me, I turned my cheek so the kiss landed awkwardly on the edge of my mouth. He looked at me for a moment, and smiled a bit sadly.

'Like that?' he said.

I thought of pretending I didn't know what he meant. But in the end I just met his (freakishly blue) eyes with my own and said, 'Yes. I'm sorry.'

Steve nodded. 'You win some, you lose some,' he said. 'I wish you happiness.'

I couldn't even fault how he handled rejection.

The next day, Saturday, I was so depressed I couldn't get out of bed. I couldn't believe the date I'd wanted so badly had gone so wrong. I wanted to tell someone – and I told myself I wanted to talk to Claire. Maybe I even believed it as I dialled her number that day.

That was the beginning of the time I was Julia, Family Friend. Claire invited me over to lunch with a few other friends of theirs. We drank a lot and laughed and laughed. I tried to picture Steve sitting with me, at Claire and Daniel's table – but I couldn't. All I could picture was Daniel. Every time I closed my eyes, all I could see was Daniel.

I told myself it was just a post-Steve reaction. I told myself it wasn't so much Daniel I wanted, but a Daniel sort of man. It wasn't Daniel I liked – I'd just realised there was more to a man than good looks. Daniel was about sex appeal and laughter. That, I decided, was what a person should look for in a man. After all, it's what Claire had chosen, and everybody can see Claire has impeccable taste. Maybe I thought that if I chose what Claire had chosen, I would have what Claire had. At the beginning, maybe it was more about wanting to be Claire than about wanting Daniel.

But the more I got to know Daniel, the more I liked him. And he seemed to like me. He was always so happy to see me, and sometimes when Claire phoned to invite me over, she'd say, 'Daniel said I should invite you,' and my palms would heat up and I'd walk with a spring in my step all day.

I'm not walking with a spring in my step now, as I face the visit with my mother.

I almost drag myself through the day, feeling slightly nauseous and tired – but tense and touchy at the same time. I snapped at Gerald when he asked me to show him again how to attach a file to an email, and I snapped at the receptionist for putting calls through to me when I was working. Even though, as she pointed out, I hadn't asked her not to.

Just before I get there, I give myself a final talking to. I always have to do this before I see my mother. Jane calls it consciously managing my expectations. She says that because there's a part of me that remembers what my mother was like before The Accident, I am constantly subconsciously hoping to see her again. And that's why I always expect more than she can give. I don't really believe that The Accident could have changed my mom that much – I can't imagine she was ever warm – but Jane's theory does make sense. And I have to admit that the thing about consciously managing my expectations does seem to work.

'She will not be happy for me,' I say to myself, standing at the gate. 'She will not hug me when she sees me, and she will not express joy that I've found Daniel. She might be mean about him being married and she will probably just not react at all. I will be okay. I will survive.'

That last part is what Jane says I must say, but whenever I say 'I will survive', I want to burst into song. Jane says this isn't a bad thing, because it makes me greet my mother with a cheerful attitude.

I ring the bell and my mother answers so quickly she must have been standing on the other side of the gate. I hope I whispered my affirmations as quietly as I meant to. I hope I didn't yell 'I will survive' out loud just before I pushed the bell. But I might have, so I start giggling.

I don't know if it's because I'm laughing, but my mother smiles as she steps aside to let me in. And then she touches my arm as I walk past, and it is as soft as a butterfly but it burns into my bare skin and I feel it etched on my arm as I walk in the front door and down the passage. My mother is not a toucher. I don't know what to do with this touch.

'Tea or something stronger?' she says as we turn towards the kitchen. We always end up standing around in the kitchen. It's not like it's one of those kitchens – like Claire's – where there's a table and chairs in the middle, and people sit around chatting and laughing. My mom's kitchen is just a bog-standard kitchen, and most of our exchanges happen with us standing propped against the melamine cupboards.

I'm about to ask for wine when I remember the baby. 'Tea will be fine,' I say, and my mom smiles again as she turns to the kettle.

When she's made the tea, she says, 'Let's go sit in the lounge – it's more comfortable.'

I just follow because this visit is feeling so different already that I don't know how to react. And I haven't even told her my news yet. 'Don't have expectations,' I whisper to myself.

'What's that?' says my mother, who's walking in front of me with the tea tray.

'Nothing, Mom,' I say. 'Talking to myself.'

Well blow me down, she turns to put the tea down on the table and smiles again.

'Are you okay?' I ask her.

'Why?'

I can't exactly say that she's smiled three times and touched me on the arm and this is so unprecedented as to be a bit frightening. Put it like that, *I* sound crazy.

'You seem a bit different today,' I say.

'I'm very pleased to see you,' she says. 'And you said you have news for me, so that's exciting.'

'Really?'

Now she pulls the face I'm more familiar with, a sort of despairing, why-is-my-child-such-a-trial-to-me face. I make a mental note to tell Jane how much more comfortable I am when she's back to sneering.

She pours both our tea and then we do our usual thing of sipping and not talking, with my mother's eyes glazed over like she isn't even in the room. I don't know how to get back to where we were. Eventually I say, 'So,' and watch as her eyes slowly refocus.

'Your news?' she says, taking a sip of tea. 'Don't keep me guessing.' She smiles again, and looks almost flirtatious.

'So,' I say. 'It's complicated.'

My mom sighs. 'Life is complicated, Julia.' And then she laughs as if she sees the irony of her of all people telling me of all people that life is complicated. But that can't be right.

'So, I met this man,' I start, and slowly, haltingly, I tell her about Daniel.

One of the many strange dynamics between my mother and I is that we very seldom lie to each other. It's not easy telling your mother that you've basically seduced a married man away from his wife and child – but not for one minute in any of this did I consider not telling her the truth.

As expected, she doesn't react strongly to anything I'm telling her. But she nods as I speak, and she says things like, 'Mmm,' and, 'I see,' and once she even says, 'How difficult for you.' I can't believe how she isn't judging me at all.

For once, it's like she's completely on my side.

Catherine

As Julia speaks, I'm having to bite the inside of my cheeks. Because when she starts talking about this couple she's met, this perfect couple with the perfect lives, I'm not thinking about this Claire-and-Daniel person, I'm thinking about Cathy-and-Mike. I'm thinking about my own perfect marriage and my own perfect family. And then when the story starts turning, and she's telling me how this Claire didn't appreciate her husband Daniel and never showed him any affection or support, I'm still thinking about Cathy-and-Mike, and I'm thinking how I thought we had forever and we didn't, and I'm wondering if Mike knew how much I loved him before The Accident, and I'm wondering what an interfering little hussy would have seen if she'd looked at my marriage. And then I pull up short because in the story I'm hearing, it is my daughter who is the interfering little hussy and she thinks she's in the right.

And I have to let her think she is too.

But I know so much that she doesn't know. I know that marriages are not about the affection revealed in front of people, and that support can be shown in one hundred different ways, and that a person outside a marriage can never judge what is happening inside that marriage – whether it is good or bad. And I know other things. I know that Julia's attraction to this Daniel is not, as she thinks, because he's different from anyone she has ever known, but because he's like her father. Like Mike. And Julia may not have known Mike for long before The Accident,

62

but she did have two years of his easy laugh and his silliness and his happiness and his irreverence. She is attracted to a bright, unusual, humorous man in a happy marriage. A man just like her father.

And the biggest thing that I know – as she is reaching the part of the story where she finds herself alone with Daniel and things take a new direction – is that you don't have a future with a man you've seduced away from a happy home. Julia's heart is going to be broken, and I know it, and I can't say anything, and all I can think is that this will change everything. She's going to need me more, not less. And I want to cry.

Then she tells me about the baby.

And the hope comes flooding back.

Daniel

Julia is at her mother telling her about us, and I'm in her flat – *our* flat – and I'm alone, and I'm thinking about what she's telling her mother, and I wish I could be there with her because she needs me.

I think back to the night it all started, when Claire went to one of her endless functions and I was at home alone with Nina. It had been a bad day, a long day – we'd lost an important client. Their CEO said it was because our agency lacked gravitas, but we all knew it was because I didn't take him as seriously as he took himself. When my buddy Ernst and I started the agency five years ago, we were very clear that we'd only work with people we had fun with. We'd both spent too many years licking arses and the whole point of our own agency was to break away from that mindset. For a long time we planned to call the agency 'Arse Lickers' in an ironic way, but our lawyer said we might have trouble registering that name. We'd also had second thoughts – it might have alienated clients. We should have known then that it's one thing to say you'll only work with like-minded clients, and a whole other ball game to do it. Maybe we should have stuck with 'Arse Lickers' just to remind ourselves where we stood.

Anyway, that's what was going on the day it started with Julia – I was learning the hard way that losing a wanker of a client also meant losing a couple of million in the bank. I didn't like that so much, and neither did

Ernst. We'd had a few tequila shots at the office to comfort ourselves, and yelled, 'Arse-licker cock-sucker wankers' really loud over our panoramic view, but we both still felt like shit.

But I had to get home to relieve Thandi, our helper, because Claire was out. I phoned Claire on the way home and I was surprised that she answered and I was so pleased to hear her voice, I started telling her about the arse-licker cock-sucker wankers. But she said, in her strict voice, 'You've been drinking and now you're talking on the phone and driving.' So I said it was worth the risk, I needed her, and she said, 'Well, I don't need to be a widow, and anyway I'm not at home, you dipshit,' which she normally only says when she's joking around, but then she hung up the call. When I tried to phone back, she didn't answer.

Just after I got home – perfectly safely – and before I could even change, the doorbell rang, and when I answered the intercom, there was Julia. I let her in, and she was all dressed up and carrying a bottle of wine and a bunch of flowers, and the silly thing had got the night of a dinner party wrong by a whole week.

Well, she was mortified but I was delighted. I *liked* Julia so much. She isn't all blonde and thin and polished like Claire's other friends. Her hair is long and dark and curly. Nobody has curly hair any more – I hear women talking about how much they pay to straighten their hair. But Julia's got hair like a gypsy. And she is ditzy and messy and always looks slightly wrongly put together, like you just know there's no way her underwear matches, and chances are that something's on inside out. I like that. So I told Julia that since she was there anyway and I was all alone, she should stay and we could have something to eat.

I opened some wine and made us some pasta, and Julia was impressed that I could cook, which I liked, because Claire just complains about how much mess I make and that it's always pasta. I was a bit drunk from the tequila, and stressed, and disappointed that Claire hadn't wanted to speak to me. I barely touched my pasta but I drank a lot of red wine. Julia, on the other hand, ate all her pasta and asked for more. I wouldn't say that Claire diets, but she's 'careful'. I liked that Julia ate like a proper person and suddenly I was noticing her low-cut top and really generous boobs. Claire's boobs are like the rest of her: text book. They are not too small and they are perky and they sit where they are meant to sit. Julia's boobs look altogether less disciplined, and deep in my wine and my stress and my misery, I had an epiphany: less disciplined was the way forward for boobs.

To avoid telling Julia about this epiphany, because I sensed it might be inappropriate, I started telling her how humourless Claire had been about me phoning from the car. Of course, looking back on it sober and knowing what I know now, it really was the same topic – Julia's undisciplined boobs and Claire's failure to talk to me.

But when I told her about the car and Claire saying that she didn't need to be a widow, Julia suddenly went pale and her eyes filled with tears. I reached across and took her hand.

'What have I said?' I asked.

That was when she told me the story of her childhood and The Accident that changed everything. While she was talking, she started crying, and she kept brushing away her tears, and saying she was sorry, she never cries about it. When the crying turned to sobbing, I got up from the table and led her to the couch and I put my arms around her – I could feel her boobs pressing against my side – and I stroked her back and held her and told her that everything was okay now.

As I was stroking her back, I kept thinking that I'd never seen Claire like that. I've never seen Claire out of control with misery – and I've been with her through the death of family and friends. But Claire's grief is neat and internal – she doesn't need me. And Julia, Julia needed me so badly that night.

I looked down at her tear-stained face just as she pulled back and looked up at me. I reached my thumb to her cheek to wipe away her tears and suddenly we were kissing and it was like we were both drowning people clinging to life, the way we clung together. And then, because I'd been thinking about them already, my hands were on her boobs and I was pulling at her clothes, and it felt just as good as I'd imagined and I couldn't or wouldn't stop, and neither did she.

Julia

I tell my mother as much as I can. There are parts I can't tell her – parts I can barely admit to myself. Like I knew full well Claire would be out that first time when I turned up for a dinner party on the wrong night. It's probably the most calculated thing I've ever done. The worst thing I've ever done, if I'm honest with myself. The worst thing, but also the best thing.

When I tell my mother that part, I gloss over what exactly happened. I don't know if it's because I'm feeling guilty, but I think her eyebrows raise ever so slightly, which for my mother is a major emotional reaction. But I could be wrong; maybe she was just trying to stay awake. She's always said that nothing's as boring as other people's dreams and other people's affairs. But when I stop, mid-story, and ask if I'm boring her, she says, 'No, no – carry on,' and it's almost as if she's interested.

The part that came after that first night also doesn't reflect well on me. The next day, Daniel came to see me at work.

'That shouldn't have happened,' he said, and I could see he'd barely slept. 'That's not the sort of man I am. That's not the sort of man Claire deserves. Or you deserve.' His eyes were filled with tears, and I reached out to him.

'You're the best sort of man,' I whispered. 'You make me feel so … safe.' I manufactured a little sob. Yes, I manufactured it. I might be an accountant, but you don't have as much therapy as I've had without

68

learning a thing or two about psychology, and the thing I've learnt about Daniel is that his drug of choice is need. He needs to be needed, and Claire doesn't need him. I saw that chink in the armour of their marriage and God help me, I took it. Every single time he looked like he was about to back away, I played the needy card. And it lured him back to my bed again and again, until in the end he fell in love with me.

'And what about Claire?' my mother asks as I'm explaining Daniel's deep and genuine feelings for me. 'She was your friend.' For a moment it feels like my mother is judging me after all, but then she says wistfully, 'It must have been hard for you to lose her. A friend.'

'It was,' I say. 'But it was worth it. Now I have Daniel and we're going to have our own baby.'

My mother barely reacts to this; maybe just another raising of her eyebrows, but it's hard to tell.

'When you meet him, you'll see,' I tell her, suddenly desperate for her approval, her understanding.

'I'd love to meet him. I'm sure he's wonderful,' she says in her calm way. She shifts slightly in her chair. 'Have you told him?'

She doesn't have to say more – we both know what she's talking about. Which isn't strange, because it has defined our lives, but it also *is* strange. Because we don't talk about it, her and I. We almost never mention the giant elephant in our psyches.

She must have told me something when it first happened – when I was two and left with my grandparents, and when she came back everything had changed. But of course I don't remember that – I don't remember a time before it was like this. Although Jane believes I do. Jane believes that if I *really* didn't remember anything, I'd be a lot better. And my mother must've answered my questions because I know the answers – I know what happened and I know where that left us. Or I think I do. And there were some things she'd have to have told me, like about my dad.

When I was about thirteen I got very depressed, and I started binge eating and vomiting. My mother sat me down one morning and said that she knew I was unhappy, and she knew it was probably her fault. She said that maybe I needed to talk to someone 'more present' than she was, and obviously more present than my dad was. Those were her words. And then she found me my first therapist, and she came to the first session with me. In the first session she said, 'Julia is unhappy and I can't help her,' and she told the therapist about The Accident as if it was something she'd read about in a magazine.

The therapist (who was very good – my mother had done her research and found the best) said, 'Why do you feel that you can't help Julia, Catherine?'

And my mother said, in this flat, bored voice, 'Because I am profoundly, pathologically depressed. There's nothing anyone can do for me, but maybe you can stop me from damaging Julia.' And then she stood up and walked out as if she'd just mentioned what she was making for supper.

For a moment the therapist looked at the door. Then she turned to me. 'How does hearing that make you feel, Julia?' she said, and we were away.

But since then we haven't talked about it. Not about The Accident and certainly not about my mother's so-called depression. And not about the fact that she loves me enough to protect me from herself. Not about that either.

'Did you tell him about Dad?' she says now.

'I told him,' I say.

She nods, as if ticking something off a list. Then she really throws a curveball. No, two.

'Why don't you bring Daniel to lunch on Sunday?' she says. 'The sooner I meet him, the better.'

And as I'm reeling from that – probably the most proactive thing she's done since I moved out, she adds the punch.

'I'm going to see Dad tomorrow and I'll tell him your news ... but maybe we can go back together on Sunday after lunch, and Daniel can meet him too.'

Catherine

After The Accident, after that terrible, endless, nightmarish time while we were trapped in the car – a time I can never forget as hard as I try, a time that used to make me wake several times a week with tears streaming down my cheeks – after that time, they took me to hospital and they sedated me. I don't blame them: I was hysterical.

When I came around, they explained to me what had happened – like I could ever forget, like I didn't know. And they told me that Mike was paralysed and brain damaged and that while he might survive and could possibly live without life support, he was for all intents and purposes a vegetable.

I was barely injured – only superficially. The truck had hit the car from the front, on the driver's side. It somehow missed me. I was badly bruised and scraped all over my body, and I had a cut on my head that necessitated shaving part of my hair and stitching me, and my muscles were very stiff from straining and not being able to move for so long. My right ankle was swollen and it would be some time before I could easily put weight on it. So they wheeled me – at my insistence – to where Mike was. And then they left me there, the nurse saying that she would be right outside the door, but maybe I needed time alone with him.

I took his hand in mine. It was completely limp, and I held it in both my hands, leaning forward in my wheelchair. And I told him what had happened – everything the doctors had told me when I'd woken up, everything I remembered, every terrible thing inside me. And then I leant my head against his side, and I wept. And while I was crying, drenching the sheets so badly they would have to change them, I felt Mike's hand squeeze mine. And when I looked up, his eyes were closed and his face was immobile, but his cheeks were wet with tears.

That's how I know Mike is alive inside that body. That's why I insisted he be kept on life support at the beginning – despite all sorts of people telling me it might be kinder to turn it off – and that's why, when he was finally able to live without the support, I tried to nurse him at home.

It didn't work though. Even though I'm a nurse, and a good one. It was too hard. Mike needed twenty-four-hour nursing, and I had to work. And Julia was upset and frightened by Mike. I tried to help her see him as her dad, just different, but she wouldn't go near him. She'd been through so much, lost so much – and I wasn't looking after Mike well. Eventually I conceded defeat and we moved him to the best long-term care facility our insurance could afford. In the beginning, I visited daily, and took Julia once a week. But even that was too hard, and eventually I started visiting less, although I always took Julia once a week. I never again spoke to Mike about those terrible hours trapped in the car on a dark abandoned highway. I never spoke to *anyone* about it. So there are things Julia doesn't know, things she can never understand about me.

But I still speak to Mike about everything else. I still know that somewhere deep inside, he's awake, living his own personal hell. When I realised how bad it must be for him – trapped in his body with an active mind – it was too late for me to help him. I had already got him into care. There was nothing I could do because I couldn't risk getting caught. My only remaining duty was to be Julia's mother, and I had to do that to the best of my ability. And that included not murdering her father – no matter how much I knew he needed me to.

When I had my epiphany about a year later – my realisation that I could kill myself if I just fulfilled my duty to Julia first, I realised that this freed me to kill Mike too, when the time came. I didn't even need to be subtle. I could kill Mike and free him from the prison of his body, and then kill myself and free myself from the prison of my pain. If the religious people are right, then it will be even better because we'll be together. But even if they're not, even if it's just nothing after this, anything would be better than this. It is true that Julia will experience huge loss, but she'll either have a reliable partner or her own child to see her through. The focus of her life won't be on being my child; it will be on being a wife and mother. That's why it is okay for me to do it then. I will have handed on the baton of Julia's happiness.

I told Mike about this as soon as I realised. I went to visit him and drew up my chair right close to his ear, and explained that as soon as Julia had a reliable partner or a baby of her own, I would free us. I said it clearly so I knew he would hear, and I repeated it a few times.

'Don't worry, my love,' I said to him. 'We just have to be patient, but I will make this hell end. I promise you. I will free you from this prison.'

The doctors and nurses at Mike's facility tell me he has no affective response – that he feels nothing and has no significant intellectual activity except that his body keeps itself breathing and moderately functioning. They tell me that nothing I say can upset him but also, nothing can please him. In the beginning they were quite gentle with their explanations, but over the years they've gotten more blunt. The doctor in charge of Mike's case at the moment seems to feel personally responsible for me, and about annually he sits me down and explains again that Mike is a vegetable and that I should move on with my life. Well, firstly, they didn't see Mike cry. Nobody believes that happened, but I know what I saw. And, secondly, there might be people who move on, but I'm not one of them. I understand that for other people there are second chances at love but that's not how it is for me. I'm not judging those people – and maybe if The Accident had been different, I would be one of them. But for me, there is only Mike. I don't need to move on.

In the early years I thought I'd meet other people like me. Sometimes I would think I had – people who drifted around in the corridors of the facility like I did. But I would watch them slowly heal, and visit their person less, and move on. I would say things like, 'I'm so happy for you,' and, 'You deserve to be happy,' but I knew it wasn't like that for me, and eventually I stopped even acknowledging these passers-through.

I can't wait to tell Mike our time is coming. I can't wait to tell him we are nearly free to die.

Julia

I love visiting my dad. It is my absolute most favourite thing in the world.
I have a slight memory of the time immediately after The Accident when
my father lived with us still. My mother always seems to suggest I was a
bit scared of my dad, but I never was. I remember standing at the door
of his room and feeling peace emanating from him as he lay there. I
remember feeling happy to be near him, and I remember feeling bereft
when he left.

And even when I visit him now, that happy feeling comes back. I
know the doctors say he's a vegetable, that he knows nothing and if
he hears us, he doesn't understand us, but that's just not true. Even my
mother feels better after she's spoken to him. He's like a wise recluse
who lives on a hill, hearing our problems and bringing peace to our lives
without saying a thing. I don't need to talk to him to know that he's
conscious and at peace with where he finds himself.

My mother doesn't realise how much I visit and how much I talk to
him. I've told him about Daniel. I spoke to him when it all started and I
was feeling confused and guilty and unsure. When I hold his hand and
close my eyes, it can feel like he's talking back to me, and I can almost
hear his voice telling me not to worry, that everything will work out and
I'm his little princess (although I don't actually know if he ever said that).

I know it's not fair – my mother has been the parent who cared for
me and worked really hard to provide for us and give me as normal a

childhood as she was capable of. But it's my dad who roots me to my life. It's my dad that I can't live without.

I've thought about taking Daniel to meet him before, but it seemed wrong somehow. I mean, it's not like Dad could tell Mom he's already met Daniel, but the nurse or someone might, and that might make Mom feel bad. Or maybe it's that I wish it *would* make Mom feel bad – because she probably wouldn't really care.

I have a fantasy that one day my dad is just going to wake up. A few years ago I talked to some doctors about it, because if you read up on the Internet it seems that people are waking up the whole time and thinking it's 1972 and wondering what they'll have for lunch. The doctors said that absolutely couldn't happen to my dad, and that it actually barely ever happens, and when it does the person is profoundly brain damaged, or wasn't actually in a coma at all, and that no one actually understands how my dad isn't dead. But I bet the doctors of the people who woke up said the same thing. After all, there's only so much medical science can explain. It's not even like he's on life support, so obviously some part of his brain is working. And the doctors have to be careful not to give false hope, so they downplay the fact that people sometimes wake up. There's a part of me that really believes it will happen for us one day, and then my mom will be alright and we'll all be happy. I believe it so much that I sometimes worry about all the personal things I've told him – I've found myself whispering, 'Don't tell Mom, but …'

I wasn't worried about asking the doctors if he'd wake up because I knew they'd have to say no. But I was too scared to ask my mother. Jane says I'm scared she'll say no too. But Jane doesn't realise that wouldn't change anything – I know my dad is still alive in that body. I know he *could* wake up one day. I think my mom also believes it.

I can't wait to introduce him to Daniel. I can't wait to place my baby into my dad's arms. Maybe that will shake him out of his coma.

Then *everybody* will live happily ever after.

THURSDAY

Claire

Thursday is the day I spend the morning at the hotel, catching up on news I can use in tweets and Facebook posts over the coming week, taking photos and checking in on event planning. It's a pain because I'm less flexible, but I also quite like it because I'm less flexible. I imagine this is how it is for women who work full time. 'No,' they can say – to the class mom request, to the coffee, to the volunteer work, to the cake sale, to the lift club – 'no, I will be *at work*.'

Once, before everything went wrong, I told Daniel about this fantasy. A life in which I could say no.

'But Claire,' he said, 'even if you were the CEO of Apple, you wouldn't say no. It's not in your nature. You'd be running Apple and still doing every cake sale and every charity event and answering every cry for help. Apple's profits would probably double with you in charge, but you'd be even more of a wreck.' He was probably right, as much as I hate to admit it.

Anyway, he's gone now. New start. New attitude. And today my goal is to say no to one request.

My chance comes early in the day – Janice corners me at drop-off.

'Claire, darling,' she says, and we air-kiss. 'How *are* you?'

I immediately know she wants something – it's the stress on the 'are', to convince me she really cares. Given that she knows sweet fuck-all about my life, an honest answer would kill her.

'Lovely,' I answer. 'And you are looking so beautiful.' She isn't really. She's dyed her hair a really strange colour and looks like a giant aubergine. 'Your hair is divine.'

Janice tosses her head. 'Do you really think so? I'm not sure.'

What I want to say was that I don't have all day to stand around giving people therapy about bad hair decisions, and that frankly she looks like a member of a hippy coven. I take a deep breath, knowing this anger is not really because of Janice at all.

'You look fab,' I say. 'Must run now.'

'Oh, Claire,' She touches my arm as I try to make my getaway. 'I wanted to ask you – we need someone on the board for my breast cancer charity. I wondered if you'd be interested? You're the best person I can think of, and I know you really care about the cause.'

This is my opportunity to say no, and a good one because I actually want to. I care about breast cancer in that I hope people stop getting it one day, and I think it's very sad that people die from it, and I certainly don't want to get it myself, but I don't want to be on the board. I am absolutely clear about this.

'Janice,' I say firmly, and then look at her big, hopeful eyes, blue irises ringed with a darker outline. 'Um … send me some info, okay? Not promising anything, but let me see what's involved.'

'Oh, thank you!' She hugs me warmly. 'You are the best, Claire, you really are.'

I feel good, but also stupid and useless and spineless. As she turns to walk away, I call her. 'Janice,' I say, 'you have really beautiful eyes. I think your new hair colour makes them stand out more.'

Janice smiles and blows me a kiss, and I wonder how much time being on the board of a breast cancer charity can really take. I've got a whole lot of extra time after all, what with being single again.

I'm intercepted on my way to the car by Liandri. She has her new baby with her, and I don't think she's brushed her hair.

'Thank you for that lasagne yesterday, Claire. It saved the day. Jan thinks I'm Superwoman for having such a divine meal on the table – I didn't tell him you're actually the Superwoman.'

I laugh. 'It was no problem, Li,' I say. 'I remember how it was when Nina was born, and I can only imagine what a second must be like.'

I'm hit by a sudden moment of sadness. Daniel and I started trying for a second baby a while ago, unsuccessfully. I guess now I'll never know what a second child is like.

Liandri looks like she might start to cry. 'It's harder than I thought,' she says. 'I just feel like everything's falling apart.'

Join the club, I want to say, but I just smile and pat her arm. 'Anything I can do, just yell.'

'Well … Could you possibly give Tatum a lift home today? I have to take the baby to the nurse and I just can't figure out how to do both.'

'No problem.' I do a mental reshuffle. I can't say no to this – I've just offered to help. And it isn't really a big issue. I'll just have to phone Nina's art teacher and explain that she'll be slightly late for art class.

Liandri hugs me, an awkward sideways hug to avoid squashing the baby, and finally I get into my car.

On the way to the hotel, I take a wrong turn and suddenly I'm in a street I don't know. I slow down to get my bearings and then I see it: a garden full of gnomes. *Full.* I pull over and I stare.

Garden gnomes are Daniel and my 'in joke'. On our first date he took me to a party. As we walked into the house, he pointed to the two garden gnomes flanking the door and said, 'You're never going to come out with me again – you'll think I'm a garden-gnome kind of guy.'

I looked at him and said, 'Oh, you're definitely a garden-gnome kind of guy.'

The garden-gnome thing gained momentum and turned into an on-going joke. Whenever we see gnomes, we stop and photograph them to send each other. In recent years, we've added 'My gnome is sad because …' So Daniel will send me a picture of a gnome saying, 'My gnome is sad because he thinks he's fat,' and then I must comfort the gnome, and say that it is all muscle, or that he looks distinguished. It's so silly. It's so Daniel. It's so us. For my thirtieth birthday he had a white-gold necklace made with a garden-gnome charm on it. The gnome is holding a diamond in his fat little hands. It is perfect.

I stare at the garden full of gnomes and I don't know what to do. After about a minute, I get out the car and take a picture. I know I shouldn't, but I do. And then I send the picture – there must be about twenty gnomes just in the frame I caught – to Daniel. And I type, 'These gnomes are sad because everything has changed.'

As soon as I press send, I regret it. I start madly pushing buttons trying to find a way to recall the message, but of course I can't, and then I see that he's read it already. And I watch as the phone shows that he's 'typing', and I'm imagining all the scathing things he might say.

And then the message comes through and it says, 'Those gnomes can't be sad. They're looking at you.'

And I sit in my car, and I cry and I cry.

Daniel

I answered Claire before I could think, but I don't regret it.

The rest of the day, I can't stop looking at the photo of the gnomes. I want to ask Claire where she was. I want to ask her how many there were, because it looks like there might be even more than I can see in the photo. But instead I just look at the picture she sent me, and I think.

Claire thought I broke her heart when I left her for Julia. But I think that when I see her tomorrow and tell her Julia is having a baby …

I think that's when it might break for real.

And no number of gnomes can fix that.

Julia

When my affair with Daniel started, I didn't think about him leaving Claire and Nina. I wanted him for my own, I wanted him to be with me, I wanted to be able to go out in public and introduce him as my boyfriend and stop in the road and kiss him. I wanted not to have to sneak around and tell lies and have furtive sex at strange times in uncomfortable places. But in all that wanting, I somehow didn't think that Daniel would have to leave Claire and Nina. That they would be left. And that I would be the baddie in that story.

That I *am* the baddie in that story.

In the beginning, I worked hard on to keep up the front of my friendship with Claire. Because if I was friends with Claire, there was nothing suspicious about me hanging around. And I still loved being friends with Claire. I still loved Claire. I just didn't love her as much as I loved Daniel. So I still went to pottery. And I still came to visit and I ate meals at their family table. And it was awful and wonderful and furtive and sexy and I felt constantly alive. I would sit across from Daniel, knowing that just hours before he had been inside me, and now he was sitting with his family, and I would get so turned on it was difficult not to pull him into the bathroom and fuck him right there with Claire and Nina sitting outside.

But Daniel hated it. He hated me being in his home and he was consumed with guilt, and across the table his eyes were dark and held none of the lust I felt certain must be spilling out of me, staining the table.

Things had to come to a head, and they did.

Daniel and I had met at lunch time. We'd rented a room – a seedy hotel just off the highway that lets you pay by the hour – and we'd pretended that I was a hooker he'd picked up, and I was wearing cheap sex-shop underwear under my work clothes and when he unbuttoned my shirt and saw it, he looked at me like he couldn't believe I was for real, and he pushed me back hard on the bed and ripped off my shirt and said, 'I'm going to fuck you so hard now,' and I was so turned on that he barely had to touch me before I came. When we were spent and my kinky underwear was lying in a torn pile on the floor and we were naked on the bed facing each other, he said, 'I think I've fallen in love with you. Nothing has ever been like this for me.'

And then that night, there I was at their table, Claire having invited me over for supper. And I was so turned on I thought I would faint, thinking of what we'd done at lunch. But Daniel was glowering and refusing to meet my eyes, and even Claire commented that he was in a very sulky mood, and he just snapped at her.

The next day Daniel phoned me. 'It's over,' he said, without any preamble. 'I hate the person I've become. I'm not doing this any more. And you need to stay away from Claire and me for a bit. Just stay away. Tell Claire you're busy. Just leave us alone.'

You'd think I would have been devastated. That I would have begged and pleaded, or even defended myself. But I just said, 'If that's what you want, Daniel. I can respect that.'

And then I didn't wait for him to hang up, I just put down the phone. I wasn't upset, because I knew Daniel couldn't live without me. I knew that all it would take was patience, and he'd call me and say he wanted to see me again. I felt calm.

I gave him a week before I thought he would cave. He lasted two days.

And when he called, it wasn't to say that he wanted to see me again.

It was to say he was going to leave Claire for me.

'I'm not a man who can have an affair and feel right about it,' he said. 'And it seems that I can't live without you. So I have to leave Claire.'

Part of me was stunned – I hadn't really thought that far ahead. I hadn't thought about where this thing with Daniel and me was going. And I certainly hadn't expected it to happen then, in the lead-up to Christmas, when every mistress knows the man goes back to the safety of his family. But it also felt inevitable. Obviously Daniel and I were meant to be together and it was just a terrible mistake that he'd married Claire before he met me. But this, I felt, was our destiny.

'I'll tell Claire tonight,' he said. 'So I'll probably have to move in to your place immediately. I don't think she'll let me sleep there once she knows.' He sounded matter-of-fact. Like he'd seen the inevitability of this path too.

'My place?' I'd never really pictured having Daniel as a fixture. The idea was strange.

'Well, I assume that's what you want,' said Daniel. 'For us to be together? I'm leaving my wife and child for you, so I kind of thought I should come to you.'

'Of course you'll come to me,' I said. 'I love you. This is the beginning of the rest of our lives.' I pushed aside any doubts. I was now in the real world of grown-up relationships; there was no space for wondering if I wanted to move in with someone after such a short time. That sort of thinking was for other people, not for me and the love of my life.

'I guess I must love you too,' said Daniel, and abruptly put down the phone. I tried not to feel uneasy.

He arrived at about two in the morning, exhausted, and he'd clearly been crying. He had one sports bag with him, and over the next few days, his PA appeared sporadically with suitcases and boxes. I presume that she'd arranged this with Claire – who was staying with her parents for the week between Christmas and New Year, and refusing to speak to Daniel – but I didn't know how or when, or what she thought of the situation. I made some space for his stuff in my cupboards, but that soon proved impractical, and he moved it into the spare room. There was a strange time when he just left his suitcases lying open on the spare-room bed, and I wondered if he wasn't sure whether he was staying. But eventually one evening, he announced that he couldn't find anything, and he didn't understand why his bags hadn't been unpacked, and with inexplicable sighing, he unpacked them. The boxes have remained where the PA and I left them, in the passage and shoved into corners of rooms. I presume he'll unpack when he's ready. I don't want to push.

I didn't ask what passed between him and Claire the night he left. I didn't really want to know. And I haven't seen Claire again. Or done pottery. I didn't really think that part through either; I didn't realise what else I would be losing.

Catherine

Usually I visit Mike on Wednesday afternoons and then at some point over the weekend, often on both days, because what else am I going to do? But I couldn't go yesterday because I was waiting for Julia, so I've taken an afternoon off today. The doctors are a bit thrown. I never take time off.

'First humming,' says Ewan Marigold, 'now afternoons off. Next thing you'll be eloping with the delivery guy from the pathology lab.'

I laugh. 'I think he bats for your team, actually,' I tease Dr Marigold, and then I blush because we've never talked about him being gay, although it's obviously not a secret because his boyfriend – a luminous Ugandan who is proof that albinism can be beautiful – often comes to meet him at the rooms. In my confusion, I blurt out the next bit: 'Anyway, I'm married.'

Dr Marigold looks at me. 'I thought you were widowed,' he says. He sounds confused, and his forehead wrinkles up like it does when he's reading the file of a challenging patient.

And it is true that I've somehow let the doctors believe this about me, that I'm widowed. I've never said it – I *would* never say it – but I also haven't corrected them when I've known they're making that assumption. My story is too painful to bring into the workplace, and visiting Mike is my private, special time. But Ewan Marigold has loosened my tongue.

It seems ages that Dr Marigold and I stare at each other. Then I shrug my shoulders.

'There's a lot you don't know about me.'

I can see he's about to ask more, so I reach out and touch his arm. I'm not a toucher, and I don't know if my gesture takes him or me more by surprise.

'It's complicated, Ewan,' I say, using his name for the first time. 'I don't talk about it.'

He glances down at my hand on his arm, and then at my face. 'Okay,' he says. 'I understand. But I'm here if you need me.' He looks so concerned, and I can only imagine what strange scenario he's constructing in his head. But I don't have the energy to explain, to expose myself.

'Thank you,' I say.

I'm planning to tell Mike the good news that Julia has found someone, that she's pregnant. I lay awake last night planning how I'll tell him that finally our time is coming, that I'll be able to end the pain for both of us. In my fantasy, I leant over and held Mike's hand as I whispered it to him, and when I got to the part where I said we could die, Mike squeezed my hand. I know it's been twenty-six years since it last happened, but that doesn't mean it won't happen again if something sufficiently exciting happens.

But when I get to Mike's room, and I sit down and take his hand and start talking, I don't seem able to follow my own plan.

'I'm so worried about her,' I tell him. 'This man is married, and by the sounds of things to a very likable, competent woman. I just can't help thinking that he's going to leave Julia and go back to his wife. And now there's a baby.'

I look at Mike's impassive face, and his chest rising and falling – miraculously on its own, the miracle that holds my hope – and I feel admonished.

'It's not that I don't think Julia is loveable,' I say, as if Mike has spoken. 'Of course she's loveable. But this man has been married. Julia doesn't know about marriage.'

I squeeze Mike's hand. We know about marriage, Mike and I. We know about true love and, God help us, we know about for better or worse. I don't think Mike ever would have had an affair, but if he had, I think our marriage would have won at the end of the day. And when Julia described this Daniel to me, he sounded an awful lot like Mike.

'Anyway, we're going to meet him on Sunday. I'll bring them here and you can see what you think.' I lean back on the hard chair. 'I just don't want her to get hurt, but I can't see how else this can end.'

I look at him.

'I'm *not* being a pessimist, so don't you go thinking that,' I argue with my silent husband. 'Believe me, I hope more than anybody that this works out well.'

Now is the time to tell him why, to explain what this really means to us. But somehow I don't. I sit there holding his hand for another hour, thinking about Julia and wondering what the future holds. At the back of my mind, I'm weighing up whether I'll be able to die soon. But mostly, I'm wondering what Julia will do if Daniel leaves her.

Being with Mike always brings me a peace, and today is no different. After sitting with him, I feel calmer, more focused. 'We'll talk about the other stuff after we meet Daniel,' I say. 'We'll know more about where we are then.' I lean down and give Mike a kiss goodbye, slightly on the side of his mouth, which I consider my own special place.

When I leave Mike's room, there's a man sitting on one of the chairs in the passage. He's crying. When Mike was first here, I often stopped and spoke to people I thought were in the same boat as me. We'd become friendly for a while, and then they would start to get better and move on, and I wouldn't, and the acquaintance would end. So I just stopped trying. These days I don't know any of the other long-term visitors; I hurry in and out of the building, speaking only to the nurses that care for Mike.

But there's something about this guy. He looks so alone, and so broken, and I know how that feels. And I've been feeling different since

Julia's news – more hopeful and more worried and … well, I suppose there's no other word for it. I feel more alive now that I can see my own death. And now here is this man, crying. I sit down next to him and pull a tissue out of my bag and hand it to him. He takes it silently, and wipes his eyes before blowing his nose with an incongruous trumpet.

'It's hard,' I say.

He nods. He looks in his fifties, like me, which means it could be anyone in here – a wife, a parent, a child. It's so long since I've had one of these conversations that I've forgotten the form.

'So,' I say, 'it's your …?' I wait for him to fill in the blank, which he does, but only after an awkward amount of time has passed.

'It's my wife,' he says, and starts to cry again.

'I'm sorry. I do know how hard it is. My husband's been in a coma for twenty-six years.'

That gets his attention and he looks at me. 'Twenty-six years?'

I nod.

'Miri's only been like this for a year and a bit. I thought that was long, but twenty-six years … I guess you're going to tell me it gets easier.'

I choose my words carefully. 'I think a lot of people do find that. But to be honest, for me it hasn't gotten easier. It's just unrelentingly painful. But most people appear to get better.'

He wipes his eyes, and seems to feel inspired by my words. 'I don't think I'll ever feel better. I'm so sick of people telling me I will.'

'Trust me,' I say with a laugh, 'I know *exactly* how that feels.'

'Thanks.' He smiles and looks like he wants to say more, but he doesn't.

I stand up, and it's awkward, I'm not sure exactly how to leave. I give him a little pat on the shoulder. 'See you,' I say.

'See you.'

I walk down the passage, wondering if he'll really never feel better, but then I sigh. Of course he will. They all do. It's just me who can't ever move on.

FRIDAY

Julia

I wake up early feeling nauseous. I'm not sure if it's the pregnancy or because Daniel seems to have wrapped his entire body around mine, but I'm hot and sweaty and uncomfortable. I try to push him away but he tightens his grip and I feel his penis stirring against my leg. I push him more forcefully and he rolls away from me, still, it would seem, fast asleep. I get out of bed and run to the toilet, but when I get there, I don't feel so sick any more. I drink some water and look at myself in the mirror. I look tired and unattractive, which is insane given how much I've been sleeping. I turn to the side and look at my stomach. There's no sign of a baby yet – maybe just a slight swelling where I used to be flatter. Claire's flat stomach probably showed the baby from the word go, but my figure is bumpier to start. I sigh in frustration, and start trying to tame my wild bed hair.

Daniel has somehow woken up and sneaked in without me noticing, and suddenly he's behind me in the mirror, and his arms are wrapping themselves around me so I can't get the bobby pins into my bun.

'You sexy thing,' he whispers, nipping at my earlobe. I try to step away but he's holding tight. 'Ah' – he pulls me even closer, which I hadn't thought possible – 'playing hard to get.'

Every instinct is telling me to push him away. I just don't want to be touched. But there's a voice in my head saying that I won Daniel by being physically available to him in a way Claire wasn't. *You made your bed …*

says the voice, and so I turn to face Daniel, and allow my body to respond to his.

Afterwards I'm glad I gave in. Sex with Daniel is always good, but it's especially worthwhile when I hear his plans.

'I'm meeting Claire for coffee today,' he says as he gets dressed, stepping around one of his boxes. I can tell from his carefully off-hand tone that he's thought about how to tell me this.

'Oh?' I say, aware that I shouldn't overreact.

'I need to tell her you're pregnant.'

'I haven't even been to a doctor,' I say.

'Well, you really should.' Daniel sounds slightly exasperated, but maybe I'm imagining it. 'Anyhow, it's really important that Claire doesn't find out from someone else, so I'm going to tell her.'

'Why's it so important?' I ask, keeping my voice level. 'Why's Claire suddenly the most important person in this story?'

Daniel turns to look at me. 'Because,' he says slowly, as if I'm stupid, 'she is Nina's mother. She is actually still my wife. And this is going to break her heart.'

I don't know what to say. I have a moment of wanting to just climb back into our bed and wake up to find none of this has happened. To wake up in a time before I met Claire, and to never, ever go to pottery. But then I wouldn't have Daniel, and Daniel is perfect.

'Okay, I understand,' I say, although I don't really. I smile. 'And this weekend we get to tell my dad.'

'Yes,' says Daniel. 'I get to meet your mom and tell your dad.'

'And *meet* my dad.'

Daniel looks at me again, and this time his eyes are a bit kinder. 'Yes, I get to meet your dad.'

I sit down on the side of the bed. 'It's all going to be okay, isn't it, Daniel?'

Daniel sits down next to me. He takes my hand. 'Eventually,' he says. 'Eventually.'

Claire

Friday morning starts at a sprint, with us losing basically everything Nina needs for the day – her lunch box, her ballet stuff, her homework book. We both race around the house looking for these things and calling them, a mad habit Nina has learnt from me. At one point we collide on the stairs, both yelling, 'Stuff, stuff, where are you?' and we collapse in a heap, laughing. I pull Nina onto my lap and squeeze her.

'No, Mommy,' she giggles. 'We're late. We gotta find the stuff. *Stuff!*'

I hold the precious weight of my girl-child. 'We're never so late that we can't stop for love,' I say.

Nina lets her body rest against mine. 'I like you, Mommy,' she says.

'I like you too, baby-girl.'

After that, we're calmer, so we find the stuff easily and leave for school.

'Don't forget you're staying with Daddy this weekend,' I tell her in the car. 'I'll pick you up and we'll pack your bags and then Daddy will come fetch you.'

'Will it be Daddy or Julia fetching me?' asks Nina, who was horrified when Julia fetched her from school.

I speak before I can think. 'If he sends Julia, you're not going anywhere.'

'Then I hope he sends her,' says Nina. She says it quietly, and she's looking out the window of the car at the passing scenery.

'Don't you like staying with Daddy? Don't you miss him?'

Nina sighs and rests her head back against the car seat. 'Mommy, I miss *everything*,' she says. 'I can't wait till Daddy comes home. His holiday is taking so long. He must just come home now.'

I don't know what to do, and my throat closes up. I can't get out the words I know I should be saying. What Nina has just said reflects almost exactly how I feel. Can't this be over? Can't Daniel just come home? Can't we pretend that none of it ever happened?

And then I think, maybe that's why he wants to see me today. Maybe he wants to beg me to take him back. Oh, I'll make him beg alright. I'll make him pay for this for the foreseeable future. But for Nina's sake, I'll take him back. I know we can fix this. What Daniel and I had, you don't get that every day.

He must have realised that by now.

'Oh, Nina,' I say. 'We'll see what happens.'

'Okay.' She goes back to looking out the window. I don't think she's going to say anything more, but after a few moments she says, 'You'll fix it, Mommy. You always do. Daddy always says you can fix anything.'

That's true, I think. Granted, Daniel's never broken anything this badly. But I *can* fix anything. Anyone who knows me will know that about me. I can fix this.

When I drop Nina at school, I'm feeling happier than I have in months. I smile at everyone, and I find time to make small talk. It slows me down, but I don't care.

I'm a fixer. And I have hope.

Daniel

I arrive early at the coffee shop where Claire and I agreed to meet. I feel like I'm waiting for something awful – the dentist or a prostate exam. I've never felt this way waiting for Claire before. Not even after I started sleeping with Julia and I felt guilty all the time.

The thing I feel now is more than guilty. I don't even have words for this thing I feel now, but it's not a feeling I ever expected. My whole life has turned into something I never planned or expected. I want to go back, but then I'd have to give up Julia, and I can't give up Julia, with her wild hair and easy manner and uninhibited sex. So I have to plough forward with this new life.

I order a cup of coffee, but when it comes I just stare at it. I can't even find the energy to get the coffee to my mouth. Am I going to destroy Claire's world? I consider putting my head down on the table and closing my eyes, but I suspect the restaurant manager might call the men in white coats. Then I start to wonder whether there really are men in white coats. I can't see that it could be true, but then who do you call when people go crazy?

I'm thinking about this, and not worrying, and I even manage to take a sip of coffee. And then Claire walks in.

Julia

To take my mind off the fact that Daniel is seeing Claire today, I make an appointment with the doctor. First, I try for the gynaecologist I sporadically use, but when I phone and say I need a check-up, the next appointment I can get with him is in three months' time, and the receptionist sounds so irritated that I don't get the chance to explain my situation. So I decide to go to the GP instead.

Dr Malcolm can fit me in immediately because she's just had a cancellation, so it seems like it was meant to be. At the same time as Daniel is probably starting to talk to Claire, I walk into the doctor's office.

'I think I'm pregnant,' I tell her when she asks what the problem is today.

'Have you done a test?' she asks.

'No,' I say. 'But I actually know I'm pregnant. I don't need a test.'

Dr Malcolm smiles. It's a warm smile, but I know she thinks I'm crazy. 'Let's start with this,' she says. 'Do you *want* to be pregnant?'

I open my mouth to answer, and I find that I don't know what to say. I certainly didn't plan this. And it's complicated everything. But I also don't want to not be pregnant because it's Daniel's baby and because I've felt a bit different since I admitted to myself that I'm pregnant. I've felt excited. 'I won't terminate it,' I say to Dr Malcolm.

She laughs. 'That's not exactly what I meant, but I guess it'll do as an answer. Okay, let's test.'

'I don't really need a test.' I can hear that I sound a bit petulant. 'I know that I'm pregnant.'

'Okay, well, humour me,' she says.

She takes some blood and puts it on a little test stick. I'm fascinated.

'Do you have to kill a rabbit now?' I ask, remembering something I once read.

'Thankfully not,' says Dr Malcolm. 'I wouldn't fancy that at all.'

She explains that we must wait three minutes for the test to show a result, and for the first time it occurs to me that I might *not* be pregnant. The test might be negative and it will turn out that in fact I am dying of a rare form of cancer. Daniel will be so cross – he's telling Claire right now. And when she finds out that I'm not pregnant but dying, she'll be triumphant. I can't believe this. What if I've set everything in motion too soon? Why do I always make such a mess of things?

I start to cry, and Dr Malcolm is unfazed. She just hands me a box of tissues.

'We'll know soon,' she says in her quiet voice.

But suddenly I'm pretty sure that I'm *not* pregnant. And I'm pretty sure I've fucked everything up.

Claire

I see Daniel sitting at the table, staring at his coffee with that look on his face that tells me he's far away. The sight is at once so familiar and so foreign that I feel a lump in my throat. I can't walk into this crying – I have to be strong and ready to heal our relationship. I take a deep breath and straighten my shoulders before I approach him.

'Claire,' he says, pushing his chair back to stand up. One of the things I like about Daniel is his old-fashioned manners. He stands up when a woman enters the room, and he walks on the outside of the pavement. Oh yes, and he sleeps with my friend.

I swallow again. This is not the time for bitterness.

Daniel looks at me intensely. 'Do you think they actually send men in white coats, or is that just something they say?' he asks in lieu of greeting. 'Like, do you think there's an actual team on standby? Maybe at the fire station?'

From anybody else, this might surprise me. But this is so Daniel. So exactly why I fell in love with him in the first place.

'I think it's just something they say,' I tell him, sitting down. 'But maybe historically it was true.'

Daniel pulls out the notebook he always carries and makes a note. I know that somewhere in the future, some creative execution of Daniel's will involve men in white coats. I love his brain, with its convoluted passageways so different from my own.

Once the note is made, Daniel comes back to me. 'So,' he says, sitting down. 'So, how are you?'

'Fine,' I lie to my husband of ten years. 'Busy. You know how it goes.'

The words are so weightless, so superficial, that I feel them float away over the sugar bowl, out the window.

But Daniel nods eagerly, like I've said something profound. 'Good, good,' he says. 'Busy is good.'

'Yes,' I say, although I don't really know what I'm agreeing with. 'And you?'

'Yes,' he says. 'Fine. Busy. Weird.'

'Weird?' At last something true has been said.

Daniel rubs his forehead with both hands. 'So weird, Claire. It's like I went to bed and I've woken up in a different life.'

'Well, basically you have,' I say, exasperated by his confusion. 'That would be because when you went to bed, there was a different woman in it.'

Daniel looks like I've slapped him for no reason. 'You're very angry, Claire,' he says, like he can't think of a single reason why this would be so.

'Yes.' But I'm not feeling angry; I'm feeling icy calm and my tone is matter-of-fact. 'I'm very angry. You slept with my friend and left me. That's kind of up there in shitty behaviour. Even my mother thinks you're a wanker.' My mother loves Daniel. She cannot believe this has happened.

'Well, that's telling me,' says Daniel.

At that point a waiter comes over and I order coffee. Daniel looks bleakly at the coffee in front of him and declines.

'So,' I say when the waiter has left, 'is there anything special you wanted to say, or are we just shooting the breeze?'

Daniel looks at me and then around the room, like he's looking for an escape route between the freelancers tapping at their laptops, and the mom-crowd who've met up after drop-off, and the breakfast meetings.

'There's something I need to tell you,' he says.

'Okay. Is it about Nina?' Obviously I know it's not about Nina. I'm waiting for him to tell me that he's made a mistake and he wants me back. That's the only thing he can be going to say, though I'm less sure now.

'I don't really know how to say this ...' he says.

'Well, I can't help you there. Maybe just close your eyes and spit it out?'

He looks at me like this is the wisest thing he's ever heard. 'You always know, Claire. You always have this great advice and know how to make things easier. I miss that.'

'Oka-ay,' I say. 'Is that what you wanted to tell me?'

He's quiet for a moment and then he actually closes his eyes, and awkwardly places his hands flat on the table.

'Julia's pregnant.'

I can't take it in.

I sit there like I'm in one of those cartoons where they hit the character over the head with a frying pan, and they stay frozen before they fall. Only, I'm stuck in the frozen part. It's like my whole body switches over into panic mode, like a rabbit, frozen still in the hope that the problem will go away. I stare at Daniel's mouth.

'Claire, say something.'

But I can't. I can't speak.

Daniel cannot be having a baby with someone else. This is not happening. I shake my head, and for some inexplicable reason Daniel thinks this is some sort of signal to carry on talking.

'It wasn't planned,' he says. 'I'm as shocked as you. So is Julia. She's quite upset, actually. But it's happened now. So there it is. A sister or brother for Nina, eh?'

I shake my head again, trying to make this end.

'She's told her mom. I'm going to meet her this weekend. And her dad. We're going to tell him.'

This extraordinary statement manages to rouse me. 'Her dad who's a vegetable?'

And then the strangest thing happens. Daniel meets my eyes and we both start giggling. Because one of the things we've talked about in the past is Julia's tragic story and her dad, who she maintains is not a vegetable. And I know my laughter is actually hysteria; a defence mechanism against the unhearable thing Daniel has just said.

'I'm not sure what I'm expected to do,' says Daniel. 'Do I shake his hand?'

We start giggling again, and for a moment it's Daniel-and-Claire against the world, Daniel-and-Claire who laugh at things that other people don't find funny. For a moment the connection is so strong it glows. And then somewhere in my laughter, reality sinks in.

Julia is pregnant. With Daniel's baby.

My husband is worrying about meeting another woman's parents.

I push back my chair, my coffee as untouched as Daniel's.

'I need to go,' I say. 'I can't do this.' I stand up and turn, then turn back. 'I guess you'd better get your lawyer to call mine.' I almost enjoy the look of panic that crosses Daniel's face. 'And if it's all the same, I'll keep Nina with me this weekend. I know it's your turn, but I don't want her to have to meet Julia's fucked-up family just yet.'

I can see from the look of confusion chased quickly by relief that Daniel had completely forgotten he was even supposed to have Nina. And that's the thing that makes me start to cry. Daniel is so deeply enmeshed in his new life that he's already left Nina and me behind.

I turn before he can see the tears, and I walk out. I hear Daniel call my name once, but he doesn't follow me, and he doesn't call again.

Julia is pregnant, and my marriage is over.

Julia

The test is positive. I'm eight weeks pregnant.

I don't know whether I'm relieved, happy or desperately afraid.

I thank Dr Malcolm, and take the pamphlets and prescription for vitamins she offers me. I promise to make an appointment with the gynae, which she promises I will get immediately if I tell them I'm pregnant.

This is real. I'm pregnant.

Daniel and I are going to have a baby together.

PART 2

May

MONDAY

Catherine

I'm visiting Mike, even though it's not my usual day. I swapped with the temp, because I really wanted to see him today and tell him the latest about the baby.

So now I tell him the exciting news Julia told me yesterday – that at the twenty-week scan they had on Friday, the baby was finally lying in a way that they could see its sex, and it's a boy. When Julia told me that, I nearly started crying. I don't know if it was joy or shock or simply all the emotions of the last few months catching up with me. I felt my eyes filling with tears and so I quickly turned away, not wanting Julia to see how her news had affected me. It's not something I can explain to her. There is too much water under the bridge.

But after I've told Mike that the baby is a boy, I seem to have nothing else to say and I sit back holding his limp hand in mine. I allow my mind to drift over all the things I am worrying about. First among them is the fact that I still haven't reassured Mike that when the baby is born, we can die. For so long that has been my aim, and Mike must know this somewhere inside him. He must be waiting in that prison of his body to hear me say the words, but I haven't. I haven't changed my mind, but everything is playing out so differently from how I thought it would that it has somehow derailed my thinking. Julia's life isn't following the script I always expected.

It's not like we don't like Daniel. I've got to know him a bit over the last few months, and I like him enormously – he's clever and funny and I can see why Julia is attracted to him. When he met me, and then Mike, he handled it so well. I had expected him to be awkward, meeting a man in a coma. It's the first time that Julia and I have introduced someone new to Mike, and I had a moment of thinking maybe it would shock Mike out of the coma, but of course that didn't happen, and afterwards I realised that Mike meets new nurses and doctors and physiotherapists the whole time.

But Daniel was respectful, and he spoke to Mike without any sign of how strange the situation was. I like him for that. But liking him doesn't change some basic facts. He had an affair and left his wife. He has another child. As far as I can make out, he's not doing anything about a divorce. And while I can see that Julia loves him – or feels something she thinks is love for him – it's not quite right, and I can't put my finger on it. I spend a lot of time thinking about them. And when I am with them, I watch Julia carefully.

I absent-mindedly stroke Mike's hand, my mind back on the baby. The baby boy.

When we were young, you couldn't see what sex the baby would be. It was a surprise when the baby came. Maybe for some people this way is better, but for Mike and me it never mattered. With this baby, with Julia's baby, I suddenly understand. I'm glad I know now, that I have time to form a mental picture before this baby is born.

Usually, I would talk my thoughts through with Mike, but it's different somehow, since Julia got pregnant. There's what I haven't yet told him about what will happen after the baby is born, and there's what I haven't talked about except that one time just after The Accident. For the first time since I met Mike, the air between us is full of things I can't say. I can't speak. Which is awkward what with Mike not being able to speak either.

To my enormous surprise, I snort with laughter at that thought, and once the snort breaks surface, a full laugh follows. I stifle it, and look at my watch.

I promised I would meet Edward at the coffee shop down the road after we've both finished our visits. I'm not sure how it's happened really, but I've allowed myself to become friends with the crying man I found in the corridor at the beginning of the year. At first I'd just sit with him for a bit whenever I found him crying in the passage – which I did most times I visited. Eventually I suggested we grab a coffee, because I was tired and thirsty, so now that is what we do. Mostly Edward tells me about how much he misses his wife, Miriam. And I nod and tell him it's perfectly normal not to feel better, and that he might never feel better. Which, ironically I guess, makes us both feel a bit better.

Edward even took me to meet Miriam once.

'Miri,' he said, 'this is Catherine, who I told you about.'

Then we both looked at Miriam for a while, and I said, 'Nice to meet you, Miriam,' even though the poor woman is quite clearly completely brain dead. She's on a ventilator and everything. Not like Mike. Edward says he can't bring himself to authorise them to disconnect her, even though that's what their children want. He says he knows she's going to wake up one day and then everyone will know he did the right thing, not giving up hope.

I think about how I wish now that I had helped Mike when I could – because being stuck in a body that can't move or speak must be the greatest hell on earth. But I don't say anything to Edward because it's different. Miriam can't even breath on her own, she's not feeling or thinking anything in there, so if keeping her alive makes Edward feel better and he can afford the treatment, well, I say why the hell not. So I don't tell him that I wish Mike could leave the prison that is his life. Instead, I pat Edward's hand and say I understand. And I do.

And I like Edward. When he manages to come out from under his sorrow, I can see the kind, funny man he used to be. Sometimes we talk about what it would be like in a parallel universe, where Catherine-

and-Mike met Edward-and-Miriam, and are all friends, and have dinner at each other's houses and maybe even go on holiday together, never knowing the tragedy we have missed.

I really enjoy my time with Edward, even though he's so sad and I'm so sad. It's just a relief to be with someone who doesn't think it's weird that I haven't moved on. Edward is incredulous that people tell him to move on. 'To where?' he asks me, and I shrug, because I've never known the answer to that question.

But I can't sit with Edward all afternoon because I'm having supper with Ewan Marigold and his boyfriend, Okkie. I don't know how it's happened that I've become a person who has two social arrangements – three if you count visiting Mike – in one day. It's almost like I'm a person with a life.

I don't know what I think about that.

Julia

I badly wanted the baby to be a boy, because then it would be something new for Daniel, not a rerun of Nina. Something Daniel and I can do together for the first time. If I had a boy, I reasoned, I won't be competing so directly with Claire.

Because, of course, halfway into this pregnancy I have lost to Claire on every level. Daniel's favourite thing if I mention any pregnancy symptom is to raise his eyebrows and say, 'Strange, that didn't happen to Claire.' Apparently Claire had no morning sickness, no swelling, no heartburn, no exhaustion, no skin problems, no cravings and no food aversions. It would seem she simply sailed through pregnancy, working up until the last minute, looking immaculate. And, of course, because I know Claire, I can believe it.

Jane says it's not Daniel who's comparing me to Claire, but me comparing myself to her. Jane says that I've fixated on Claire as a symbol of everything perfect, and that this is understandable given my guilt about her. Jane also says she doesn't think Daniel realises what he's saying. She asked me to bring Daniel to a therapy session so we can talk to him together about it, and I thought that was a great idea. But when it came to the crunch, I couldn't suggest that to Daniel because Claire would never have needed so much therapy and even if she did, she'd never drag him into it. Jane pointed out that if my theory is that Daniel needs me to need him, then asking him to help me should trigger his kindness. I can see the logic, but I still can't ask him. When I mentioned therapy the other day, just in passing, he pulled the same face he pulls when he's telling me what Claire never does, so I knew what he was thinking. I said, 'Anyway, I'm stopping all that because now I have you, and that's enough.'

He really liked that, and we ended up having sex on the kitchen floor, but now I have to lie about going to therapy.

So when the doctor said that the baby was a boy, and showed me and Daniel the baby's little willy on the scan, I was really happy. Daniel looked bemused though.

'God,' he said, 'I never really thought about a boy.'

But that evening at home he was full of smiles and held my hand and said he'd have to learn to be a more butch dad, and play rough games with the baby.

'I've read that it's very important for fathers to teach their sons the limits of rough play,' he said, and I felt overwhelmed with love that he'd researched it.

And then I told my mother, and that was the usual mess. She's been slightly more animated recently and I almost thought she was excited about the baby. She even sometimes phones me just to ask how I'm feeling, and she never used to. So I got it in my head that maybe she was excited to know the baby's sex, although I guessed she wouldn't have a preference. Well, when I told her, she just turned away as if I'd been talking about the weather, and said something noncommittal like, 'That's nice then.' I don't know why I felt so disappointed – I should really know by now.

And then in the middle of all that's going on – being pregnant, and feeling sick and inadequate all the time – the worst thing that can happen at work has happened: we have a new project with Steve's company. And last time I saw him was on that terrible date, and now I have to work with him again. Halfway through a pregnancy, with a baby bump twice the size the books say it should be, and spotty skin and greasy hair (because no matter how much I wash it, it somehow stays greasy) and swollen ankles. It's not like I want him to be attracted to me or anything – I have Daniel, and things with Steve wouldn't have worked anyway. Probably. But still, I don't want him to look at me and wonder what he saw in me and want to vomit. That doesn't mean I feel anything for him.

I even told Daniel I would be seeing him, because couples shouldn't have secrets. My mom tells my dad everything, and he's in a coma. I definitely don't want to be one of those couples who skirt around issues. Except for the lying-about-therapy thing, but that's different.

'Just so you know, I've got to do some work with Steve again,' I said, stroking my tummy as we were watching TV.

Daniel had his laptop balanced on his knees. 'Who's Steve?'

'Oh, no one really. Just that guy I dated before I met you. Well, one date. One bad date. Nothing you should be jealous of.'

Daniel looked at me curiously. 'Did you sleep with him?'

'God, no,' I said. 'Of course not. What do you think I am?'

'You're a very sexual person, Julia. I can't expect you to have no past.'

I suppressed a burp – reflux is a bitch. 'Well, I didn't sleep with him.'

But now Daniel had some idea in his head, and he put aside his laptop. 'But you did sleep with other men before me,' he said, slipping his hand into my shirt and squeezing my breast. Which was agonising because it was so tender. I concentrated on not swatting him.

His voice was husky. 'You're so hot and horny,' he whispered in my ear. 'Maybe you should tell me about those other men. Tell me what they did to you. Tell me how many there were. Tell me how much you loved it.' He was nuzzling my neck and making me feel like I couldn't breathe, and then he looked up. 'Maybe there were women too?' He eyed me and tweaked my swollen nipple.

'No,' I said. 'No women.'

'You're a vixen,' he said, as if my answer was somehow sexy, and started pulling at my clothes. While he got on with things, I planned the baby's room in my head. I've been thinking shades of cream with green edging, not the stereotypical blue. I sighed and moaned at opportune moments, and he didn't seem to be able to tell the difference.

'Christ, you are so hot,' he said afterwards.

I nodded, feeling like I'd lost something and I didn't know what.

The next morning at breakfast, I say, 'So you're okay about me working with Steve?'

'Who's Steve?'

'No one. Forget it.' Although clearly he already has.

Claire

I'm late again dropping Nina at school and it's the worst day for this to happen. Straight after drop-off I'm meeting the other moms involved in planning the school fête, and they're all waiting, sipping their lattes, and I feel like they can look through me and know that I'm falling apart. But I say nothing, and they all leap up when I arrive and there's a lot of cheek kissing and hugging and moving around the table making space for me.

I wonder what everyone knows about me and Daniel. On one hand, I think I'm going to die of embarrassment when people find out not only that Daniel has left me, but that I haven't told anyone. I just couldn't talk about it at first – and anyway, it was Christmas and who talks to anyone around that time – and then time passed, and suddenly it was awkward to tell people because so much time had passed, and I was embarrassed and inexplicably ashamed. And now I'm even more embarrassed about having said nothing. But I know rumours must be out there. It's impossible that nobody has said anything, that nobody has seen Daniel and his pregnant girlfriend out and about, that people aren't speculating. Joburg can be a very small town. But nobody has said anything to me, and I almost feel hurt. These women are supposed to be my friends, but they haven't even broached the subject of my failing marriage. Nobody's asked if I'm okay, if I want to talk, except that bloody Mrs Wood.

But I smile as I sit down, and I order a skinny latte, and Janice comments that I hardly need it to be skinny and I briefly consider throwing her own skinny latte in her face, but instead I laugh and say, 'Habit,' and the others all laugh too, like I've said something genuinely funny.

A woman called Tiffany is the head of the fête committee. Her daughter's in a higher grade – I can never remember what grade or what the daughter's name is. Daniel knows Tiffany's husband, and over the years we've been at the same dinner parties. I should know her daughter's name. And she probably knows that my husband is living with another woman. I smile at Tiffany and she seems to take that as a sign that we're ready to begin.

'Ahem,' she says, tapping her knife on her latte cup, 'let's start, ladies.' She laughs, a strange snort, and says, 'I feel like a CEO,' and then does the snorty laugh again. I remember that I quite like Tiffany.

'So,' she says, 'who wants to kick off with some ideas?'

I sit back, because it's always me with ideas and I worry that I dictate to people, that I don't give other people a chance. But they all turn towards me.

'Claire,' says Tiffany, 'please tell me you've had your trademark brilliant idea.'

I sigh. 'I'm sure other people have lovely ideas. You all have such great taste and are so clever.'

The others look around and some shake their heads. Janice is suddenly fascinated by the sugar bowl. A woman called Marion I know from the PA has an urgent need to look for something in her bag. Nobody volunteers anything.

'Okay,' I say, bowing to the inevitable, and not sure if I'm pleased we'll be using my ideas or irritated that nobody else has bothered to have any. I haul my laptop out of my bag and open it. 'I've put together a Pinterest board, but the idea I had for our theme is "Old School Charm". Old-fashioned sweet stalls with jars, lots of bunting, blackboards as stall labels …' I start showing them the ideas I've pinned, and they all nod approvingly. Now that I've set the tone, other people contribute their thoughts, and Tiffany takes careful notes. By the end of the meeting we have a plan and a series of long to-do lists.

Afterwards, Tiffany hugs me warmly. 'I don't know how you do it, Claire,' she says. 'I don't know what we would do without you.'

'Oh, nonsense,' I say. 'Such a pleasure.'

As I turn to walk out, my cellphone beeps. It's a message from Daniel. Given how often he messages me, he is apparently unable to remember our child-sharing arrangements from one second to the next. I open the message.

'I thought you might want to know that Julia is having a boy.'

I stop in my tracks.

A boy. A little boy with Julia's beautiful hair and Daniel's brooding eyes. He'll be devastating. I feel sick.

I take a deep breath and push back my shoulders. The one good thing about communicating with Daniel is that he's the one person I don't have to pretend with any more, the one person I literally could not care about hurting – he has hurt me so badly.

Tiffany is still watching me, so I give a little wave before I type my answer.

'I don't give a fuck if your husband-stealing mistress is giving birth to a two-headed elephant.' I push send and smile.

TUESDAY

Catherine

I loved having dinner with Ewan and Okkie last night.

It was at their apartment in a gentrified part of Newtown with spectacular views over the city, and furniture I didn't realise actual people had in their homes. Okkie cooked a traditional Ugandan meal and we talked about everything – about Mike, about growing up gay, about growing up with albinism in Uganda, about studying medicine and practising medicine, about my years as an emergency nurse. Ewan couldn't believe that I'd given it up, so I explained a bit about The Accident, but obviously not everything. Never everything.

Okkie and Ewan are one of those couples that bounce off each other – they are funny and clever and say smart things that make me laugh. And suddenly I was also funny – I also had smart comebacks and clever thoughts. At the beginning of the evening I had thought that they'd regret inviting an old bore like me. But at the end of the evening, Okkie stretched out his long body, pushing back from the table.

'You are such fun, Catherine,' he said. 'I'm so glad Ewan made friends with you.'

It's been a long time since someone called me a friend. And even longer since I have been considered fun. But it's true that once, long ago, in the time of Mike-and-Cathy, I was a fun person. I was a person who had friends.

The last friend I had was after The Accident. It was a friendship born of grief.

The truck that hit us that night, that pinned us in the car for hours before help came, had a driver. A driver who, it emerged, was killed on impact. While I suffered through my private hell that night, a dead man I would never know lay near me. But he left a wife – a bright, clever, beautiful young wife who was bereft without him. And who carried, on his behalf, the guilt of what he'd done to me and my family.

The first time we met was at the hospital, when she came to my bedside and introduced herself, and then sat crying next to me.

'It's okay,' I said, although it wasn't. 'It wasn't your fault.'

'It was,' she sobbed. 'He was rushing to get home to me.'

I closed my eyes, unable to bear the idea that if this woman had not been loved, The Accident would not have happened.

'I'll never get over him,' she said. 'And I'll never forgive him for what happened.'

And with those words she won me over – and ensnared me. She would never be the same and I would never be the same, so we would be each other's friends. Our destroyed lives would degenerate together.

In the beginning it was exactly how I imagined. Nerina and I would meet, and we'd talk about how awful we felt and how we cried at night and how we hid our pain from our daughters – because Nerina also had a young daughter. We assured each other that we understood each other's grief because nobody else did. We both refused to go to support groups in the beginning, because we had each other and we felt unique in our misery and loss – both coated with guilt and horror.

Nerina came to my house and I went to hers. We met each other's daughters. We cried ourselves dry on each other's couches. I didn't need other friends, because I had Nerina.

And then, about six months after The Accident, Nerina told me she was going to a support group, and she asked me to join her. I felt hurt that I wasn't enough for her, that our friendship wasn't the only support she needed. But I agreed to try.

The support group was full of people who had ghastly stories, terrible losses. We sat in the ubiquitous circle, and each person shared their pain and what they called their 'journey'. And a pattern emerged – a pattern of recovery and healing. People talked about how, with time, it was getting easier. There was even a mother who'd lost two children, both to cancer, who said that she knew one day she'd be able to remember her children with peace, and she just wished that day would come. And I couldn't understand them at all. I knew that for me there was no journey towards peace and healing and happiness. For me there was just learning to live with the pain well enough to take care of Julia. That was all I could do. Until that moment I'd thought there must be lots of people like me – going through the motions, but dead inside. All the support group showed me was that I was alone.

As the stories moved around the circle, I became petrified that Nerina would tell her story, because her story was my story and Nerina knew everything. *Everything.* I did not want my story to be shared with these people. I was relieved when a few people shook their heads and remained silent, and then it came to Nerina and she opened her mouth to speak and I felt suffused with dread. But she said, 'Not this time,' and the circle moved on.

When Nerina and I got into my car – she avoided driving whenever possible – I was about to say, 'Well, that was ghastly. Never again,' but Nerina spoke first.

'That really helped,' she said.

'What?'

'It helped hearing that people feel better. That I will feel better. It gave me hope.'

I turned to look at her.

'Watch the road,' she said calmly.

'But what if we don't feel better? Those people … It was weird.' I couldn't verbalise it.

'We *will* feel better, Catherine,' she said. 'That's how grief works. We'll always be changed, but one day we won't wake up and want to die. I know that, and so do you.'

But I didn't know that. I was pretty sure, even then, that I would never feel better.

'Maybe it's different for me with Mike ...' I said.

'Maybe, but there was that guy whose wife had been demented for so long, and he's got a whole other life now.'

I didn't want to be like that man. I didn't want a whole other life. I wanted the life I'd had, the life Nerina's husband had stolen from me.

'Well,' I said, 'I'm not going back.'

'Okay,' said Nerina. 'But I am.'

It's not that Nerina and I stopped being friends then and there. We still saw each other for a while, and she phoned crying just like she always had. But over the next few months she started talking about feeling better. She started using phrases like 'moving on' and 'getting closure'. She went to a therapist, and I think the therapist told her I was bad for her, because she started contacting me less and less.

And I was glad. I didn't need friends. I couldn't have friends – I was too damaged. I had Julia, and I had Mike, and that would be enough.

And it was. Until now.

Suddenly I'm a person with friends again – not one set, but two. I know for other people this sounds like a poor allocation, but it's a bounty I had never expected to enjoy again. It makes me feel good, but also strange and guilty.

It makes me think that other people might say I'm moving on. But I know it's because of the baby; it's because I know I can die soon that I'm free to relax and make friends.

Nobody said life made sense.

Claire

The day starts badly. Nina's school has a sports day so I'll have to spend the afternoon watching. Which means less time to work, and I'd hoped to drop off a casserole at Ivy from pottery, because she's had a hip replacement and I'm worried she has too few people – except the other pottery widows – to help her. I sigh, thinking how in the old days I could've asked Daniel to take Nina to school to buy some time ... and then I realise I still can.

I think about phoning, but I have an absolute fear of hearing Julia's voice in the background or even worse, having her pick up the phone – as unlikely a scenario as that is. So I message him and I'm really nice, remembering that my last message wasn't exactly supportive.

'Any chance you could take Nina to school this morning? Bit swamped,' I type.

Within seconds, my phone beeps: 'Not today. Xx'

What the fuck? He hasn't even given a reason, and he has the audacity to send kisses. But then I wonder why I'm even surprised. It's typical Daniel – if something doesn't suit him, he just doesn't do it. He doesn't explain – he just says no. There must be a million examples of me asking for his help and him – charmingly, sweetly – shrugging it off. Even if he still lived with us, he wouldn't have taken Nina. He would have smiled, and laughed maybe, and said, 'Not today, babe,' and it would have turned out that he wanted to go to gym, or pick up a coffee, or he had a mad hankering for a scenic drive before work, or really just fancied a bit more sleep. Only occasionally was it an actual excuse – a meeting, or an appointment. I chose to see it as charming that he never lied. And I would shrug and smile, and rearrange my day to accommodate the task, telling myself that it wasn't that big a deal.

And suddenly I'm furious about all those excuses, all that selfishness. Daniel's charm no longer affects me.

'Julia is SO welcome to you, you selfish fuck,' I type.

I imagine Daniel's incredulity – he won't understand what's just happened. He'll look at his phone with his mouth slightly open, like a wounded puppy. I laugh out loud.

'You're so happy, Mommy,' observes Nina, dipping toast into her soft-boiled egg.

'Of course I am, Neens,' I say. 'I get to take you to school today.'

Nina nods, as if that does indeed explain everything. 'Poor Dad,' she says. 'He's really missing out these days.'

This time my laugh has a slightly hysterical edge. 'He really is,' I say, deciding to stop by the delicatessen after dropping Nina to buy Ivy a casserole . There's no rule that says helping has to be hard work. In fact, I'll also get one for my next-door neighbour, who was complaining how much she hates to cook the other day. Maybe I'll discreetly leave the shop's card in the bag. Give her an idea. And I'll put it all on the credit card that Daniel still pays. I don't even think he knows he pays it, because it goes through the business accountant. In the beginning I felt bad and only used it for Nina's things. But fuck that. In fact, I might take myself shopping for new clothes before sports this afternoon.

And because I'm now in a good mood, I send Daniel one more message, reminding him about sports day. He won't come, but it's not my fault.

Julia

I dress carefully this morning, knowing I'll be seeing Steve. It's not like I actually look good in anything – even my maternity clothes don't seem to fit me properly. If something fits my growing waist, then it's too tight on my boobs, and if it fits my boobs, then it billows – but in a frumpy-watermelon way, not in a boho-chic way. And the maternity fashions all seem focused on the wrong colours for me, so I look even more washed out than I actually am.

In an effort to hide my pregnancy acne and skin discolouration, I put on too much make-up and look like a clown. So I scrub it off, leaving my face glowing red and one of my many spots bleeding. I toy with the idea of becoming a religious Muslim for the duration of my pregnancy so that I can explain hiding my face with a scarf.

Eventually I kind of give up. I put on comfortable pregnancy leggings, even though I think they smell vaguely of pee, and pair them with one of Daniel's shirts and a string of fake pearls. I leave my glowing-red face, but add lip gloss. Looking in the mirror, I accept that Steve is not going to break down in tears at the thought of what he's missed. In fact, he might do a little happy dance. Who could blame him?

I arrive at work late and the meeting's already started. Gerald looks flushed and agitated when I walk in. My unofficial role in the firm is the people pleaser – the one who makes the small talk and adds the corporate gloss. In his dun-coloured cardigans peppered with dandruff,

Gerald is not going to win big contracts no matter how good he is at his job. And Steve's company is the biggest contract we've ever landed. We need to keep it.

Gerald jumps up when I enter the meeting room – a dull room furnished with what seems to be someone's old dining-room table, and which is currently dark because it hasn't occurred to Gerald or his secretary to open the blinds. I stroll over and try to make it look perfectly normal to start a meeting by letting in a bit of natural light.

'Oh,' says Gerald, delighted. 'That's what's wrong.'

I turn to face the room. Steve and his boss, Malcolm, are staring at me. I try to summon efficient Julia from somewhere in my psyche, and walk over to shake hands. The two men stand up, and we do firm, business-like handshakes all round, saying things like, 'Good to see you again.' And I can see that Steve, who is taller than I remember, is taking me in, in all my bloated pregnant glory. Suddenly I worry that he won't even realise that I'm pregnant; he'll just think that I'm really fat. Gerald soon sorts that out though.

'Julia's pregnant,' he says.

We're all a bit taken aback.

'Congratulations,' says Steve after what seems like hours.

'Yes,' says Malcolm. 'How wonderful.'

'Thanks,' I say, 'but please don't think that it will in any way impact on our service to you. Has anyone offered you something to drink?'

Of course no one has, so I bustle about organising teas and coffees with Ann, the secretary, who looks at me like I'm speaking a foreign language when I ask her to get them, and I end up writing down the order for her outside the door.

I come back in to the meeting room, where once again there's an awkward silence – Gerald's speciality.

'So,' I say, opening the file in front of me, 'let's talk.'

The meeting goes smoothly after that. Steve is mostly quiet, but Malcolm is obviously happy with what I'm saying. There's a stutter when

Malcolm closes the papers in front of him, and says, 'We're very happy with the work this firm has done so far – but it has been mostly Julia servicing our account. What's going to happen when she's on maternity leave?' He directs this question at Gerald, who looks as if he's never heard of such a thing.

'Maternity leave?' he echoes.

'Yes,' says Steve, in that dry voice I suddenly remember. 'You know, that thing where you're legally obliged to let people look after their newborn babies.'

I stifle a giggle – Gerald is looking appalled.

'Maybe,' continues Steve, 'you're planning to have Julia come in with the baby? Feed and change it between tax returns?'

Gerald looks at me hopefully, but I shake my head and turn to Malcolm.

'As you can probably tell,' I say, 'we haven't actually discussed the details of my maternity leave. However, I can assure you that Gerald is completely familiar with your company and in fact does most of the hard work on this account.'

That's not entirely true, but he is familiar with it, and he could do the work in his sleep. We just have to hire someone who can help him with working a computer. I decide not to mention that.

After the meeting I say goodbye as quickly as I can, and race to my office, relieved. But Steve follows me.

'So,' he says.

'So,' I answer, and I sit down at my desk with a sigh.

'I don't mean to pry or be inappropriate, but I'm guessing *this*' – he indicates my body in a vague gesture – 'has something to do with *us*. Or with what turned out not to be us.'

I force a smile. 'In a way. Although it only happened afterwards. I'm sorry.'

'There's nothing to be sorry for,' he says. 'You're glowing – pregnancy clearly suits you.'

I laugh. 'I am so *not* glowing,' I say. 'Well, not in a good way at least.'

'You look beautiful to me. Your partner is a lucky man.'

'Yes,' I say, but there's doubt in my voice and Steve raises an eyebrow. 'It's complicated.' And I'm thinking that Daniel hasn't ever said pregnancy suits me.

'What can be complicated about having a baby with a wonderful woman?' says Steve. 'Whatever the history is, I'm sure he's delighted.'

'I guess he is.'

'Well,' says Steve, 'I'm looking forward to working together again. We just better make a plan as to what will happen when you go on leave. I'm not sure I can handle Gerald for four months. Maybe we can hurry the work so I don't have to face that.'

We both laugh, and I remember how easy his laugh was. I remember how easy working with him was, except for the part where I became obsessed with him. But that's over now, and suddenly I'm looking forward to the next few months.

Claire

Somehow I get everything done. The last two of the weddings from the 'big batch' are this weekend, so I double confirm every detail and check in with both brides so that they feel cared for. Both want to chat, but I manage to cut them short, and there are no last-minute crises, which is almost unheard of for these weddings. But I also have to start mapping out the huge Farmer's Market Festival the hotel throws on its grounds every year – and I'm a bit behind schedule with that. Then I realise that some of my ideas for the school fête can double as ideas for the market – so I create a new Pinterest board and transfer some of the pins before sending the link to the hotel manager. Finally, I draw up a schedule of weddings at the wedding venue over the next two months – very few, as is usual at this time of the year – and I draft some tweets and Facebook posts about our new idea: 'Last-minute winter weddings'.

Then I go to the deli and buy casseroles for Ivy and my neighbour, and three for the freezer. I drop one off at Ivy, and I make us both a cup of tea. Ivy is cheerful in the face of her post-operative recovery, and is talking about starting yoga when her hip stops hurting.

'People do all *sorts* of things with their new hips,' she says. 'I want to be in on the action.'

I agree that I might do some yoga classes with her, and she claps her hands in delight and is soon tapping away at her phone to invite the other pottery widows. But talk of mutual friends leads us to Julia.

The widows are among the very few people who actually know what Julia did to me, and they were horrified when I told them. Grace was the saddest: 'She seemed like such a *nice* girl,' she kept saying. And Ivy, who I'm closest to, was the angriest: 'Little fucking bitch,' she said in her sweet-old-lady voice. 'Ah well,' said Liz, the widow who mourned her husband least – 'You're probably better off without him. Nothing like a man to cramp your style.' And then the three of them cackled like witches and even I laughed.

'Do you miss him?' Ivy asks me this morning, and it's a hard question. Late at night after a long day I miss him. I miss laughing with him, and the silliness, and that when he listened, he really listened. I miss sex. I miss knowing what tomorrow looks like.

But it's also easier. I just get on with things – I don't have to worry about where Daniel is and what meals he'll be home for and when he's doing what. As I saw this morning, it's not like he was ever that much help.

'Less than I should,' is what I eventually tell Ivy.

'Always the way,' she says philosophically. 'But he probably misses you.'

'Ivy,' I say, 'he's got a nubile young girlfriend who's funny and interesting and who thinks he's God. He's escaped the drudgery of daily fatherhood, for now at least. Compared to Julia, I'm old and I'm boring and I nag. I doubt he misses me at all.'

Ivy looks at me. 'You underestimate yourself, Claire. You're a very special person.'

'Daniel used to think so,' I say. 'Just not any more.'

Ivy nods, too wise to try to convince me otherwise. 'Then he's a fool, Claire. And there are lots of other men out there.'

'So, *so* not interested, Ivy.' Of the many scenarios I play out in my head at night, finding another man is not one of them.

After Ivy, I grab a sandwich for lunch, and then head back to the school for sports day. On the way, Daniel messages me: 'Can't make sports day. Sorry, babe.'

I'm actually quite impressed he thought to let me know. I'm less impressed that he's calling me 'babe', and that he doesn't think he maybe needs to up his game with Nina now that he sees her less.

I park at the school, and sit for a moment composing various responses in my head. Then it strikes me that I spend the most enormous amount of energy thinking of how to communicate with Daniel. So I just type, 'Whatever,' and send it.

But I feel heavy as I get out of the car. I'm tired deep down inside me, and now I have to face all these women. I sigh and hitch my bag over my shoulder.

There's no other option, so I glue on the smile.

But when I get to the field, I find myself faced with a choice after all. Most parents are casually sitting on the large steps designed for spectators. I can see Janice and Tiffany and a group of other moms I call friends sitting there together, and Janice waves to call me over. I can see from this distance how happy she is to see me – no doubt she has some charitable event she needs to discuss with me. She really is a very giving, involved person.

As I walk towards them, I notice that there are also a few parents scattered on the benches that run down the side of the field, basking in Joburg's warm winter sun. Up in front of me is a mother from our class called Laurel, sitting alone on a bench. Laurel doesn't like me, I don't think. I once saw her roll her eyes when I spoke at a class meeting, and she barely greets me even though I always say a chirpy, 'Hi there,' when I pass her. I don't know what I've done to her, but I try to shrug it off – we can't all like everybody. But as a result, I've avoided Laurel when I can.

But today the idea of sitting with someone who doesn't like me – who doesn't *want* anything from me – is strangely attractive. I approach the bench.

'Hi, Laurel. Can I sit here?' I say. I feel a bit nervous.

Laurel turns to me, and her eyes widen slightly.

'Claire,' she says, almost like she's identifying me to herself. She pulls her bag towards her to make room for me next to her. 'Sure, no problem.'

I sit down. Laurel is watching the girls, who are already on the field. The Grade 1s are sitting in their houses on the bandstands across the field. I squint till I find Nina, and wave. She waves back, with a big smile, and I feel warm. I blow her a kiss, and settle back on the bench. Out the corner of my eye, I can see Janice on the steps. She looks confused and I know I've done the wrong thing – I'd better get up and join them. Janice doesn't deserve to be hurt, and I can't possibly explain it all to her. Laurel's eyes follow mine.

'Your friends are over there,' she says as if she can't see me looking at them.

'Yes.' I try summon the energy to move.

'They look a bit anxious without you …' Laurel pauses for a moment, then adds, 'Actually, they *always* look a bit anxious without you.'

'How do you mean?'

'Like they're not sure what to do without your guidance,' she says. 'Like they don't know how to live when you aren't there to show them.'

'That's a bit harsh,' I say.

'Yes,' agrees Laurel matter-of-factly. 'It probably is.'

I look at her. 'You don't like us. You don't like *me*.'

Most people would splutter and protest if you said something like that. But Laurel doesn't.

'I don't know you,' she answers, unfazed. 'But you seem too good to be true. You always look lovely, you're cheerful, you organise things and I understand that you even work. Nobody's that good. I wonder about you.' Her voice is calm and level. There's no nastiness in it.

'You're very honest,' I say.

'Sorry.' She sounds abashed for the first time. 'I *am* too honest. People don't like it – my husband's always telling me to tone it down. I'm sorry if I've hurt your feelings – I'm sure you're very nice.'

I laugh. 'Actually, you *don't* think I'm very nice,' I point out. 'You just told me.'

She looks at me properly for the first time. 'And you don't mind?'

'You really *don't* know me,' I say. 'If you get to know me, and you still don't like me, maybe then I'll be bothered.'

'Okay,' says Laurel. 'When should we start?'

'Start with …?'

'Getting to know each other.'

I smile. 'It's okay. You don't *have* to. And there's a danger you might end up liking me, and then you'll turn into one of them.' I indicate Janice and company. 'You'll have to sit and talk to us and be on committees and, God help you, buy tickets to Janice's charities. Plus we have a uniform, you know.' It's true that Janice, Tiffany and I are wearing almost identical outfits, probably from the same shop. My tirade started as a joke but now I'm feeling defensive, and I don't know if I'm more angry at Janice and Tiffany, or Laurel, or myself.

Laurel chuckles. 'Shit, it's a real danger because I already like you better.'

My anger evaporates. 'You see?' I say. 'You're going to wake up in the middle of the night with a mad urge to buy a jacket exactly like mine. And theirs.'

'It *is* rather nice … So,' she says when she's recovered from laughing, 'why *aren't* you sitting with your sheep?'

I think carefully before I answer. 'Because they need me to be a certain person, and I'm not sure if she's still here.'

Laurel is interested now, and turns to me. 'Why?'

I pause for only a moment. 'Because my husband fucked one of my best friends and now they're having a baby and I don't know who I am any more.' I smile tightly, looking at the little girls on the field running a relay. 'You see,' I say. 'I'm not what I seem.'

I'm taken aback when Laurel laughs.

'That's nothing,' she says. 'I'm sleeping with the netball coach.' She indicates a slightly butch woman standing on the sidelines of the race track holding a flag – and carefully not looking at Laurel. 'You want to talk about not knowing who you are any more? I can talk about that all day.' She laughs. 'Unless Sandy calls. Apparently when Sandy calls, I'm unable to talk sense about anything.'

I'm staring at her open-mouthed. 'Really? Or are you just trying to shock me?'

'Are you shocked?' asks Laurel.

I'm still not sure if Laurel is baiting me. 'Of course I'm shocked! You don't expect to sit down next to a virtual stranger and discover she's doing the netball coach.'

Laurel throws back her head and laughs. Her salt-and-pepper hair catches the sun, and I'm suddenly aware of how careful my appearance is. Sandy-the-netball-coach turns to look at us, and I can see instantly that Laurel isn't lying.

'Oh my God,' I say, nudging her. 'It's true. You devil.'

'So,' says Laurel, 'if your sheep can spare you, want to go grab some supper tonight and talk about how we don't know ourselves?'

I look at Laurel. 'You know what, that sounds like a good idea.'

Julia

When I get home, I'm in a good mood for a change. The nice things Steve said to me have made me feel more attractive than I have for a while. And working with people other than Gerald always energises me. I even manage to stop at the shops on the way home to buy some food for supper. And Daniel's home when I get there, which is also a pleasant surprise. But Daniel is all glowering and sulky, and even though I try lift the mood by giving him a glass of wine and telling him to put his feet up (feeling like I'm Claire), he stays grumpy.

'Want to talk about it?' I say.

'About what?'

'About your bad mood.'

He sighs, and does seem to relax slightly. 'It's Claire.' He closes his eyes and puts back his head. 'She's so unreasonable.'

I feel a curl of hope begin to unwind in my chest. I've been very careful not to push Daniel, not to ask him when he's going to start his divorce proceedings. I tell myself it's enough that he's moved in with me, that it will all happen in good time. But it bothers me that he's never mentioned it in the five months he's been living with me, that there's been no talk of divorce and us getting married. He's lucky I'm not one of those people who feels strongly about being married when my baby is born – especially under the circumstances – but I still think about it. Quite a lot.

But obviously it's now happened. Suddenly it feels as if this is what all my anxiety and ambivalence has been about: I need Daniel to commit to our future by divorcing Claire. Once that happens, I will feel fully committed to Daniel.

I sit down next to him, and put my hand on his leg.

'Did you talk to her about the divorce?' I ask, trying to make my voice gentle.

Daniel opens his eyes. 'What?'

'Is she being unreasonable about the divorce?'

'What divorce?' says Daniel, his brow furrowed.

'The divorce you need to get so we can be together properly,' I say. I don't want to say the word 'married'. I don't even really need us to get married. But I'd prefer it if my live-in partner and the father of my child wasn't married to someone else. I like the sound of that in my head, so I say it aloud: 'I would prefer it if my live-in partner and the father of my child isn't married to someone else.'

Daniel looks at me like he's never seen me before.

'Oh,' he says. 'Of course. Yes. That's reasonable.'

'Yes,' I say. 'I think so. So will you talk to her?' Because clearly he hasn't.

'Yes, I guess I will. I guess I have to divorce Claire.' He sounds a bit incredulous, so I nod as if I'm dealing with a partially retarded child.

'Good,' I say. 'I'm glad we've got that cleared up.'

I wait a moment to see if Daniel wants to talk more, but he's closed his eyes again, so I get up and go to cook supper. But there's a spring in my step that wasn't there before.

It really has turned out to be a very good day.

Daniel

I don't want to divorce Claire.

Holy Christ, I don't want to divorce Claire.

How did this happen?

WEDNESDAY

Claire

I wake up with the most shocking hangover, convinced that the noise coming from next to my bed cannot possibly be the alarm. I've only just fallen asleep. But Nina is squirming next to me, and then emerges from under the duvet.

'School time!' she says brightly, which sends a shooting pain through my right eye. This would be the one morning of all mornings that she has decided to be perky first thing. 'Time to move it, move it.' She's stealing my lines.

I went out for dinner with Laurel just like she suggested. I could have asked Daniel to have Nina for the night, but that felt too complicated so I arranged a babysitter instead. I'm deeply regretting that now, but I had absolutely no idea how crazy the night would get.

I consider phoning Daniel to fetch Nina for school, but then he'll see the state I'm in, and that can't be a good idea either.

We started out at a lovely Italian restaurant I've been wanting to try. I wasn't sure how much I'd be drinking, and it was in a part of town I've never been to before, so thank goodness I took an Uber. I was scared we'd arrive at dinner and have nothing to say to each other and the rapport of the afternoon would be gone; I was scared Laurel would regret inviting me and write me off as another sheep. I haven't, I realised, made a new friend since Julia. And look how that turned out.

But it wasn't like that. We spoke like old friends from the moment we sat down, and we laughed and laughed and laughed. I laugh less without

Daniel, so it was intoxicating. And so were the two bottles of wine we shared. By the time we'd finished eating, I was very drunk.

'Let's go dancing,' said Laurel. 'When last did you go dancing?'

I thought, but I couldn't remember. It'd been a very long time.

'Where?' I asked. 'I don't even know where the places are.'

'Downstairs,' said Laurel. 'Sounds like it's pumping.' It's true there was a base reverberation coming through the floor.

Obviously I was going to object. School night. And I hadn't been to a club for years. I started to shake my head.

'Worried what the sheep will think?' said Laurel, seeing my hesitation.

'Fuck you,' I laughed. 'Let's do it!'

Which is how it came to be that half an hour later we were standing at a bar with three tequila slammers lined up in front of each of us, spurred on by a pair of men young enough to regard us as old. We looked at each other and shrugged before slamming back those tequilas. The rest of the night was a blur, but the young men never left our sides. I have a fuzzy memory of one trying to kiss me, and me explaining at great length about being married and being old and boring, but he still looked at me all doe-eyed and said, 'Whenever you're ready.' Oh Lord, I think I gave him my phone number.

And now I have the mother of all hangovers.

Somehow I manage to scrape myself together, and feed and dress Nina, who is annoyingly upbeat and filled with inane clichés I can't think where she's learnt. We get to school late again, and running to the classroom makes me want to vomit, but Mrs Wood seems to have given up hope in this respect, and just shrugs when Nina comes in.

I'm trying hard not to think about everything I have to do today. As I walk back to the car, I bump into Tiffany and Janice.

'Well, you and Laurel certainly seemed to have had a good time last night,' says Janice.

'I didn't even realise you were friends,' says Tiffany.

They are both wearing odd expressions, like they've carefully curated their faces. Maybe I just think that because of what Laurel said about them.

'How on earth do you know?' I say, forcing a smile.

Janice swipes at her phone. 'You posted about a million pictures on Facebook.'

I never put anything on Facebook. I look at it occasionally and 'like' things other people have posted, but I'm not a Facebook person really. I take Janice's phone, and sure enough I seem to have posted a whole lot of pictures between 11pm and 2am, all of me and Laurel and the two young men dancing, and taking stupid selfies, and generally falling about.

I don't know whether to laugh or cry. 'Oh God,' I say. 'I didn't even know I knew how to do that.'

Janice laughs, obviously deciding that the correct reaction is Good Sport. 'What? Have fun or post things on Facebook?' I can almost feel Janice crafting the story she will tell about 'How Absolutely Hilarious Claire Is'.

'Both!'

'Well, it looks like you had a ball,' says Janice.

'Ask us along next time,' says Tiffany. 'I haven't partied like that in years.'

'It was very spontaneous,' I say, a bit defensively. 'And the way I'm feeling today, I doubt I'll ever do it again.'

They both laugh, and I can see they've decided not to be offended.

Then Janice says: 'What did Daniel think about you being out so late? Dirk would go ballistic if I did that.'

I know I should just tell them. This secrecy is getting ridiculous. But if I say anything now, then there's going to be a whole intense conversation and they're going to want to go somewhere and talk, and all I want to do is to climb back into bed.

'Oh, you know Daniel ...' I wave my hands vaguely, hoping that I'm indicating Daniel's generally relaxed attitude. I must succeed because they both nod.

'You're so lucky, Claire,' says Tiffany. 'But you deserve it.'

They both hug me, and I feel awkward because I don't think I bathed when I came home and I must smell of alcohol and clubs. I say as much, and they seem to think that's hilarious.

'You're such a hoot,' says Janice.

'Always up to something,' says Tiffany.

I sigh inwardly. I have a feeling that wild girls' nights are on the cards for both of them.

Julia

I feel like seeing my dad today, and I know Wednesday afternoon is when my mom always goes, so I decide to pop in at lunch because I might bump into my mom when she arrives.

'I'm going to see my dad at lunch,' I tell Gerald. 'So I might be a little late back.'

'Right,' says Gerald, who's been treating me like royalty since I saved the meeting with Steve's company yesterday. 'Your dad's in a coma, right?'

'That's right, Gerald,' I say, because he seems to need to revisit this information often. 'But he can hear what we say, so we visit.'

'Right,' says Gerald.

'Right,' I say, because the habit seems to be catchy. 'Bye.'

I'm really looking forward to having this quiet time to speak to my father, to tell him my news and to feel what he thinks. His presence is always so powerful and so peaceful. I love the way I know he's there, at peace with the world like a Zen monk. Maybe I should start telling people that my dad *is* a Zen monk. It would be closer to the truth, really.

But when I walk into his room, it's about as un-Zen as can be. My mom is there, but she looks cheerful and a bit manic, so basically totally unlike herself. And there are two men – one caramel coloured and one with the stark pale of albinism.

'Who are these people?' I say to my mom, who looks flustered by my appearance.

'My friends,' she says. 'Ewan, Okkie, meet my daughter, Julia.'

I don't know which one is which, and I don't care.

'What's going on?' I ask, not even looking at the strangers. 'Why are they here?'

I take in the room. There's a basket of food on the ground, and a bowl of chips balanced on my dad's knees. Not Zen then.

'Are you having … a picnic … on Dad's body?'

'Don't be ridiculous,' says Mom, grabbing the bowl of chips.

The caramel-coloured man steps forward, his hand outstretched so that I'm forced to shake it.

'I'm Ewan Marigold,' he says. 'I work with Catherine, and she mentioned that she wouldn't be able to see your father today because she saw him on Monday. So I suggested we all come and have lunch with him.'

Mom turns to me and her eyes are shining. 'And then I remembered, Julia, how much Dad loved having spontaneous lunches. Sometimes he'd wait outside the hospital with a basket of food, and we'd spend my lunch break in the park. He loved doing that.'

My mother never tells me anything about my father before The Accident. I have a tiny list of things that I've gleaned about him, and now I have this new thing: he loved spontaneous lunches. It makes me feel uncomfortable, even though it's a nice thing.

Then the other man steps forward. 'I'm Okwango,' he says. 'Ewan's boyfriend. But people call me Okkie.' He too sticks out his hand. 'We are so excited about your baby.'

'My baby?' I echo, like it's news to me.

'Your mother told us,' says Ewan. 'It's so lovely. She's so excited.'

I look at my mother, incredulous, and she blushes. I can't even process her right now. I search my mind for what's bothering me and eventually realise: my mother is acting like a normal person. With emotions. And friends. Quite exotic friends at that.

'Are you drunk?' I ask her. It's the only explanation.

'Don't be ridiculous,' she says, but her eyes stray to a bottle of wine sticking out of the food basket. And she sees me watching her, and she giggles. I need to sit down.

And just as I'm feeling like the world can't get any weirder, a man's head appears around the door.

'Hi there, Cath,' he says. 'Heard the laughter – thought I'd say hi.' The man is about my mom's age. He's good-looking, like an ageing rock star. But like an ageing rock star he looks tired and worn out. Maybe he *is* an ageing rock star, given how weird this is.

And then my mom walks over to him, and takes him by the arm, pulling him into the room. I've never seen my mother touch a stranger – not even my friends when I was at school – so my mouth falls open. And then she starts introducing this ageing rock star to the other two, and the room is full of people shaking hands and saying, 'Nice to meet you,' and, 'Heard so much about you,' but I've never heard about any of them. It's like I've stumbled into a cocktail party I wasn't invited to. I wonder what the nurses think.

I sink into a chair and look at my dad. His face is restful. He's lying there still and peaceful, like he always does. He's not judging my mother for her outlandish behaviour; he is, in fact, Zen. I focus on him and let the room wash over me.

And then there's a new flurry, and Ewan and Okkie are wiping the crumbs out of the chip bowl, and the ageing rock star says something about going to see someone called Miriam, and my mom kisses my dad goodbye, and in the chaos gives me a kind of affectionate pat on the shoulder, and then they all start saying how late they are for work, and they leave en masse.

And I'm left, like the flotsam of the party, looking at my peaceful father.

'What the fuck was that, hey, Daddy?'

I can almost feel him laugh.

Catherine

I had no intention of seeing Mike today. I saw him on Monday, and that had me staring into space thinking my own thoughts. I couldn't take off another afternoon anyway, and I promised myself I would see him on Thursday evening. It's tough knowing he's awake inside, and that he waits for me and misses me, and I can't get there always. I used to go every evening – even if it was sometimes only for a few minutes when Julia was little – but over the years that has lessened. But if I'm honest with myself, with all these worries about Julia, I've seen Mike less in the last few months than I ever have before.

But I know he understands. Even though we haven't talked about it, he must know that I'm preparing for us to leave the world together. And to do that, I need to make sure that Julia is okay.

I was thinking these thoughts when Ewan came out of the consulting rooms mid-morning.

'Wednesday, Catherine,' he said. 'Off to see Mike this afternoon?'

'Not today,' I answered. 'I took my half-day on Monday so I'll miss today.'

I must have sounded upset about it. Or maybe Ewan Marigold is just the sort of man who is always looking to help people.

'Okkie and I are going out for lunch,' he said. 'Do you want to join us?'

'Won't I be intruding?' I said. 'Third wheel?' I feel like this a lot –

like I would be more socially acceptable if I had Mike alongside. I even spoke about it with Okkie and Ewan that night at their place. And Ewan obviously remembered, because next thing he said, 'I have the best idea. Let's visit Mike. We need to meet him, and what better time.'

And then before I could even answer, he disappeared.

After his next consultation, he stopped by my desk.

'So,' he said. 'Dr Vermeulen's daughter is coming in for an hour, so we can take a long lunch and she'll man the desk. And Okkie's bringing a picnic we can take to Mike.'

I don't know how he organised all that and saw a patient in the space of one consultation, but it was too late for me to voice any objections. I'd never done anything like this before, so I had no idea what Mike would think. But, I reasoned, maybe it would startle him out of his coma. Maybe this was the kind of thing that I'd missed. Mike was a social guy when he was awake, so why would that have changed? And suddenly I remembered how much Mike loved surprising me with picnics. It was his thing. I haven't thought about it for years. It seemed so obvious suddenly, so I smiled warmly at Ewan. 'That'll be great,' I said.

And it *was* great. Mike didn't wake up, but Ewan and Okkie are so easy and fun that I relaxed. And then Julia arrived and I felt almost like part of a normal family, introducing people, and when Edward popped in it was complete. A really good afternoon.

But it's left me feeling flat and doubtful. Suddenly all the choices I've made all these years, the careful way Julia and I have lived to avoid pain, seem hollow.

I should have found a way to keep Mike at home with us.

I should have had a busy, happy life going on around Mike, with guests and Julia's friends. *My* friends.

I should have pulled myself together, and held the grief further apart.

I should have had therapy.

I tell myself that I did the best that I could, that my grief was too heavy, that I was too broken from those hours in the car. I did my best.

And as I listen to my inner voice, I realise something. I'm thinking about my grief and my pain – my whole identity – in the past tense.

And once I realise that, I don't know what to think.

Claire

I was intending to carry on with my day through the hangover. I have a meeting with a client and I need to plan a Twitter schedule and also bake some scones for the PTA meeting this evening. But when I get into my car, I can't face any of it.

I cancel the meeting, let the PTA know that neither I nor my scones will be able to make it tonight, and I head home, intending to sleep.

I actually change back into my pyjamas – I don't like sleeping in clothes and I really like my pretty pyjamas – and I climb into bed. But then I can't sleep because my brain is all over the place: last night, Daniel, Janice and Tiffany, work. Nina, always Nina. And then my phone beeps and I'm almost grateful I have a legitimate reason not to sleep.

It's a message from Laurel, and I open it expecting a standard, 'Thank you, had a nice time', sort of message. But instead it says, 'Received a Facebook friend request from every single one of your sheeple. What to do?'

I laugh. 'Accept them,' I type back. 'They're nice if you give them a chance.'

She's typing an answer before I can even think about putting down the phone. 'Will I have to wear the uniform?' she asks.

'Oh, definitely. We do inspections every Thursday. Hey, did we get run over by a truck last night?' I type. 'I feel terrible.'

Laurel takes a few minutes to respond and I wonder if I've somehow said the wrong thing. But then her message comes.

'Sorry. Had to have a vomit. You were saying …'

I laugh out loud, and send a crying-laughing emoji. As I'm waiting for her to type, another message comes through on a number I don't know:

'Hi Claire. Rob here. From last night. Want to go out some time?'

I quickly message Laurel: 'Which one was Rob?'

'Why?'

'He wants to go out some time.'

'He was the really hot one.'

I turn to my photos of last night. The guys look equally hot.

'Can't tell which is hotter,' I type. Then I pause. Why does it even matter – it's not like I'm going to go out with anyone. 'Just realised it doesn't matter,' I message Laurel.

'That's the spirit,' she answers. 'Go out with either!' She follows that with a whole lot of eating, drinking, dancing emojis.

'As if,' I type.

I'm about to respond to this Rob person when my phone rings. It's Daniel. But there's no point putting it off.

'You seem to be having a fun time,' he says before even saying hello.

'Sorry, what?'

'Facebook,' he says. Christ, is everyone in the world glued to Facebook twenty-four seven, waiting for Claire Marshall to post something?

'Can I help you, Daniel?'

'No need to be grumpy.'

'I'm not grumpy. I'm tired. You know, from having a rare bit of fun last night.'

'Who're the guys?' asks Daniel. I can hear that he's keeping his voice carefully neutral.

'Just some guys,' I answer. 'Did you phone me for a reason or just to interrogate me?'

'Just showing some interest,' he says.

'Well, don't,' I say.

'Okay, well, I wanted to know if you could keep Nina this weekend. Julia's really frazzled and having Nina around is very tiring for her.'

I pause. 'I'd love to help out your pregnant back-stabbing mistress, Dan,' I say. 'But I've got a date with one of those guys from last night. So you'll just have to take care of your daughter.'

'Which guy?'

'The hot one.'

'Oh,' he says, and I'm tempted to ask him if he knows which one that is. 'Which night?'

I improvise. 'We haven't decided. Both, maybe.'

'Isn't Nina more important than a date with some gigolo?' asks Daniel, and I remember how irritating he is when he uses a calm voice when he's upset. 'And just so you remember, we're still married.'

'Isn't Nina more important than Julia's precious moods?' I ask. 'And being married didn't bother you when you started fucking Julia, so spare me.'

'I can hear you're upset,' says Daniel, still using his I-am-reasonable-and-calm voice. 'We can talk when you're more rational.'

'It's like you can't recognise that *you're* actually the person one hundred per cent in the wrong here,' I say. My voice is also calm now, because I'm more incredulous than angry. 'Like you think *you* can have sex and a baby with another woman, but *I'm* the irrational one. I actually don't know who you are any more, Daniel.'

He is silent for a moment, and when he speaks, his voice is sadder. Like he's about to cry. 'I don't know either, Claire. I don't know how we got here.'

For a moment I feel sorry for him. But then I remember.

'Ask Julia,' I say. 'Ask Julia how you got here.'

I don't feel like speaking to him any more, so I put down the phone.

Julia

I'm in a strangely good mood after the lunchtime visit to my dad. After-wards, I went and bought some attractive maternity clothes so I can feel better about myself. I also bought some pricey liquid foundation the shop assistant swore will hide my pregnancy-raddled skin. And to top it off I bought a pair of enormous sunglasses that glamorously hide my blotchy cheeks. Back at the office, Gerald didn't say a word about the fact that I'd basically taken a three-hour lunch. He smiled anxiously, and I went into my office and ploughed through more work than I've managed in the last three months.

When I get home, Daniel's already here. He's standing at the entrance like he's been waiting for me, looking uncharacteristically worked up.

'I tried to get Claire to keep Nina this weekend,' he says before I've even put down my keys. 'But she was totally unreasonable about it.'

'Why did you want her to have Nina?' I say, pushing past him to offload my shopping and myself on the couch.

'Well, you're feeling so sick,' he says, following me. 'You need to rest.'

'Actually, I'm feeling better than I was.' I realise as I say it that it's true. I've got through a day without feeling sick or wanting to vomit or thinking I might fall asleep at my desk. Granted it was a weird day with my mother's behaviour, but still. Maybe I should ask my mom to behave strangely more often. It seems to give me energy.

'Well,' says Daniel, 'Claire was totally unsympathetic about how you're feeling.'

That stops me in my tracks. I look at him. 'You told Claire that *I* didn't want to have Nina?'

Daniel shrugs.

'But, Daniel, I would *never* stop Nina visiting. I love having her here, and that aside, she's your daughter.' I feel fury building up inside me. 'I cannot *believe* you would make Claire think I am so selfish. I cannot *believe* you would make me look so bad. I actually don't even know why you're discussing me with Claire at all.'

'Anyway,' says Daniel as if I haven't spoken, 'Philip's invited me to the cricket on Saturday and I have a brunch on Sunday with a client from the States.'

'None of which I'm invited to?'

'Well, someone has to look after Nina,' he says, but he looks shifty. I wasn't invited anyway.

'So it didn't suit you to have Nina, so you tried to blame it on me.' I'm not asking him. I'm just stating it as it is.

'Claire is very unreasonable,' Daniel repeats, as if in justification.

'For Christ's sake,' I explode. 'You left her for another woman who is now pregnant. How reasonable is she supposed to be?'

Daniel looks like I've slapped him. 'Whose side are you on?'

Part of me is tempted to reassure him, but suddenly I'm tired. *'Mine,'* I say, and my voice isn't even angry. 'I'm on *my* side, because no one else is.' I walk past him into the bedroom, close the door, and kick the box, which still hasn't been unpacked. Then I send two messages I never would have imagined sending.

The first is to my mom.

'I liked your friends,' I type. 'I think Daddy enjoyed having lunch.'

And then I take a deep breath and type a message to Claire. It's the first time I've communicated directly with her since Daniel left her.

'I just want you to know that I didn't ask Daniel to cancel Nina. She is always welcome. Daniel is busy so she'll mostly be with me, but if that's okay, I would love her to come stay this weekend.'

I push send. I plan to wait for an answer, but instead I fall asleep fully clothed, and I don't even wake up when Daniel covers me with a blanket and climbs into bed next to me.

Claire

When the phone beeps, I almost don't look at it. It feels like it's been beeping at me all day. Over and above the usual emails and meeting requests and school WhatsApp groups, I've had Janice already planning a girls' night, as predicted.

I know I'm being mean, but in her position I'd have been more subtle – waited a few weeks before trying to resurrect the event I was left out of. I feel a bit irritated with her for being so clueless, but also protective of her for being so transparent. And I've had Laurel sending me texts all day that make me laugh, because she doesn't ask me for anything. She's just really funny. Mostly about my friends, so I feel a bit guilty enjoying it so much, but she is so right. And I've had this man called Rob who won't take no for an answer.

After I spoke to Daniel, I briefly considered actually going on a date with this Rob person. At the very least it would solve the mystery of which is 'the hot one'. But the truth is, whichever one it is, he's too young for me. And more specifically, the thing Daniel pointed out is true: I'm married. I know I have the moral high ground here, that if I want to sleep with an entire rugby team I'm actually free to do so. But still. And even though it must be coming, we haven't spoken about a divorce.

And I'm a mother. I'm not some fancy-free person who can take on a toy boy. I told Rob all of this, but he seems to have taken my explanation as an invitation to chat because he keeps texting reasons why we should 'hook up' – his words, not mine. I'm not even sure if 'hook up' means have coffee or have sex. At this stage it doesn't matter, because I'm saying no to both. But it is kind of flattering the way he keeps at it, without being disrespectful. After all, I *am* his elder.

So I presume that the new message is one of these things, and my head is pounding and I'm so, so tired, so I ignore it for a bit. But then I think that maybe it's Laurel, and maybe that will cheer me up, or maybe it's something really urgent, so I look at it. And it's Julia.

My first reaction is that I cannot believe her cheek. If she needs to say anything to me, she can say it through Daniel. I almost delete it without reading it, but my curiosity gets the better of me.

After I read it, it's like I'm feeling so many different things at once that I can't feel anything. It's even more conflicted than how I feel about poor Janice's girls' night out. There is anger with Daniel. No, not anger – that's too mild. It is intense, burning rage. But there's also a streak of amusement in the rage, because it's so typical of Daniel to try to rearrange the world to suit himself without actually taking the blame. And there's shame that I've been so harsh towards Julia in my thoughts. And pity – pity for Julia, that she's found herself in this strange hinterland of my marriage. And admiration that she has the guts to send me a message, because that can't have been easy. Part of me wants to pick up the phone and just chat to her, pretend that nothing's changed, and have a few laughs. Maybe tell her that everything's going to be okay. Instead, I just text her.

'Thanks for letting me know. It probably makes more sense for me to keep Nina this weekend, but I appreciate what you've said.'

I want to say more, and I stare at the message for a long time before I send it. But there's no point – Julia and I can never be friends again. We must just be civil for Nina's sake. This is a good thing Julia has started.

Once I finally send the message, I sigh. Now I need to plan a fun weekend for Nina. Before Daniel left, I didn't feel this particular pressure. Our weekends kind of happened. And in a way they still do, but I'm more aware of the hours. I'm more aware of planning, making sure we're busy, being the better parent.

After I send the message to Julia, I can't settle. All evening I'm jumpy with Nina, who then insists on having four stories read to her before bedtime, and after I get her to sleep, I keep checking my phone. I don't expect to hear from Julia again – and I can see she hasn't even read the message. For a moment I think it's because she's too busy fucking my husband, but then I realise that, given the message, it's more likely they're fighting. That should make me feel better, but it doesn't.

Eventually, despite the hangover and despite feeling tired and groggy, I sit down with my phone and diary and laptop. First, I send out some messages to make arrangements for the weekend. Then, I do some of the work I should have done today. When I realise that sleep is still eluding me, I end up baking scones anyway, and I divide them into batches. Ivy could use some, and so could Liandri. And I can freeze some so that we're ready for any surprise visits.

When the scones are done, I finally feel ready to go to bed. As I lie down, the phone beeps again. It's that Rob character.

'Just think about it.'

That's the thing, I muse, muting my phone. I haven't thought about him for hours. I'm knee-deep in surviving my life.

THURSDAY

Catherine

I am not one of these people who is always on their phone. I don't do any of these social media things that people seem so fascinated by, and I don't have lots of friends who message and WhatsApp me. I have a phone because of Julia, and because the home might need to contact me about Mike – although that has never happened in all these years. But they might. Like if he wakes up – I'd be really sorry to I miss that call and only get there a few days later. Can you imagine? So, I have a phone.

But this morning there are not one but three messages for me. 'An embarrassment of riches' is the phrase that goes through my head, and then I feel confused that I am regarding this as 'riches' rather than a bother and a distraction.

The first message is from Julia. She sent it yesterday but I didn't notice it. It says that she liked my friends and that she thinks Mike enjoyed the lunch. First, I laugh out loud with delight. At the sound, I look around. When last did I laugh by myself? The sound echoes off my walls, looking for a place to hide. But I am really so happy that Julia has said something nice about my friends. Or maybe I'm just happy that she sent me a message that wasn't about a practical arrangement. I'm not sure when last that happened either. And I still feel sort of amazed that I am a person with friends.

I type, 'They're not friends, they're just some people,' but that feels ungracious and untrue, so I delete it. I type, 'They liked you too,' but that

154

sounds trite and a bit dishonest because Julia didn't really interact with them. She just sat there all bug-eyed. I giggle again.

I try, 'Thanks,' but that sounds too bland – I want to communicate how happy she has made me. I decide to wait till I know what to say.

The next message is from Okkie. This is the first time Okkie has contacted me directly. He says, 'Thanks for letting us meet Mike. Xx.'

I feel so touched, and kind of awed by a life in which I have this gay Ugandan man as a friend.

'Thanks for wanting to meet him,' I message back.

Why is it easier to speak to Okkie than Julia? That can't be right. I try for a moment to think what to say to Julia, but nothing comes, so I look at the last of my three messages.

This one is from Edward, inviting me to a family lunch on Saturday: 'I'm thinking that if they meet you, they'll understand better about people in our situation,' he explains.

I'm a bit thrown. What exactly is he asking me? To come to lunch and be miserable so his family can see that this is normal? To come to lunch and be sociable so they can see that *I* am normal? To come to lunch and speak with expertise about the dull, lonely life of a person married to a person in a coma? To give them hope?

'I'll phone you later,' I type back to Edward. Maybe I'll feel more comfortable if he can explain what he wants from me.

I turn back my attention to the challenge of Julia's message. I ask myself what I *really* want to say. What I really want to say is that I love her. So I write it.

'Thanks. I love you.'

But this isn't how Julia and I are. We don't do 'I love you's' and hugs and things. I'm worried it sounds insincere. I'm about to delete it but my finger slips on the screen and the message is sent. I think about messaging her again, telling her to ignore the last message.

But on a balance, that would probably be weirder.

Claire

Thank God I'm feeling better today. I get Nina and myself up well in time for school, and Nina also seems easier than usual. There's a moment when she can't find her pink-striped panties – the only pair she will currently wear – but by some miracle I convince her that the blue-striped panties will do. This is an achievement I have never managed before.

I pack up the scones for Ivy and Liandri, and I pop one into Nina's lunch box, together with her usual sandwich and snacks. I don't know if she'll like it, but it's nice to give her something different.

I'm hoping that by getting to school a bit early, I won't run into anyone I know, because I want to use this energy to get back on top of my work. But when we pull into the car park I see Janice's car is already there. I wonder if I can dodge her, but the thing about Janice is that she always finds me.

I take Nina up to her classroom, and Janice isn't there, so I spend a few minutes catching up with the new art on the walls, letting Nina show me hers. This she does with expansive arm movements and announcements of, 'This is my one. It's the best.' But eventually I have to leave, and as I'm walking down the path, I spot Janice lurking at the end. I take a deep breath.

She feigns surprise when she sees me, and we air kiss.

'I'm so sorry I haven't got back about the girls' night,' I start, but Janice interrupts me.

'Oh, Claire,' she says, touching my arm. 'I'm so sorry but that's off.'

I'm not really sure how to react but she barely gives me time to.

'I was telling Dirk about it last night, and he got upset when I said I needed some excitement. So he's taking me to Italy for a week without the kids.'

I'm about to comment that it really isn't the same thing at all, and how typical of a man not to get that a night with friends fulfils a totally different need, but then I notice that Janice is beaming.

'That's lovely,' I say. 'I love Italy.'

'It will be so glamorous and romantic and spontaneous,' says Janice. 'And I'll post lots of photos on Facebook so you can all share it with me.'

Of course, I realise – this isn't actually about spending time with friends. It's about doing something that other people will look at with envy.

'I'm rather jealous,' I say, suspecting that's what she wants to hear. 'I *love* Italy.'

'You must give me a list of your best places,' says Janice, her smile so wide I'm worried it will damage her. 'And I'll tag you when we go.'

'Lovely,' I say. 'You're a lucky girl.'

'I know!' She's actually hugging herself with glee. 'And it's all thanks to you.'

'Oh, nonsense.' I want to say it's all thanks to her overwhelming need for attention, but instead I say, 'It's thanks to your lovely husband. I can't wait to see the pics.'

Janice almost skips off, no doubt to find someone else to tell her news to, and I'm left feeling strangely empty. I might question Janice's motivation, but it *would* be nice to be jetting off to Europe with a husband who wants to make me happy. I know Janice is excited for reasons I don't really get, but she's excited, and her husband did that for her. Maybe he even knew exactly what she needed to get out of the trip. Daniel used to be like that with me. He was always surprising me and whisking me off to interesting places. And it would always be fun because he'd be attentive and amusing and sexy and charming. Recently I've been thinking so much about the bad side of Daniel that I've forgotten the things I fell in love with – the humour, the spontaneity, the quirkiness. Life with Daniel was never boring. I can't say the same about life alone.

I'm so deep in thought I don't see Laurel till she's almost on top of me.

'Dear Lord,' she says. 'I just bumped into Janice.'

'Yes.' I smile. 'She's going to make sure she bumps into everyone this morning.'

Laurel laughs. 'I wish I'd known that a week in Italy was a viable alternative to a girls' night. I would've dumped you like a hot potato.'

'Then I'm glad you didn't know. I had fun. Even if the hangover and the fallout from Facebook have been terrible.'

Laurel suddenly freezes. 'Sandy's coming,' she hisses. 'Do I look okay?'

'You're mad,' I say, because I don't really know what I think. It's not that Sandy is a woman; it's that Laurel is married, and my husband also left me for another woman.

Laurel cocks her head. 'You don't approve?' I'm not sure if her tone is amused or defensive.

'It's hard for me,' I say. 'Remember, I'm the cuckold in my situation. I think you need to make a decision.' I'm smiling but I know I look sad. 'I guess I don't approve of the lies. I suppose that proves everything you always thought about me.'

Laurel glances up to make sure Sandy is still far enough away. 'I actually agree with you, Claire. I just don't seem able to implement it.'

'That's always the bummer,' I say. 'I'll leave you to it then.'

'Coffee later?' says Laurel.

'Lovely,' I say, and I mean it. 'Call me when you can.'

We give each other a quick hug, and then Laurel walks towards Sandy, and I head back to my car. And just as I start to breathe a sigh of relief that I can get on with my day, I bump into Tiffany.

'Hon,' she says, 'you're just the person I needed to see.'

My brain darts around – have I promised to action something for the fête that I've forgotten about? Have I promised to support some cause?

'We're having a little dinner party on the fifteenth,' says Tiffany. 'I'd love it if you and Daniel could join us.'

Of course this isn't the first social obstacle I've faced. In the last few months, I've been to two dinner parties, pretending that Daniel is busy at work or away. I've been to a lunch on the same pretence, and made excuses for a few other invitations. But suddenly I'm tired. I've never had much patience for people who lie, and yet here I am, living a lie every day. And why? Because I'm scared of what people will think? I've always thought I don't really care what people think, that I'm secure enough in my own self. I guess that's not really true after all, because why else have I kept such a big secret?

I make a decision.

'Tiffany,' I say, 'I would love to come to your dinner party – you always throw such a fabulous do. But Daniel and I have separated, so he won't be able to join. I understand if that throws your plans and you don't want me to come alone. So let me know.'

Tiffany's mouth falls open, but I don't let her speak.

'Gotta go, chat soon,' I say, almost running away.

I know Tiffany will spread this news faster than I can say 'Boo', and some people are going to be upset that I haven't told them personally. So I quickly type a message on my phone and send it to about ten people I consider reasonably close friends: 'Just to let you know, Daniel and I have split up. I haven't wanted to talk about it, and still don't really want to. But just so you know. Xx.'

I push send. And wait.

Julia

I wake up feeling that strange grogginess that comes, ironically, from too much sleep. My bladder is bursting – I don't think I've slept through the night without a bathroom visit for the last four weeks. There's a pain in my ribs. It feels like the baby has wedged his foot into my bones, which can't be possible because, depending on which source you read, he's only the size of a banana or a mango. I don't know who regards bananas and mangos being a similar size – is my baby a fat mango or a skinny banana? I grab my phone as I run to the toilet, wanting to look up the baby's developmental stage of the day. Could his banana feet be stretched out of his mango body and hooked in my ribs?

But there's a message from my mother that makes me sit down hard on the toilet seat.

'Thanks. I love you.'

I must have misread who the message is from – maybe it's from Daniel, or a friend. But no. It's from my mother.

My mother has never in my life told me she loves me. I mean, I know she does, insofar as she is able, which isn't very far. Jane says I don't give her enough credit, that her whole life is a testament to her love for me, and that some people can't express emotions. Which is crap, because she tells my dad she loves him every time she says goodbye. But even if we're giving her the benefit of the doubt, she still never says it to me. Especially not as a throwaway response to an SMS. It's just not something that happens. But it has.

And then I realise: something must be wrong. Very wrong.

I phone her, right there, sitting on the toilet.

'Is Dad dead?' I say as soon as she answers.

'What?' Her voice is sleepy. I've woken her. That's never happened before either – my mother isn't a big sleeper.

'Is it you? Are you sick? Is it cancer?'

'Julia,' says my mother, her voice stronger. 'Have you been drinking? Or have you taken something?'

'Of course not – I'm pregnant and it's 6.30am.'

'Then why are you sounding so crazy? Of course Dad is not dead. Of course I don't have cancer.'

'Then why did you send me that message?'

And suddenly it's quiet between us. Because I've bought truth into the spotlight – that a message from my mother telling me she loves me can only signify a crisis.

'Oh,' she says. 'That.'

Neither of us know what to say, obviously. Eventually I break what feels like several years of silence. 'So, you're okay?'

'Yes,' she says, 'I'm fine. And so is Dad.'

'Okay. Well, just checking. Bye then.'

There's another short silence.

'Bye,' says my mom.

Only after that do I look at my other messages. Claire has responded with her perfect blend of politeness and graciousness. I read her message several times, but I can't fault her.

When I get to the kitchen, Daniel is drinking a cup of coffee. I don't want to be cross with him any more, but I find I still am. To try change that, I touch his shoulder and he reaches for my hand.

'I told Claire the situation,' I say. 'She's keeping Nina this weekend.'

Daniel lets go of my hand. 'You spoke to Claire?'

'Well, I messaged her and she messaged back. We all need to be civil if we're going to put Nina's interests first.' Which is a bit ironic, because of course it's Claire and me who are putting Nina's interests first – Daniel's just doing whatever pops into his head.

'You think I'm a bad person,' he says, looking at me in that intense way he has.

I have to think about that. 'I guess I'm just finding out you're not quite the saint I thought you were,' I say slowly. 'I guess that's part of getting to know someone.'

Daniel stands up and I think he's angry; I think he's going to walk away. But then he puts his hands on my waist – or the place where I used to have a waist – and he says in a husky voice, 'What did I do that made you think I was a saint?' His one hand creeps round to my breast, and the other one pulls me against him so I can feel his erection. 'I'm no saint,' he whispers. 'I am so bad.'

I really, really don't want to be turned on by him. I really want to be angry. But apparently, along with my new energy, I've finally hit the stage of pregnancy I've read about where you're interested in sex again. Very interested.

I resist for a moment, but I can't. 'Show me,' I whisper. 'Show me how bad you are.'

So he does. And I'm late for work. On the good side, I'm in a better mood than I've been in for weeks and it's taken my mind off my mother. On the bad side, I'm still cross with Daniel. Apparently great sex doesn't make that go away.

Claire

When I sit down to work, I realise that I'm not as in control of my diary as I usually am. I haven't written in some of Nina's school things, and I need to fill in the change to the childcare arrangements. When I open the diary, the first thing I see is that Nina's on holiday next week. I'd completely forgotten because it's not the usual holiday time, but an extra week off because of some course the school is sending all the teachers on. So now, not only do I have to keep her entertained all weekend, I also have her at home all of next week. It suddenly seems too much – and for a moment I just want to give up. But it's not my style, and I have no real choice.

'Nina is on holiday next week. Want to take her for a few days?' I text Daniel, even though this kind of thing isn't in the agreement set out by my dad's lawyer. This separation business should also work for me. And anyway, Daniel needs to make up the time he's missing this weekend.

'Sorry, babe,' he texts back almost immediately. 'Busy week.'

He's still calling me 'babe'. I look around my office as if there's someone I can tell, but the downside of self-employment is that there never is. 'Babe,' I spit at the computer, which remains impassive.

Between Janice going to Italy, and telling Tiffany and everyone else the truth, I'm exhausted. I wish I was going to Italy like Janice. I wish I was going anywhere. Me and Nina, and fuck the rest of the world.

And then I have an idea. That's exactly what we'll do.

I go online and scout around. A week in Mauritius, at a child-friendly resort – that's exactly what the doctor ordered. Exactly.

I phone my mom. 'Mommy,' I say, 'I need a break.'

'Well, of course you do, my love,' she says. 'I keep telling your father you're working far too hard and that bastard putting you in this terrible position … I don't know how you do it. I just don't. *What* can we do? Should we take Nina? Do you want to go to the farm?'

My parents own part shares in a trout farm, and for a moment I think maybe that's a more sensible plan. But now I have a vision of myself sipping pina coladas on the beach while Nina frolics in the sea – possibly with dolphins.

'I was thinking Nina and I might go to Mauritius for the school holiday next week,' I say.

'That's an excellent idea,' says my mother. 'I should have thought of it myself. I'll tell your father to put some money into your account immediately. And don't skimp, darling. Go somewhere fabulous. Not a cheapo. Daddy will pay.'

'Thanks, Mommy,' I say, feeling guilty. My parents are predictable in their ability to throw money at a problem, and I've fallen into the lifelong habit of counting on it.

'Which reminds me, darling,' says my mother. 'Daddy and I were talking about it, and Daddy says that if that bastard's being difficult about money, you mustn't stoop to fighting about it. We'll look after you if he's too cheap to do so.'

Since the split, my mother's referred to Daniel only as 'that bastard'. It's supportive and irritating at once, which is probably an apt summary of my entire relationship with my mother.

'He's being perfectly generous,' I say. 'And I actually earn money too. But not enough for a week in Mauritius on the spur of the moment.'

My mother, who's never earned a cent of her own money, laughs. 'And why should you spend your money on something like that?' she demands, genuinely outraged. 'Daddy would *love* to help you.'

We talk a bit more, and when we finish I feel my usual mix of guilt and love and quiet horror at my parents' lifestyle. Which I realise is hypocritical under the circumstances. Before I can have too many mis-givings, I find the package I want and mail the agent. Nina and I will leave for Mauritius on Saturday.

I will, of course, need to tell Daniel and get him to sign the requisite affidavit so I can travel with Nina alone. I download the form from the government website, and fill in the details. Then I email it to him.

'Please sign this,' I say.

He can piece the rest together himself.

Julia

I'd forgotten this was one of the days I'd be working with Steve. But Steve hasn't forgotten that he's working with me, because he arrives at the office with a decaf coffee (because he's sure I wouldn't be drinking caffeinated beverages at five months pregnant) and a selection of croissants (because he knows pregnant women get very hungry) and a pair of warm slippers (because he's heard that pregnant women get cold extremities and swollen ankles). As he hands over his gifts and explanations, we both look down at my feet. They are possibly the only part of my body that are still their original shape.

'Ah well,' says Steve, 'maybe they're cold?'

He looks so hopeful that I assure him they are very cold, Arctic even, and desperately in need of slippers. To prove this, I immediately take off my smart high heels – which, to be honest, *are* pinching me.

At this point, of course, Gerald walks in to the meeting room, carrying various files. He looks at my feet in their new sheepskin slippers, and then at the shoes lying next to them. 'Um ...' he says.

'Is there something you need, Gerald?' I say.

'I brought the files you'll be working on.'

'They're on the computer, Gerald,' I say. 'But thank you. That was kind of you.'

Gerald smiles and adjusts his rather incongruous tie. 'Well,' he says. 'I'll leave you to it then. You're in good hands, Steve.'

For some reason, both Steve and I find this very funny, and Steve laughs and pats Gerald on the back, and tells him he's sure he's in wonderful hands, and Gerald goes off smiling like he's pulled off some major corporate coup.

'He's an odd chap, your boss,' says Steve.

'He is,' I say. 'But he's awfully clever, you know. Just not quite of this century.'

'Or this planet, really,' says Steve with a smile.

We both sit down and open our laptops, and I expect that we'll start working. But apparently Steve's in no hurry.

'So, tell me about the baby,' he says. 'Tell me what's been happening in your life. Clearly quite a lot.'

And so I tell him. With all the complications, even though I know how bad it makes me look. And he's interested and curious, and asks questions and says nice things about how it's not my fault, these things happen. For the first time in ages, I feel like I'm speaking to a friend who's completely on my side. I've thought of trying to reconnect with my friends – especially Heleen, now that we have something in common again – but the whole living-with-a-married-man thing is a bit hard to explain, and I'd feel judged even if I'm not.

Steve's not even slightly bitter that he's basically one of the victims of my relationship with Daniel. And he laughs when I'm funny, and I can't remember when last someone did that. Daniel used to laugh with me a lot, and make me laugh. But now, I realise, we're either fighting or having sex. And while we once might have laughed during sex, that doesn't happen any more. And then I find myself wondering what dating Steve would be like. If I was having *his* baby, would we still be laughing together? It so easily could have happened like that.

The thought makes me feel disloyal to Daniel, so I pull the laptop towards me.

'We'd better get to work,' I say in the middle of a story Steve is telling about some friend's pregnancy.

He looks a bit baffled.

'Sure,' he says after a pause. 'Let's do that.'

FRIDAY

Claire

Now that I've booked the holiday, I'm frantically trying to get on top of everything before we have to leave. I realise that I really didn't think the whole thing through, and between work and the arrangements I've made for next week, I'm going to spend the whole day sorting things out, and cancelling appointments and playdates I set up literally hours before. People will think I'm losing it. Not to mention the packing.

I try to get Nina to school early – partly to have more of a morning, partly to avoid bumping into people and wasting time talking. It's because I want to be quick that Nina has other ideas.

'It's show-and-tell today,' she announces as she eats her breakfast.

'No, it's not,' I say from the kitchen, where I'm packing her lunch box and school bag. 'Show-and-tell is on Mondays. See.' I point to the board where we've written all her school commitments.

'It's *today*,' she says, nonplussed. 'I must bring something from Egypt.'

'From *Egypt*? You want me to find something from Egypt at the last minute?'

Nina nods and carries on eating her toast.

'Sweetie, we don't have anything from Egypt,' I say after a quick think.

Nina spits out the mouthful of toast and shouts, 'It *is* today. I *must* have it.' Having made her point, she calmly puts the half-chewed toast back in her mouth.

I rack my brain. Egypt? Pyramids? A sphinx? For the first time in my life I wish I owned one of those touristy papyrus things with Egyptian hieroglyphics. Like they have on the wall in the house next door.

Bingo.

I message Lynette, my elderly neighbour, and ask if Nina can borrow her 'beautiful Egyptian artwork'. I'm worried Lynette won't be awake – it's early – but she messages back in seconds, and offers to bring it round. I feel like Supermom. Like I have literally saved the world.

'Lynette is bringing something perfect,' I tell Nina.

Nina looks at me. 'For what?'

'For your Egypt show-and-tell.'

Nina shrugs. 'Oh, that,' she says. 'It's not important.'

I consider throwing something at her, but the doorbell rings.

Lynette is at the gate, and thrilled to be helping. I thank her effusively, deciding that it's better to keep her away from Nina, who might not show sufficient gratitude. I use the opportunity to tell Lynette that we're going away, and she wants to talk about Mauritius. I know she's lonely, but I have to get Nina to school, and before I know it, I've arranged to pop by for afternoon tea. Which is literally the last thing I can manage. But the promise gets Lynette out, and Nina and I finally leave for school.

On the way, Daniel messages me: 'What hotel are you staying at in Mauritius?'

I want to tell him it's none of his business, but I need him to sign the affidavit. So, when we're stuck at an endless red light, I simply message him the link to our package. Hopefully he'll realise that I can't be bothered to give him the information myself.

At school, things go downhill.

Nina and I bump into Janice outside the classroom. 'We're going to Mauritius,' Nina tells Janice before either of us can say anything. 'Mommy decided yesterday.'

Janice looks gobsmacked. I'm quite sure she's rehearsed a little speech about my separation from Daniel and me not telling her. And this must look like I'm raining on her Italy trip. I've probably offended her on so many levels that she'll never talk to me again.

I go for honesty.

'I'm a mess,' I tell her. 'I'm sorry I didn't tell you about Daniel for so long. And I'm sorry I'm going to Mauritius. I'm just a mess.'

Janice is looking at me like I'm crazy. 'Claire,' she says, taking my arm, 'I totally understand why you didn't want to talk about Daniel. We all do. We respect that.'

As she says this, I realise it's true. While most of the friends I messaged yesterday came back with things like, 'So sorry. Xxx', no one asked questions and no one made me feel bad. That was all in my own head.

'As for Mauritius – why on earth are you apologising? I think it's a magnificent idea. You be sure to take lots of pictures, you hear?'

I nod, speechless.

'Now,' says Janice, 'what can I do to help you? It must be madness with this last-minute planning, and I know how busy you are.'

'Janice,' I say, 'you know what? You've already helped me. So much.' I give her a hug.

'Can we go in now?' demands Nina from waist level, and we moms both laugh.

When I come out of the classroom, I bump into Laurel.

'I overheard your conversation with Janice,' she says after we greet each other. 'You're right. She's actually a very nice person. I misjudged your sheeple.'

'I probably misjudged them too,' I say.

Laurel laughs. 'So,' she says, 'Mauritius?'

'You should come with,' I say, inspired. 'Please come with me?'

Laurel laughs. 'That would be so fabulous,' she agrees. 'But I can't.'

'Sandy?'

'Nothing that exciting. We're going to Max's folks' place at the coast. Family holiday. His sister's kids' school is also closed for this stupid course, so apparently that was taken as a sign that we should all go away together.'

'Sounds fun,' I say.

'Not to me,' laughs Laurel. 'But what can I do? And the kids love it – all the cousins together.'

Now I'm worrying that I've made a mistake. What is Nina going to do on an island with just me? But it's like Laurel reads my mind.

'You and Nina are going to have a ball, Claire. And you need the break.'

It would seem that absolutely everyone in the world thinks I need to go to Mauritius. I decide to stop feeling guilty, and just get ready.

Catherine

I phone Edward in the morning during a lull at work.

He explains that he's having his brother and his wife, Lizette, and Miriam's brother, to lunch on Saturday. Tomorrow.

'Please come, Catherine,' he says. 'There are too many men, and Lizette will feel awkward. She finds me ridiculous anyway, thinks I should buck up.'

'She doesn't sound very nice,' I say, wondering if I want to spend an afternoon with her.

'Oh, she's fine. A bit annoying, but I liked her well enough before. She just can't understand grief. Her greatest loss in her life so far has been her dog.'

'Surely she's lost parents?'

'No,' says Edward. 'They're obscenely old and obscenely healthy. They're not even a burden to her. I think she thinks I've done something careless, letting Miriam get damaged and dependent. But other than that, she's actually quite nice.' We both laugh, and I have a strange thought: *Edward's going to be okay.* I don't know where it comes from – being okay is not something I expect of people. It's not something I think people should necessarily aspire to.

'And Miriam's brother?' I ask.

Edward sighs. 'He's a really nice man. I've always liked him. In fact, I was friends with him first at Rhodes – that's how I met Miriam. But he worries about me all the time. It gets tiring.'

'What about his wife?'

'Ah,' says Edward. 'Poor man. His wife left him about ten years ago for a trainer at the gym. It was the most shocking scandal at the time, because we all liked her so much. And Larry was devastated, of course. Plus, she left him with two young sons. She just walked out on the family.'

He sighs again, obviously reliving that time. A part of me is interested that he's even able to engage with another person's historic suffering. Again, that unbidden thought: *He's going to be okay.*

'Okay,' I agree. 'I'll come. I'm visiting Mike in the morning and I'll come straight from there. Want me to pop in and see Miriam?'

'Please would you,' says Edward. 'I usually go, but I have to get ready for this lunch. She's going to be so worried – I always go on a Saturday.'

I know better than to say Miriam doesn't know whether he's there or not. I mean, she can't even breathe on her own. But I want to reassure him.

'You know,' I say, 'I don't think they feel time the same way an awake person does. I mean, I don't think they know what day it is. They just know that we visit. I don't worry when I change days. As long as I go often.'

Edward is quiet for a moment. 'You're probably right,' he says eventually, but I know he doesn't agree. He just doesn't want me to feel bad. We're so gentle with each other, us damaged people.

'Either way,' I say, 'I'll pop in and chat to her. She'll be glad of a visitor whatever day it is.'

I can hear the relief in Edward's voice. 'Thanks, Cath. It's so wonderful having someone who understands.'

I suddenly realise Edward has probably never had to cook a lunch on his own. 'Oh, can I bring anything tomorrow? A salad or dessert or something?'

He laughs. 'Actually,' he says, as if reading my mind, 'I'm quite the chef. I've always been the one who cooks for company. Miriam used to tease me.'

'In that case, I'll be sure to tell her you're toiling over a hot stove.'

'Oh yes,' he says, sounding happy. 'She'll like that.'

We make final arrangements about times and I get his address – I've never been to his house before and I'm relieved that it's not too far from me. I can have a glass or two of wine.

'I'm looking forward to it,' I tell Edward.

And to my surprise, I actually am.

Julia

I'm working with Steve again today, and I dress carefully.

'You look good,' says Daniel as I get ready to leave the apartment. It's the nicest thing he's said to me for ages, and I perk up.

'Thanks,' I say.

He strolls over to kiss me goodbye, and pulls me in hard, slipping his tongue between my lips. 'Do you have to go to work right now?' he says. 'Or could I quickly fuck you against the wall?'

I know this worked for me just yesterday. But right now it feels like the baby is sitting on my bladder, and all I can think about is how I don't want to have to change clothes. But I have kind of an idea that if I refuse sex, I'll be like Claire. Only without the good bits. And I don't even know why I have it in my head that Claire refused sex, because Daniel's never said so. But if she didn't, then why is Daniel with me at all? And that thought worries me. Do I believe that Daniel is only with me for the sex? That he'll leave if I say no?

While I'm evaluating my inner world, Daniel's concerns are more corporeal, and he's edging me against the wall, taking my silence for consent. For a moment I let him carry on, kissing me and touching my breasts and pushing me against the wall. And then the baby does that strange wiggly thing, like bubbles in my abdomen, and I'm absolutely sure I'm going to wee, and anyway I can almost feel my linen maternity pants creasing in real time.

'I'd love to, babe,' I say, trying to sound as though I mean it. 'But I have an early meeting. Can't be late.'

'Are you sure?' Daniel's still holding my breasts and nuzzling at my neck. 'Can't you feel how much I want you?'

The truth is I *can* feel, and it's not really doing anything to ease the whole needing-to-wee situation.

'I want you too, babe,' I say huskily, but I push him away. 'It's just that I've got to get to work. Later.'

I do a strange sort of manoeuvre to get past him and out the door, and try to throw a sultry look back at him, but suspect I just look relieved. Then I realise I haven't wee'd, but I can't go back in because he'll think I'm up for it. Rather than risk that, I drive to work as fast as I can, and by the time I get there I'm so desperate that I virtually throw bodies out of my way to make it to the toilet. But it's completely worth it.

My next stop is the meeting room where, despite the early hour, Steve has already set up. He's working hard and doesn't notice me walk in. I watch him for a moment, his head bent over a hard-copy ledger as he tries to reconcile what he's reading with something on his screen. His shirt sleeves are pushed up over his wrists, and he's wearing his glasses. He looks like The Dad in a 1950s movie – an impression enhanced by the dust motes dancing in the few sun rays that have managed to squeeze through the perpetually closed blinds.

I cough, and he turns around.

'Julia,' he says, beaming and standing up. 'I got here early to get a head start, and here you are – early too.'

I smile. I'm not going to explain that I ran out the house to avoid sex with my boyfriend, the father of my unborn child.

'I am,' I say. 'I needed to wee, so I drove super-fast.'

Steve laughs, and pushes his glasses up his nose.

'I bought you something,' he says, reaching under the table. He's not joking: he pulls out three shopping bags. 'Now I hope this isn't inappropriate, and you're totally not allowed to tell a soul, but I'm a sucker for baby stuff.' He opens a packet and pulls out a denim jacket for the tiniest human being you can imagine. 'I mean look at this,' he says. 'How is a person supposed to *not* buy this?'

He looks so serious that I start laughing. 'You like buying baby stuff? Men don't like that shit,' I say.

'I know. That's why you have to keep my secret. If this gets back to the guys, I'm basically dead.'

I stroll over to where he's now pulling out a set of tiny newborn onesies. 'So ... how often do you indulge?'

He drops his voice as if his rugby mates might be listening at the door. 'I have to wait until I know a pregnant person – it'd be creepy if I bought stuff for no particular baby. But the moment there's an actual baby, I just go nuts.' He takes a floppy-eared rabbit out of the bag. 'Rabbit.' His voice is steeped in satisfaction.

I saw the same rabbit in a shop, and in fact considered buying it. But it was ridiculously expensive.

'Steve, you've spent a fortune. I can't accept all this.' I'm touching the soft clothes as I speak.

'No, you mustn't think of it like that,' he says. 'It's like you're doing me a favour. Indulging my addiction. Plus, you're now burdened with my secret. So we're quits.'

I don't know what to say. Currently, this is basically the baby's entire earthly possessions. I finger a soft jersey. 'If you're like this now, what on earth will you be like for your own baby?' I laugh, and then we catch each other's eye and there's a moment of complete awkwardness, because we both know that in an alternate reality this could've been his baby.

Steve blushes, and then laughs. 'Oh, I'll be impossible with my own baby. In fact, I hope I have twins so I can buy double.'

We both contemplate the baby stuff that's now spread over the table.

It's suddenly so real, so tangible. There's going to be a baby who will wear these clothes and hold that rabbit. Tiny little fingers will wrap around the rabbit's ear. A little mouth might suck on it. Or on the dummies Steve has also bought.

I start to feel a bit faint, and sit down.

'Wow. I'm having an actual baby.'

'Are you okay?' says Steve. 'You look a bit pale.'

'I'm not really sure I've properly grasped this baby thing,' I say. Not worrying about how foolish I must sound. I expect Steve to laugh, but he doesn't. Instead, he crouches down next to me.

'It must be overwhelming. It must be the biggest thing ever.'

'That's just it,' I say. 'It is. But I don't think I've really grasped that until now.' I gesture at the baby stuff. 'I've just been thinking about Daniel, and us, and what that means. I haven't thought about an actual baby. I'm not sure I can cope with an actual baby.'

'You'll be brilliant,' says Steve. 'You're going to be an ace mom.'

'You're just saying that.'

'Okay, I have another secret. You might have gathered from this,' he says, waving at the baby clothes, 'that I really want to have a baby at some point. So when I meet a woman, I get to know her a bit before I ask her out formally. And I only ask a woman out if I think she'd be a good mother. It means I don't date a lot, but I don't want to waste my time.' He pauses. 'And I asked *you* out. So I'm not just saying it. I really think you'll be a good mom.'

'You only date women you'd have a baby with?'

'Well that's putting it strongly. Let's rather say I only date women who I think there's a possibility I could have a baby with.' He grimaces. 'And I'm not always right, but in your case, I'm sure I was.'

'You're kind of an odd guy,' I say. 'Not as straightforward as you seem.'

'Oh,' says Steve. 'I'm very straightforward. To a fault. I'm the quint-essential what-you-see-is-what-you-get kind of guy. I've been told it's not very sexy.' He looks genuinely upset as he says this.

'You know what, Steve?'

'What?'

'I only date sexy guys. And I dated you. So fuck those people who don't see it.'

Steve laughs. 'Well, this is a pretty unusual start to a meeting,' he says. 'Baby clothes and angst, all before coffee.'

'In that case, we'd better get some coffee. And possibly do some work.'

As I pack up the baby clothes I wonder what Daniel will say. He hasn't bought a single thing for the baby so far, and he might feel that it's his prerogative as the father.

On the other hand, he probably won't.

Daniel

Claire's message weighs down my phone. A trip to Mauritius without me. Claire with Nina and an affidavit from me allowing them to go.

I *love* Mauritius. Claire knows I love Mauritius.

I follow the link she sent me and suddenly I know what Claire expects me to do. Everything makes sense.

With a smile, I print out the affidavit. I take it down to the local police station, where I wait almost an hour to have it commissioned. Usually the inefficiency would annoy me, but today I feel strangely at peace.

I get the document signed, and when I get back to the office, I get the driver to drop it off at Claire's place.

Then I buzz my PA, and tell her what needs to be done.

SATURDAY

Claire

When I got home yesterday to find the affidavit from Daniel, I breathed a sigh of relief. I realised that part of me had expected him to object, to stop me taking Nina out of the country without him. You're always reading stories about women whose mean ex-husbands prevent them from travelling with the children anywhere, and they have to take them to court and all sorts of things.

But Daniel's signed the document without any fuss. There's a small part of me that feels sad. Daniel loves Mauritius, and he loves family holidays. We'll never have one of those again, and he's obviously made peace with that. It's just another of the many milestones I'll have to face in this new life without Daniel by my side. I'm sad, but I'm also a bit exhilarated.

Nina is beside herself. She's ready to go to the airport hours before we need to leave. I have to persuade her not to travel in her swimming costume and the large straw sun hat my mother once left here. Nina's furious, and I placate her by allowing her to wear the hat.

While I do the last of the packing, I tell her to phone Daniel to say goodbye. She likes phoning Daniel – the increase in the number of phone calls she's allowed to make alone is, in her opinion, a positive side effect of our new situation. I hear her voice rise and fall as I pack, and I wonder what she's saying to him. They never used to talk this much when we all lived together. I grimace. *Another* silver lining. It's starting to feel a bit strange – exactly how many silver linings are there in this story?

When she finishes, she reports back.

'Daddy is very strange,' she observes.

'Why, sweetie?'

'He kept laughing and saying stupid things that didn't make sense. Daddy is so stupid. *So* dumb. I'm going to phone him and tell him that.'

I let her go. It'll keep her busy. I laugh to myself. We haven't even left, and already I'm feeling so much better.

And Daniel really can't be told often enough how stupid he is.

Julia

I wake up happy. I don't feel nauseous and I don't feel tired. Best of all, I feel happy. Last night was the best.

I got home and decided to leave all my baby gifts in the car, because I wasn't really sure how Daniel would react, and why borrow trouble? I opened the door and Daniel had transformed the apartment. There were candles everywhere and rose petals leading from the front door to the table. The table was beautifully laid, and there was a huge teddy bear sitting on my chair, wearing a T-shirt that says 'Baby's First Teddy'. I suppressed the thought that actually, by a few hours, it wasn't.

As soon as Daniel saw me, he came rushing over from where he'd been cooking, carrying a martini glass.

'A virgin cranberry martini,' he said. 'For my beautiful Julia.'

'Wow,' was all I could manage.

'You sit down while I finish with supper. Put your feet up. Relax. You work too hard.'

I didn't know what to make of it. It was like he'd accessed the disloyal thoughts I've been having about him and decided that he'd show me how great he really is. And I'm certainly not complaining. Maybe he'll finally started the divorce proceedings, I thought. Maybe he was going to propose! That gave me a small frisson of excitement. And apprehension. I supressed the memory that Daniel had proposed to Claire on top of the Eiffel Tower. 'So cheesy!' Claire had laughed when she told me, but to me it had sounded romantic.

I looked around my small, over-crowded flat. Daniel's boxes are still not unpacked, lurking like malevolent spirits everywhere I look. They're now dusty and the edges are scuffed from us tripping over them. Whatever's in them doesn't seem important enough for Daniel to actually need. But other than the boxes, my place is nice. And I've made it feel like home, even more so since Daniel's moved in and the spectre of Claire's perfect house has loomed over me. There are lovely new scatter cushions that I paid too much for, and curtains that Heleen made for me, and an orchid on the coffee table, because Claire once told me there's no design dilemma an orchid can't fix.

It wasn't Paris, but it would do.

But as it turned out, Daniel didn't propose to me. In a way that made it better, because then I didn't have to compare it to Paris. As it was, it was just a wonderful, romantic night, exactly like I imagined life would be with my perfect match. Romance for no special reason. Just because.

And we ate a delicious meal, and Daniel didn't even blink when I asked for third helpings – he just smiled and said, 'Got to keep my little boy growing.' And when I actually burped at the table, he looked at me as though I'd performed a magic trick. So I almost immediately squashed the thought that Claire would *never* have burped in front of him. Obviously he was fine with it.

And after dinner we made love in a good, ordinary, romantic way. None of this up-against-the-wall, dirty-talk stuff. Just ordinary sex, with loving words. And yes, maybe it wasn't as earth shattering as the other type. Maybe it was even a bit boring. But that was a good thing – that's the type of sex one should be having with the father of your child when you're twenty weeks pregnant. It made me feel like at long last I was safe with Daniel.

So today I wake up happy. And even though Daniel is busy all weekend, like he said he would be, I don't mind. He sends me text messages during the day, checking in on me. At first, it's sweet. It's like we've turned a corner; like he's made the decision to be with me in his heart. But as the day goes on, it gets a bit irritating. He's gone weeks without contacting me all day, and now my phone is beeping every ten minutes. I go from feeling like the star of a romance movie to the victim of a stalker – but I push that feeling down. This is how it's supposed to be. This is love.

Eventually, I send him a message: 'Stop worrying about me. I'm fine. Enjoy yourself.'

And it's a good time to smuggle Steve's baby presents like contraband into the house. First, I put them in the cupboard in the nursery, which is what I'm calling the spare room, but then I think Daniel might look there. After all, it is where half his clothes still are. So I put them under my bed. But that's insane, so I put them back in the nursery, in the cupboard he never uses, and realise that I can always tell Daniel I bought the stuff myself. I feel a twinge of guilt at the thought, and think briefly of Steve and his strong hands and his love of buying baby things. Steve will make someone a great partner, I think. It's just not going to be me. I've made my choice.

I try to phone my mother, but she's out. So I stay at home, researching schools and births and early childhood development. I'm going to be ready for this baby. I feel grown up about my life.

Daniel is late home, but he texts several times more, so I don't worry.

'I'm okay, stop stressing,' I tell him, every time. He's obviously not used to being with a strong, confident woman like me, is all I can con-clude, trying hard not to picture Claire.

I'm fast asleep when he gets home.

I hear him bashing about getting changed, making the most enormous noise and pulling things out of the cupboard. I smile to myself – he must be very drunk. But I don't let him know that he's woken me, because as lovely as last night was, I don't really feel like sex. And he might.

So I let myself fall back to sleep, holding my baby bump and thinking how lucky and happy I am.

Catherine

On Saturday I wake up feeling good. I have a visit with Mike and then the lunch with Edward and his family. It feels good to be full of plans. I think about phoning Julia before the day starts, but then remember how I hated my mom nagging at me when I was a young adult. Obviously, after she died I would have given my right arm for a dose of her nagging, but you can't tell them that, can you? It's one of things people must learn for themselves, when it's too late. Anyhow, last time I spoke to Julia she was fine, and she'd let me know if there was a problem. We don't have one of those mother-daughter relationships where we need to yabber about nothing all day. It's probably my fault. I haven't been the small-talk type since The Accident.

For a moment I remember how I used to speak to my mother about everything, and I feel a pang of longing. It's been years since I had space in my grief to miss my parents; it feels strange.

I dress carefully – I don't want to look too smart for lunch, but I want to look good. I'm glad that I've finally started going to the hairdresser again, and my hair is glossy, with all the grey coloured away. I take the time to apply the make-up I spontaneously bought last week when I was in the shop getting shampoo and deodorant. I even threw in some ridiculously expensive perfume. It's been years since I bothered with all that, and I'm surprised by the face that looks at me from the mirror. It looks like a person with an interesting life.

I find that I'm wanting Edward's family to like me. I'm wanting them to see that even if you're a broken half-person, you can still look okay. Maybe then they'll have hope for Edward.

I explain all this to Mike when I get to the hospital, speaking easily and laughing as I hold his hand. When I run out of words, I just sit for a bit, stroking his hand, trying not to think too much. Mike and I have been through so much, and I owe him that final release from his prison, but right now I can't get a grip on my plan for us to die. When Julia first got pregnant, it felt so important. And it *is* important. I *will* be free when the baby is born, and I must free Mike. But for now I just want to sit, holding his hand, telling him about my day and absorbing his peace.

When I am done chatting to Mike, I go down the passage to Miriam. I know for most people this would be strange, but I treat her like I would Mike, even though I know that it's different because obviously she's nothing like Mike. Nobody's home, basically, but out of respect to Edward's grief, I speak to her as if she's as alert inside as Mike is.

First, I tell her who I am again, in case she *is* awake inside there and has forgotten me. I tell her a bit about Mike and about Julia and the baby she's expecting. It feels quite cathartic speaking to her – I'm less self-aware than I am with Mike. Maybe because Miriam is a vegetable. I tell her about the lunch, and who will be there. I ask her what she thought of these people when she was up and about, and I wonder what they'll make of me.

'Edward's cooking,' I say. 'He says he was always the one that cooked, but I bet you helped more than he realised. I bet he's going to find it really hard without you.' I laugh.

And as I laugh, Miriam's hand flies up next to her and then drops, and her heart rate monitor goes up. An alarm must sound at the nurse's station because they come racing through, and suddenly she's surrounded by personnel. I tell them what happened, and one of the nurses painstakingly writes it up in her chart. But Miriam's back to normal now, and the nurses decide that they'll speak to the doctor on his rounds rather than calling him.

'Must I tell her husband?' I ask. 'Should I get his hopes up?'

One of the nurses I know well shakes her head. 'It happens, Catherine,' she says. 'It was just muscular.'

I nod. I know that. But I can't help thinking that even Mike has never done anything that dramatic. And if it *had* been Mike, I'd want someone to tell me. I decide to play it by ear – I can't tell Edward in front of everyone, and I don't want to tell him before his lunch because he'll get all distracted and worked up, and will probably want to come see her immediately. That's what I'd do.

On my way out, I pop my head back into Mike's room.

'Miriam just moved,' I tell him. 'Do you want to match that? See her and raise her?' I wait a minute, and nothing happens. 'Okay. Just thought I'd check.'

When I get to Edward's place, Stan, his brother, and his wife, Lizette, are already there. Stan is like a shorter, washed-out version of Edward, but Lizette could never be described as washed out. She has big hair, blonde, and bright-red lipstick. When Edward introduces us, Stan stands up and shakes my hand. Lizette remains seated but pats the seat next to her.

'I'm not the sort of person who beats around the bush,' she says. 'We're very curious about you.'

I smile and sit down next to her. 'I'm sure,' I say. 'But really, I'm not very interesting.'

'It's not like me to be blunt,' she says, contradicting her first statement, 'but Edward tells us your husband is also a vegetable, just like Miriam.'

I look at her to see if she's being deliberately rude, but her pale-blue eyes are open very wide, and she's looking at me with curiosity. At that moment, Edward arrives with the gin and tonic I requested, and rolls his eyes at me. 'Lizette,' he says, 'I've explained that they're not vegetables. They're in prolonged comas.'

'Edward' – her tone is apologetic – 'you know I'm not the sort of person who wants to upset people.'

Stan pats her hand. 'Nobody's upset, love. Just try not to refer to people's spouses as vegetables, okay?'

Lizette nods. 'That's very fair,' she says. Then she turns back to me. 'So, what happened to your husband that made him a vegetable?'

I feel a laugh building up and I catch Edward's eye and see that he's also laughing. I guess that's all we can do.

'It was a car accident,' I say.

'Oh, how awful. Car accidents are terrible. *Terrible.*' Lizette says this like she has just realised the truth of it, and she shakes her bouffant sadly. 'Don't you think?'

'Yes,' I say. 'I'd have to agree.'

She perks up 'I *knew* you would,' she says, like we've just agreed on a very obscure point. 'I'm sure we're going to be great friends. I'm the sort of person who has a feeling about these things.'

I'm tempted to tell her that I'm not 'the sort of person' who has friends, but that would upset her, and anyway I'm not even sure it's true any more. So I smile, and sip my gin before asking Lizette what she does, allowing her to give a soliloquy on the sort of person she is, which only requires me to nod and smile.

As Lizette is telling me that she's not the sort of person who likes death – because of course the rest of us are simply mad about it – another man enters the room. He is tall, with grey hair and bright-blue eyes. Stan jumps up and shakes his hand, and Lizette stops mid-sentence to embrace him warmly.

Edward waits for Lizette to let go – which takes slightly longer than it should – and then introduces me. 'Catherine, this is Larry, Miriam's brother.'

I stand up and shake Larry's hand. His skin is warm and dry, and his grip is strong.

'Catherine visited Miriam this morning,' says Edward.

'Oh,' says Larry. 'And how was she?'

I could tell them about Miriam's strange arm movement at this point, but it's too private. If I am going to say anything, I need to tell Edward by himself.

In my confusion, I instead say, 'She's fine.' Larry looks a bit taken aback, and I realise of course that she isn't at all fine. 'You know, for a person in a deep coma,' I add.

Larry nods, but I can see he thinks I am bats.

Edward, however, is smiling. 'Catherine's husband is also in a coma,' he says, much like you might mention a shared profession or hobby. 'So she knows all about what I'm going through.'

'I'm so sorry,' says Larry. 'How long has he been in a coma?'

'Twenty-six years.'

Lizette turns to Stan. 'That's a terribly long time, you know.' Stan pats her shoulder. 'It is, love. Poor Catherine.'

Lizette looks at me with her wide eyes. 'Catherine's not the sort of person to wallow in her grief,' she announces. 'Catherine's the sort who keeps her chin up.'

We all look at her. I'm stunned that anyone who has spoken even three words to me can hold this opinion. Larry and Edward look interested, although Edward must surely know I am an absolute expert in wallowing in my grief.

And Stan's chest swells. 'Lizette's the sort of person who has a good grip on other people.' He is so proud and she looks so happy that you can't even be angry with them. I catch Larry's eye for a moment, and I could swear that he winks at me, his eyes glistening with humour. I must be mistaken, but I allow myself a small smile.

At lunch, Larry and I are seated together, and as he offers me some wine, he mutters, 'I don't know about you, but I'm the sort of person who needs a drink to get through all this self-analysis.' I turn to see if he is being serious, but as our eyes meet, he starts to laugh.

'Oh, that's nasty of me,' he says. 'Pretend I never said it.'

I smile. 'She is awfully sure of what sort of person she is.' We are speaking softly so Lizette, who is lecturing Edward, won't hear us.

'Once …' says Larry conspiratorially, 'once I had a sip of wine every time she said, "I'm the sort of person" or anything similar. I got absolutely shit-faced. Miriam was furious with me.'

I laugh out loud. 'I'm almost tempted to try. It must have been hilarious.'

'Hilarious and kind of terrible,' says Larry. 'I wasn't in a good space. And then when I got drunk, I kept starting my own sentences with "I'm the sort of person …", and Miriam thought I was doing it deliberately. But here's the terrible part: I wasn't. It's just contagious. Like a cold.'

Lizette intervenes. 'Have you caught a cold, Larry?' she asks. 'I'm not the sort of person who gets sick, but when I do, I always take lots of vitamin C. You should try that.'

Larry smiles easily. 'That's a very good idea, Lizzy. I'll definitely try that.'

Lizette looks thrilled at this, and I realise that Larry is a very kind man, despite his teasing.

'I think Lizette's the sort of person who likes to help people,' I say.

'Oh, I am, Catherine, I am,' says Lizette, delighted, while Larry snorts on his wine.

The lunch is easy after that – the tone is set. We all gently tease Lizette, who loves it and has no idea she's being teased. Stan probably knows, but he seems to be a man who is happy if his wife is happy, merely reigning her in with a pat on her arm or a quiet comment when she gets a bit overexcited. She always takes his criticism well – 'You are so right, darling' – and then blithely ignores it.

Somehow, Larry and I manage to speak a bit in-between all this. I tell him about Julia and he tells me about his two sons, who are in their late teens and who live with him. They haven't seen their mother since she left with the gym instructor and they won't even speak to her on the phone. Larry is matter-of-fact about it, which means I am matter-of-fact when I tell him about Mike and the bare bones of the accident – the version I always tell. The sanitised version. But Larry is an insightful person.

'So, you were stuck in the car, conscious, for hours?' he asks. Somehow, people don't usually pick up on this.

'Yes.'

'That must have been a living hell.'

'It was.' I close my eyes and I am briefly back there, but I force the memories away. I'm having a good time. I do not need to go back. There's no point.

The reason for Larry's insight soon becomes clear: he's a psychologist. When he tells me, I feel a hint of discomfort at having exposed myself. But he explains that his work now is mostly corporate – he does executive life coaching.

'After my wife left me and I didn't see it coming,' he explains, 'I didn't think I could hold myself up as a bastion of human understanding.'

Edward is listening in. 'You're too hard on yourself, Larry. Miri always says so.'

Larry reaches across the table and for a moment the two men grasp hands. 'I miss her too,' says Larry.

'I know you do,' says Edward. 'But she'll be back. I know it.'

Larry nods. 'Can't keep a good woman down,' he says, and Edward laughs. I have a brief vision of that flying hand.

It's an easy afternoon, despite all the heavy topics and the trickiness of Lizette. But I feel comfortable with Edward and Larry, like the three of us are old friends. I find myself wondering if Larry really believes Miriam will wake up, but then I think about how she moved and I feel a strange discomfort. I will have to tell Edward, I resolve. But not today. I will call him tomorrow.

I feel better after making that decision.

Since The Accident, during the few times I have forced myself to socialise, I have usually found myself wishing away the hours and longing to leave. But today ends before I am ready, and suddenly everyone is saying goodbye and hugging and promising to stay in touch.

'I'm not the sort of person who makes empty promises,' Lizette assures me as she takes my number.

Larry says goodbye to me last.

'It's been really lovely meeting you,' I say, and he looks so uncomfortable that I wonder if I have misread him completely and he doesn't like me at all.

But then he speaks. 'I know you're married and all,' he says. 'But would you, maybe, like to have dinner sometime?'

'That would be lovely,' I say. 'I'd really enjoy that.'

I can't believe how I have suddenly started making friends, and that it feels so good. I wonder what Mike will think.

It's only when I'm driving that I think about Larry's wording more carefully. If he was asking me to dinner as a friend, why would he mention that I'm married?

Oh God, I think. Have I just agreed to go on a date?

The idea should make me uncomfortable, but the truth is, it doesn't. I feel strange: a bit excited, a bit apprehensive and very amazed. Someone – a rather attractive someone – wants to go on a date with me.

I start to smile, and I am still smiling when I drive past an accident scene. I can't stand accident scenes. I've been known to actually stop and vomit after driving past one. And this one is bad – there are two cars, and both are completely destroyed. There is glass and metal all over the road, and as the emergency services slow cars down and wave us round, I see a body bag on the road. I wait for the usual feelings of horror and revulsion and fear. But they don't come. And within a few minutes I'm smiling again, thinking about my day.

I don't like to say it. I don't like to even think it. But my last thought as I fall asleep is that maybe I'm finally getting better.

Maybe I've done what all those books and friends and things told me was possible.

Maybe I've learnt to live with my grief.

Claire

When Nina and I touch down in Mauritius, I know I've done the right thing. For the first time since this all started, I feel a weight lift from my shoulders. I don't have to worry about running into Daniel. I don't have to worry about seeing Julia and her baby bump. I don't even have to worry about my friends and what they're thinking about me and how I should act. I can just be. I can't remember the last time I could just be.

Nina looks around the airport with wonder. 'Are we staying here, Mommy?' she asks.

I laugh. 'No, baby. This is the airport. We're going to a hotel. It'll be even better.'

At that moment, I see a bored-looking man standing holding a sign with my name. He has two beautiful floral leis draped over his arms. I walk towards him and he perks up.

'Mrs Marshall.' He drapes a lei around my neck. 'Little girl,' he says, putting one on Nina, who is entranced. 'Welcome to Ile de Maurice. We will make sure that you enjoy your stay.'

I look down at Nina, who looks so happy and entertained, and I silently thank my father for paying for the best sort of Mauritian hotel.

'I think we're going to have a wonderful time,' I say. 'I don't think we're going to want to leave.'

Part of me thinks that the good feelings must fade, that something must go wrong. But we get to the hotel and it is perfect and beautiful, and Nina is delighted. We have a swim in the warm sea, and then I have a gin and tonic while Nina has a chocolate milkshake, and we watch the sun set over the sea from the edge of the pool.

'This is a really fun place,' says Nina.

'And you haven't even seen all the fun stuff there is for kids,' I tell her.

'It feels nice being here with my mommy,' she says.

I'm so happy in that moment. Everything's going to be okay. I'm going to be okay without Daniel, and so is Nina. This holiday for the two of us was the perfect idea.

The perfect beginning to a new, happier chapter in our lives.

SUNDAY

Julia

Daniel's not in bed when I wake up. I hadn't really expected him to be, because I knew he had plans. But it feels very early, and the bed feels cold, like he hasn't been there for a while. Daniel might be selfish about doing his own thing, but he's even more selfish about getting his sleep. He doesn't get up early on a Sunday for anything. I lie in bed for a moment, holding my baby bump, trying to persuade myself that my uneasy feeling is ridiculous.

Eventually my bladder persuades me that it's time to get up. I pad through to the bathroom. Something is off, but the baby is sitting on my bladder, so I attend to my most urgent need first. I want to brush my teeth because my mouth feels dry and unpleasant, but when I reach for the toothpaste, it's not there. And my toothbrush is alone in its cup. The toothpaste and Daniel's toothbrush have vanished.

It feels like time is slowing down.

I open the bathroom cupboard and take inventory. Daniel's deodorant is gone. His shampoo is gone. His razor is gone. But his other things – a spare razor, some painkillers, the special soaps he likes to stockpile – are still there. I wonder if there's any chance I'm dreaming, but a sharp kick from my baby assures me that I'm awake.

'This isn't happening,' I say out loud, but I go over to our cupboard in the bedroom. When I started getting the nursery ready, we finally found a way to squeeze most of Daniel's clothes into my cupboards. This mostly involved me giving away a lot of my own clothes, and storing the rest on the top shelves in the nursery. I even took a suitcase to my mother.

At first I feel relief: Daniel's clothes are still there, his suits lined up in a regimented row, ubiquitous jeans neatly folded over hangers. Collared shirts like a small linen rainbow. I can smell Daniel wafting off his clothes.

I open the cupboard on the side, the one with shelves. Daniel's shelves are always organised and neat, but now the T-shirts are all over the place, and his few pairs of shorts are gone. Like he grabbed a few T-shirts from the middle of the pile and didn't have time to straighten it up. Because it doesn't matter.

I look at his underwear drawer. Almost empty. Underpants gone, except for a pair that are almost worn out, which I've been begging him to chuck. He always agrees, but doesn't do it. The socks are still there.

I look down at where he keeps his shoes. Work shoes, present and accounted for. But his two pairs of slip slops and his sandals are gone.

It's like he's left me, but only for the weekend. And not very well at that, given that even warm Johannesburg is now chilly with early-winter cold.

'Maybe he was drunk,' I say to no one. Then I remember all the bashing I heard when he came home last night. And that I'd thought he must have been drunk.

He got drunk and when I told him not to worry about me, when I didn't return all the love he was showering on me, he decided to leave. Only he was so drunk, he packed for a month of warm Sundays.

This is not a problem, I think. One phone call and he'll understand how much I need him, and we'll laugh at all this. We'll be telling our baby about the time Daddy packed his slip slops in the middle of winter. This is one of those stories couples need. I'm almost happy that this has happened.

I pick up my phone and call Daniel, but it goes straight to voicemail.

'Daniel,' I say, 'I'm sorry if I didn't make you feel loved yesterday. Please come home now.' I laugh. 'And anyway,' I say, 'you need a jersey.'

I put the phone down, wondering where Daniel slept last night. Or did he sleep with me, and then wake up drunk and leave? As I'm trying to figure it out, my phone beeps.

I'm surprised – it's a message from Daniel – even though his phone was off a moment ago.

'I'm sorry, Julia. This is what I need to do.'

I immediately dial his number, but it goes straight to voicemail again. I look at his WhatsApp profile: he's offline.

I sit down slowly on my bed.

Daniel has left me.

The realisation comes slowly, but I know that it's true.

But where would he go?

Like a punch, I know. He's gone back to Claire. Without even thinking much about what I'm doing, I dial Claire's cell number. Her voice goes straight to voicemail too.

That's all I need. I feel sick, and only just make it to the toilet before I vomit. Daniel has left me. They must be together, laughing about foolish Julia.

I don't know what to do next, so I lie down in my bed. My bed, I think, that was never really our bed. I expect to lie there tormented, but I fall asleep.

When I wake up a few hours later, I know what I need to do.

I need to go to my mother.

Claire

I wake up with the sun streaming through a gap in the curtains onto my bed. Nina is curled up in the bed next to me, fast asleep, her mouth slightly open, with a small patch of drool pooling on the pillow. We went to sleep late, and the sun already seems to be high in the sky. I watch her sleep for a while – wondering when last I took the time to just breathe her in. I've been so focused on survival since Daniel left that I've barely been present in my life. I lean down and inhale the smell of little girl and shampoo and a slightly sour morning breath.

'What are you doing, Mommy?' Nina says without opening her eyes.

'Smelling you,' I say.

'You are very weird, Mommy,' says Nina, still lying with her eyes closed. 'Are we still in Maurish?'

'We are. I'm thinking we should get up and have some breakfast and go exploring. What do you think?'

'What do Maurishes have for breakfast?'

'I'm not sure, but I think you can pretty much have anything you want.'

Nina opens her eyes. 'Anything?'

'Well, not chocolate. Or Coke.'

'A whole plate of bacon?'

'Sure.'

'And messed eggs?'

'Definitely.'

'And choccie milk?'

'Pretty sure we can get that.'

Nina smiles. 'Let's go, Mommy. What are we waiting for?'

'Maybe we should put on some clothes instead of pyjamas,' I suggest.

'That's a bad thing about hotels, eh?' says Nina, making me laugh.

We get dressed and go to the hotel dining room, where we opt for an outside table overlooking the pool and the sea. I take Nina into the restaurant and show her how the buffet works, and what all the different choices are. We debate which fruit juice looks nicer, and whether we should start or end our breakfast with pancakes. Eventually, after Nina decides to start with pancakes and I opt for a bowl of fresh fruit, we go back to the table. The waitress brings me some tea, and Nina a chocolate milk. I feel completely relaxed as I take my first sip of tea.

'Mommy,' says Nina, 'can I have juice *and* milk?'

'Sure, baby,' I say. 'Can you get it yourself, do you think?'

'Yes!' yells Nina, excited by this high level of responsibility. I smile as she runs into the restaurant, her hair swinging behind her, catching the sun.

I close my eyes for a moment. This was totally, absolutely the very best thing I could have done for Nina and me. It's almost that being in a different country from Julia and Daniel has liberated me. Freed me to be myself; and to finally see clearly that I'm happy on my own. I have a good life. Daniel is charming and funny and charismatic, but life with him was always all about him and his needs. It's taken him leaving me to see that, but now I realise that I'm actually happier without Daniel.

I stretch, eyes still closed, making a promise to myself that this is the beginning of everything.

A shadow falls over the table and I open my eyes, squinting as I readjust to the light.

'Morning, babe.' Daniel is looking down at me.

Catherine

I wake up late, screaming.

My body is drenched in sweat, the sheets are tangled tight around me, and my face is wet with tears.

And I am screaming so loud that it hurts my throat.

I used to have nightmares about The Accident all the time. But they were always watered-down versions, or versions where help came, or versions where I was in the time before The Accident and I could still make it not happen.

The nightmare is like watching a film. A film that you've watched before, but in which you still think you can change the ending. It starts when we drop off Julia at my parents.

In real life, Julia was two, and she was angry that we were leaving her but excited to have Granny and Grandpa to herself. Mike and I argued about whether leaving Julia out of the trip was the right thing to do. Mike had won an incentive week in a private game reserve that we would never have been able to afford ourselves, and it was a great opportunity, but not great timing given Julia's age. We'd been arguing, in our gentle way, ever since we'd made the decision to go ahead and book it. I was adamant that Julia was too young for hours of looking at animals. A four-year-old could be entertained and would like the animals, but it was too much for a two-year-old, I said. And malaria, I argued, although Mike very reasonably pointed out that we were not going to a malaria area.

In the dream, just as in life, I get my way. Julia is taken to my parents. Mike is not happy with the decision. He wants Julia with us. Fighting was never our way, but he is scratchy, unsettled. In the dream I reach over and say, 'It was the right decision, Mike. It was the only right decision we made.'

We dropped Julia in the afternoon. It took longer to settle her than we'd expected, and we were worried about the time when we left. Before we went, I phoned the game lodge from my mom's phone. They said not to worry, we could check in any time, the reception was open twenty-four hours a day.

'It's probably better,' Mike said in real life, and he also says it in the dream. 'It's more comfy driving when it's cool.'

In the dream I say, 'No, Mike, we mustn't go.' But he doesn't hear me because, I realise with the clarity of dreaming, he can only hear when I say the things I actually said in real life.

I try anyway. 'Mike, this is dangerous. We mustn't go.'

But he smiles at me, and starts driving. I try to scream, to reach out and grab the wheel, but I can't stop him. This is going to play out, no matter what I do. So I turn my head and watch Mike, absorbing every feature of his conscious face and trying to will myself awake, the part of me that knows I am asleep.

And then it is dark, and we are on a lonely road, and Mike is leaning slightly forward.

'Drive carefully,' I say. 'There's no rush.'

And Mike can hear that, because I said that in real life. Even in real life, I knew.

We see the truck approaching from a long way away. In real life, of course, it was barely of any interest, except that we hadn't seen much traffic on that road for a while. In the dream, I know what's coming and I start to scream, to beg Mike to stop, and I start trying to clamber over to the back seat to avoid the biggest mistake of them all. But that dream thing happens, the one where you can't scream or move, no matter what you do.

In real life, I never found out why the truck swerved. But in the dream, I see it. A rabbit darts into the road, and the truck swerves to miss it. Even as it happens in the dream, I wonder if perhaps this is a real memory finally coming out. Was there a rabbit? Did everything happen because the truck driver – a young man called Ralph, who was rushing home to his wife and daughter – did not want to hurt a rabbit?

The truck swerves onto our side of the road and in the dream, as in life, everything becomes loud and black and hard and I don't know what's happening but I do and I can't stop it and I'm screaming.

But I don't wake up. Not yet. That would be too easy.

The truck hits the driver's side, almost ploughing through us. The wonder is that they weren't killed on impact. Like the truck driver. Because on the driver's side of the car was Mike. And behind him sat our four-year-old son, Jack, who we had thought was old enough to enjoy the trip to the game reserve. Jack, our first child.

Jack, the brightest, funniest, best-looking little boy that ever lived.

Jack, who was asleep at the back of the car when the truck hit.

And even though I know what will happen, the dream plays out like in life and I scream, 'Jack, are you okay?' and he says, 'What happened, Mommy?' and my heart releases because he's alive and that's all that matters and someone will come and help us soon.

And then I look over at Mike, and he is very still, and there is blood trickling out of his nose. But I can see that his chest is moving slightly and I know he is alive too. And even in the dream I think, *This is terrible, but we will be okay.*

But I am completely pinned to my seat. The airbag is holding me in, and a piece of metal from the truck has landed across me. I try to fight it, to get to Jack, but I can't. Eventually, I work my arm free, grazing all the skin off my forearm in the process, and I reach behind me to Jack. He finds my hand.

'Jack,' I say.

'Mommy,' he says, 'Mommy, I have blood.'

'Where, baby?'

He laughs. Actually laughs. 'Everywhere, Mommy!'

'Does it hurt, love?' I say, because I'm starting to feel my own pain – in my foot and along my side where something has grazed me and my arm that I have just hurt.

'A bit now, Mommy,' he says. 'My tummy is a bit sore, Mommy.'

'Okay, Jackie,' I say. 'Mommy's here. Someone will come help us soon. It's gonna be okay, my baby. It's gonna be okay.'

But nobody comes. And I start to think about how empty the road was as we drove, and I manage to move my right arm, the one that is still caught, so that I can see my wrist. It is 10pm. If the roads were already empty, it's unlikely they will get any busier now.

In real life, I hoped. In the dream, I already know.

'Mommy,' says Jack. 'I'm really sore. And sleepy.'

I squeeze his hand.

'Jackie, my baby, my love,' I say in the dream, just as I said in real life, 'I think it's better if you try to stay awake.'

So I talk to Jack and I try to sing and I try not to think about the fact that Mike hasn't moved and the whole world is quiet. And after we have sung a few songs, Jack says, 'Mommy, I want a hug.'

Now I'm crying, like I was in real life. 'Me too, Jackie,' I say. 'But I'm stuck. Someone will help us soon. Just imagine Mommy is hugging you. Imagine my arms are around you.'

But Jack starts to cry and I am crying, and he says, 'I'm so sore, Mommy. I want to sleep.'

'No, Jack,' I scream. 'You mustn't sleep. You must stay awake. You must stay with me.'

But that's just the dream.

In real life, I let him sleep. I said, 'Okay, baby, you go to sleep. The people will be here to help us soon.' And he falls asleep, and his hand slips from my grasp, and for a while I can hear him breathing.

And then I can't.

And in the dream and in real life I scream his name and I scream and I scream.

And in real life, nothing happened. It was another two hours before a car came to a screeching halt beside us and called to me, and then drove as fast as it could to the nearest house and phoned for help. But that was real life.

In the dream I just scream and scream and scream and then I'm awake and my pillow is wet with tears and I'm shaking and screaming and crying.

And I know that this has all been a terrible mistake, thinking I could ever be better. I want to die. Maybe if I die, I will be with Jack again, and hold him, and apologise. Or maybe I won't, and there'll be nothing but oblivion and I will never have to feel this pain again.

I try to get my breathing under control and I make some decisions.

It is time for me to go.

Julia has Daniel and she is having a baby and she will be okay. Yes, she will be a bit thrown by her parents dying just as she is having a child, but Julia is hard. She'll get over it. I wasn't a great mother but I made her self-sufficient. I always knew she would have to be one day.

It is time for me to die, and take the memory of Jack with me.

Because Julia doesn't know about Jack.

Of course, when it happened, when I fetched her from my parents eventually – me broken and grieving and raw – Julia asked about Jack. But I just said, 'He's gone,' and then I wouldn't talk about him again. To anyone. Not to my parents. Not to Julia. Not to friends – all of whom I eventually pushed away – not wanting anyone who knew Jack near me, reminding me. As if I could forget.

I never decided that I would bring Julia up not knowing that she had ever had a brother. I just didn't talk about it. And then she started to forget. And I never reminded her. And then my parents died too, soon after each other, taking away the last people who might have reminded her, because Mike's parents died before I met him. And suddenly it was too late to remind Julia about Jack and it was easier for me not to talk about it, even though I thought about him all day, every day. And there was no one in our lives who would talk about Jack – my parents were dead, and Mike couldn't speak, and the others were all gone. Even if we did bump into an old friend, as sometimes happened, they never said anything directly. 'How *are* you?' they would say, searching my face with their eyes. Because people don't just blurt out your loss – they avoid it or use euphemisms, so they could have been speaking about Mike, from Julia's point of view. And so Julia grew up thinking that she was an only child, and that the reason I mourned so deeply was because of Mike.

But Mike isn't dead. Jack is.

And I was bereft. And I wanted to die. For twenty-six years, I have wanted to die.

And now it is time.

I reach under my bed to where I keep my box of photographs and mementoes of Jack. When Julia was a child, I kept them up high, at the back of a shelf. But now that there's no danger she will stumble across them, I keep them near me again.

For a long time I thought I should perhaps leave the box lying around. Let Julia finally discover the truth. But now I know that I can't. The very first thing I need to do is destroy the photographs. After that, I can kill Mike and then myself. This what I have always wanted, and as I sit holding the box, I am still crying. I stroke the lid. I will not look at his photos now, or his tiny shoes or his first lock of hair or his birth certificate. I will do that for the last time just before I destroy them. I would do it now, but first I have to get the means to kill Mike. I have to think carefully about how to do it.

I take a deep breath. I will be okay; this will all end soon. And Julia will be okay too. And Mike will be free.

The time has come.

And as I breathe in again, and wipe my tears, the doorbell rings. I'm not expecting anyone and I can't see anyone like I am. So I ignore it, even when it rings again.

And then my phone rings and it's Julia.

I answer.

'Mommy,' she says, and I can hear she's crying. 'Mommy, where are you? Mommy, I need you. Please, Mommy – I need you.'

PART 3

September

MONDAY

Catherine

Today is Julia's last day of work before her maternity leave. I suggested to her that it was a bit strange they were making her go in just for a Monday, but she said it is impossible to explain anything involving flexibility to her boss, and it was just easier to end on the date they had agreed. I hear Julia's alarm go off and wait for the sounds of her getting up. I wait five minutes, but there is no noise from her room. Or the spare room, depending on how you look at it.

Eventually I pull myself out of bed, and go down the passage to check.

She's fast asleep, on her back, her mouth slightly open. Her full-term pregnant stomach is enormous beneath the blankets, and her legs look incongruous where they peep out from the tangle.

When Julia was a baby, before The Accident, I used to watch her sleep all the time. I don't know why – I never really watched Jack sleep – but there was something about Julia's vulnerability that touched me. After The Accident, I stopped. The only child I wanted to watch sleep – to watch gently breathe – was Jack. And he was dead and would never breathe again. And then forgotten, by everyone except me.

But now I watch Julia sleep, the giant mound of her unborn son rising and falling beneath the blankets, and I am again struck by her vulnerability.

'Wake up, sweetie,' I say, but I know I'm speaking too softly and she won't hear me. I am tempted to climb into the bed and cuddle her – which I haven't done since Jack died. But since she's been back, as her vulnerability and her baby bump have grown together, I have found myself wanting to reach out to her in a way I never have before.

'Julia,' I say, louder this time, 'Julia, time to get up. Last day of work before maternity leave.' Across the decades, words echo back: last day of school before holidays; last day of holidays before school; last day before we leave you at Granny and Gramps, and take Jack on holiday. Last day.

Julia moans and turns over, her back to me. 'Just five more minutes,' she mutters.

'Julia.' My voice is strong and strict. 'Get. Up. Now.'

This is talk my baby understands, that she knows, and she groans and sits up.

She complains the whole time about how terrible she looks, so pregnant. But to me she has never been more beautiful. I feel sad for Daniel that he's missed this, but that only lasts a minute before I feel angry at Daniel and his stupidity, and instead, I feel sad for Mike that he can't see this, even though I tell him all about it.

And Jack. Since the day Julia turned up on my doorstep that day I had decided to die, I have thought about Jack almost constantly. Often I find myself about to say something before I remember that Julia still doesn't know anything about him. Sometimes I open my mouth to tell her, but the words won't come out.

Julia rubs her face. 'Maternity leave,' she says.

I smile. 'From tomorrow. This party is going to get started pretty soon.'

She takes a deep breath. 'Okay,' she says. 'I can do this.'

'You can do anything.'

'Including have a baby on my own and totally screw up my life?' She's smiling, but I can see it is forced.

'Julia,' I say, 'we are not doing this again. A baby is always a good thing and your life is not screwed up.'

Losing a baby, that screws up a life – is what I want to tell her. Having a baby does not. The only problem I can see with having a baby is that you might lose it. But I can't think like that.

I turn to leave her room.

'Mom?'

'Yes?'

'I couldn't have survived this without you.'

My heart swells with a feeling I have seldom felt: pride at being a good mother to Julia; pride at having done exactly the right thing. I want to tell her that it is my pleasure, my joy. But I don't want to make her feel like she is weak.

'You would have been fine, Julia,' I say. 'You're a strong woman.'

And then I go into the bathroom and I cry, and I don't know if it is from joy or sadness or fear of what is to come.

Julia

As my mother leaves my room, I smile. Her answer is so typical – emotional outpourings don't go very far with her; no hysterical declarations of love. But in the last four months I've been back living here, I've learnt to read my mother better, and there is a shift in her. There's a tiny bit of softness showing through her hard shell, and today I see it in the moment when she pauses before she answers me, the love showing in the way she holds her shoulders.

I didn't expect myself to be back living with my mother, twenty-eight years old and pregnant with a married man's baby. That was not on my script. Even that morning when I arrived on her doorstep, I wasn't expecting to stay. But Daniel was gone. Of course, I knew that he'd gone to Claire. I hadn't realised that he'd actually followed her to Mauritius. And that he wasn't invited. He'd just gone. But I knew I had lost him.

I wasn't going to stay with my mother. I arrived on her doorstep, expecting that she would, in her strange, unemotional way, comfort me and help me back onto the path of my life. I thought I would spend an hour or two with her telling me stiff-upper-lippish things, and then I would return to the business of Daniel leaving me in the same way I've had to handle all the other challenges of my life – essentially, but not entirely, alone.

But there was something different about my mother that morning. For a start, she was in her pyjamas and she looked like shit. My mother never looks like shit. She never looks great either, but she always brushes her hair and teeth and dresses in neat, clean clothes. Recently, she'd started to look really good – she'd actually had her hair coloured and cut, and her clothes seemed to be a bit smarter. But that morning, she looked terrible – her face was splotchy and ravaged. If it was anyone but her, I would've thought they'd been up all night crying. But that obviously couldn't have been the case, and I will admit that I was too distressed to think about it much more.

But that wasn't the really strange part. The really strange part was how she reacted to me. She opened her arms and let me throw myself into them, and then she led me into the house, stroking my back and making soothing sounds. And then she made me a cup of sweet tea, and one for herself, and we curled up on the couch together and I told her everything. And she didn't give me any practical advice. She just stroked my back and made supportive noises.

When I'd finally cried myself out, I looked at her and said, 'So. What must I do?'

And then instead of Catherine's Practical Step-by-Step Life-Advice Guide, I got a shrug. 'You're really sad,' she said. 'I think maybe you should just stay here.'

'With you?'

She smiled. 'Yes, with me.'

'But you like being on your own,' I said.

'Do I?' She looked confused, almost, and – I don't say this lightly – almost vulnerable.

'Well, that's what you always tell me,' I said. 'And you never lie.'

'No,' she said. 'Well, then I guess it must be true. But for now I think it would be good for you to stay with me. And maybe it would be good for me too.'

'How would it be good for you?' I asked, dragged out of my problems despite myself.

'Life is more complex and multi-layered than you think, Julia,' said my mother, who never philosophises.

'Everything happens for a reason?' I hazarded.

'Don't be ridiculous,' said my mother, and even though she sounded really angry, I felt comforted. That was more like it. 'Anyway, Daniel will come crawling back, and you will sort things out.'

I sighed. 'He's gone back to Claire, Mom. Why would he want me when he can have her?'

'I'd choose you any day,' said my mother with a smile. And then she repeated it, like she was saying it to herself – 'I'd choose you any day' – and her eyes sort of turned inwards and I thought that maybe the shock of saying something so parental had made her feel peculiar, so I quickly started asking about the practicalities of me staying.

So that is what I've done. Almost despite myself, as the last four months have played out, I've gone back to my girlhood room – which my mother insists on calling the spare room – and I've stayed with my mommy.

Claire

The alarm goes off when I am so deep in a dream that I react like someone has shot me. I sit straight up in the bed and yell, 'What!'

Nina is curled up next to me, as usual. 'You need to stop doing this, Mommy,' she says without opening her eyes. 'You can't get a fright about waking up every day. Waking up just happens and happens and happens.'

I don't know what it is. I never used to sleep so deeply. And I certainly never used to greet each day with a shout of surprise – so predictable now that it bores my seven-year-old daughter.

I try to claim back the parent role.

'Up we get, Neens. New week. Got to get you to school early for the special concert rehearsal.'

'I know,' says Nina, her eyes still shut, her body unmoving.

'Plus, it's ballet after school.'

'It is,' she agrees.

'And then a playdate with Lulu.'

'Lulu's so boring,' says a still-sleeping Nina, who spent most of last week begging me to invite Lulu to play.

'And after that Daddy's taking you out for supper,' I add.

Nina opens her eyes and sits up. 'But I am not going to sleep at him,' she tells me.

'That's right,' I agree. 'Because—'

'Because,' she interrupts, 'Julia could have that baby AT ANY MINUTE. And Daddy must be able to drive to her AS FAST AS HE CAN. And he can't leave me alone. And I can't go with because the baby being born will be GROSS.'

I laugh. 'That's exactly how it is. You've got it.'

'And none of us know when that damn baby is going to come,' she adds.

'Don't say "damn", Nina.'

'That's what Daddy calls it. He says "that damn baby" every time.'

I try not to laugh. 'Listen, Neens, just don't. That damn baby is going to be your brother, whatever we all think of that. And that's pretty exciting, so let's not say "damn".'

'Can I take it for show-and-tell when it's born?'

'Let's call it "he". And you'll have to ask Julia about show-and-tell.'

'Can I phone her now?'

I look at my watch. 'Too early, baby,' I say. 'It's her last day of work before her having-a-baby holiday. Let's rather phone later.'

'Okay,' says Nina, and without me having to say anything more, she gets up and goes to her room to get dressed.

I get out of bed, and pull my diary towards me from where I left it on my bedside table last night. The day is jam-packed. The week is jam-packed. I smile – this is the way I like it. And this is the way it's been since Laurel and I started our business last month. It's not like my work has changed that much. But before I was just a person called Claire who did PR. Now I'm one half of CL Events. And I have a business partner. It was Laurel's idea, when she broke it off with Sandy.

'My problem is that I'm bored,' Laurel said. 'I have an MBA from a top university, and instead of working a high-powered job, the main challenge of my day is figuring out what to make for supper. No wonder I'm having a sordid affair with the netball coach.'

'I'm not convinced,' I said. 'Maybe if Sandy was a man. This thing with Sandy seems bigger than boredom.'

'But that's just it,' says Laurel. 'A man would have been boring. I've *done* men. I needed a new challenge. I should have started doing mac-ramé. Instead I started doing Sandy.'

When we'd both finished cackling, Laurel looked serious. 'I want to show you something.' She took out her laptop. 'Look at this.'

'This' was a business plan with graphs and predictions and financials of how my business could grow.

'Basically,' said Laurel, 'with your skills and connections, you could start an empire.'

'An empire sounds a bit tiring,' I said.

'That's why we'll do it together,' said Laurel.

And after a bit of thinking and talking to other people, that's exactly what we did. The only person who doesn't think it's a great idea is Sandy, who's been thoroughly dumped. She phones Laurel all the time, and sends her flowers. Between the flowers I get from Daniel and the flowers Laurel gets from Sandy, our small offices in Parkhurst always look fabulous. We're not sure what we'll do when they both give up, as is inevitable. Laurel says I'll have to get a new boyfriend to fill the gap. She doesn't know what she'll do.

'Can't Max fill the gap?' I ask. 'He is your husband, after all. He should be glad to have you back.'

'Max never even knew I was missing,' said Laurel a bit sadly. 'I'm not entirely sure that Max realises I'm working again.'

But that isn't true. Laurel's husband Max pops into our offices with lunch for her at least once a week, and he has referred two clients to us already.

'Just appreciate the bloody man,' I tell Laurel often. 'Just appreciate what you have saved.'

'Mommy,' says Nina, now in her school uniform, interrupting my thoughts as I start to get dressed.

'Yes, baby?'

'Tell me again why Daddy can't live with Julia?'

'Because Julia got really cross when Daddy met us in Mauritius. And she was quite right.'

'Not as cross as you though.' Nina starts giggling. 'You were so, so cross. You said all sorts of bad words. You threw the sugar bowl at Daddy's head.'

Some children might have found this traumatic, but Nina found it hilarious. I even took her to a play therapist after it all happened, but the therapist confirmed that Nina seemed remarkably unscarred. Even at the time, while Daniel and I stood yelling on the deck of a five-star hotel, Nina was doubled over with laughter. And she loves retelling the story. I realise that's the only reason she's asked about Julia again – for the chance to retell the story of the flying sugar bowl. Soon she'll be listing all the words we said.

'Enough, Neens,' I say. 'Hurry up and get ready. Concert practice, remember?'

'You called Daddy a—'

'*Enough*, Neens,' I say sternly. 'I don't want to hear those words out of your mouth again. Get ready!'

But I'm laughing as she leaves. Daniel's face *was* priceless.

Daniel

I wake up and look at the ceiling. It's still the same one. The wrong one. Or maybe it's the right one, but with no one next to me in the bed, I don't know any more.

I'm hoping that the fact that Julia hasn't thrown me out of her flat means she's picturing coming back to me when the baby is born. I'm also hoping Claire will take me back.

I reach for my cellphone and go onto the Internet. My browser goes straight to the same-day gifting service, that's how much I use it. I organise to send them both flowers. Sometimes I have the energy to send them different things. Not today. I send them both sweet peas. I know Claire loves sweet peas – she always says so. And surely Julia would too? I mean, who wouldn't love sweet peas? Anyway, it doesn't matter. It's not like they're going to compare notes.

I contemplate getting up. But it seems like a lot of hard work, so I roll over and close my eyes. As I drift back to sleep, I realise I have no idea what a sweet pea looks like. When I wake up, I think I'll google it.

When I wake up, I'll google everything.

Julia

Steve is already there when I get to work.

'I thought we finished three weeks ago?' I say, smiling.

Finishing the work for Steve's company before my maternity leave became the biggest goal of my work life. Steve didn't seem in any hurry, finding queries and wanting to double-check things, but I just ploughed right on. His boss was thrilled by our exceptional turnover time and service delivery. Gerald gaped at me like he'd never seen a person before – but that might relate to his utter discomfort with my enormous belly. Only Steve was less than thrilled. Hurt, almost. Until I told him he could still visit if he wanted to, and even take me out to lunch. What with me being hungry all the time.

'It's your last day,' he says now. 'And I knew our dear Gerald wouldn't have done anything. So I've arranged a special farewell.'

'Oh Steve, we're not that sort of company,' I say, appalled at the thought of a baby shower involving Gerald and his nervous secretary. 'It will be ghastly.'

'That's why I'm taking you all out for lunch and Gerald is paying,' says Steve. 'There'll be no jolly games or anything like that.'

'Lunch?'

'Yes,' says Steve. 'Because you really, really like lunch.'

We both laugh – my appetite has become our standing joke.

'I do,' I say. 'But it's 8am. Surely we're not going for lunch now?'

'True,' says Steve, looking crestfallen. 'This is true.'

'And you don't actually work here,' I point out.

'No,' he says. 'I don't.' Then he smiles. 'But, you see, I came to check that—'

'That I hadn't had the baby in the night?'

'How did you know?'

I laugh. 'Because it's the third time in the last two weeks you've had an uncanny feeling that I've gone into labour.'

'It felt definite this time,' says Steve. 'And I'm not sure you'll remember to call me if it happens.'

'Oh, I'm sure calling you will be the furthest thing from my mind,' I say. 'But my mom has your number on her "Baby news" list, and my mom will *not* be swept away with emotion.'

'She might be, you know,' he tells me.

We've been through this, but Steve's still convinced that my mother is a normal person. He bases this on the fact that I'm living with her again. He feels that a person as hard as I claim my mother is would have sent me back to my own house.

What makes it stranger is that he's actually met my mother, and he still thinks she's a warm person. 'Achingly vulnerable', was how he described her.

'And you're achingly blind,' I snapped back, but he's immovable.

A thought strikes me. 'You haven't invited my achingly vulnerable mother to this lunch of yours, have you?' I ask.

'Listen, I'd love to stay and chat, but I have an actual job to go to.'

'Oh, crap, you have.'

Steve smiles. 'I like your mom,' he says, like that's an answer. 'See you later.' And he's gone.

Before the door has even closed, the delivery guy steps into my office carrying a huge bouquet of sweet peas – I didn't actually know you could fit so many in a bunch. He knows me so well by now he just hands them over without comment.

'Thanks,' I say. There's an awkward pause while he waits for a tip. If I tipped him every time, I'd be broke, but it's my last day at work so I might not see this same delivery guy again. 'Here—' I give him fifty rand, 'you've been great.'

A smile transforms his face. 'Thank you,' he says. 'And good luck. Maybe you can take flower-guy back when the baby comes.'

'But then the flowers would stop,' I point out.

We both laugh, and I feel good. I can't believe I can joke about Daniel, but then there's a lot I can't believe about how things have changed in the four months since he left.

As if summoned by the thought, my phone beeps. It's a text from Claire.

'Sweet peas,' it says. 'You?'

'Also,' I type back.

'Lazy arse.'

'The laziest,' I reply.

'Nina might call this afternoon about taking the baby to show and tell after he's born. Okay?' texts Claire.

'Hilarious,' I answer.

'She's excited.' I suspect Claire's lying, so I'm not really sure what to say. After a few moments I just type: 'xx'.

Claire

I put down my phone.

I would never have predicted that Julia and I would ever speak to each other again, let alone have such an easy comradery. The reality is, like it or not, that we're friends again. We'll never be friends exactly like we were before, because you can't sleep with someone's husband and expect to waltz back into her heart – but we *are* friends. And our children – again, whether we like it or not – will be siblings.

When Daniel showed up in Mauritius, I knew our marriage was over. Maybe if he'd come back to me in a different way, at a different time, he could have persuaded me. But following me to Mauritius was so invasive. *So* all about his needs and not about mine. And when I saw him, I felt nothing but irritation and anger. I realised that if I was still in love with him, I would have felt glad. It would have been the stuff of fantasy.

But as it was, I threw the sugar bowl at him. To Nina's great amusement.

And strangely, it was his attitude to Julia that cemented it.

'What did Julia do when you left?' I yelled at him.

He looked sheepish. 'I don't know.'

'What do you mean you don't know? You can't get on a plane to Mauritius to see your wife without your pregnant girlfriend having something to say about it.' I looked at him and he looked at me. 'Oh my fuck,' I said, 'you just left.'

'I sent an SMS,' he said defensively.

'You know what, Daniel? Go home. Just go home. Maybe you can still salvage things with Julia. Because you can't with me.'

And I actually thought that was what had happened, that Julia had taken him back.

But then the flowers started to arrive. Truth to tell, I wouldn't be surprised if he'd sent me flowers and notes begging forgiveness while still living with Julia. But one day my flowers arrived with a note addressed to her: 'Julia, if not for me, for the baby. Xx Dan', said the card.

So I phoned her.

Julia sounded tentative when she answered. 'Claire?'

I cut to the chase. 'I've just got some flowers addressed to you.'

'Hang on,' she said, and I heard rustling in the background. 'Oh my God' – she came back on the line – 'my card is addressed to you. It says: "Don't throw away what we had."'

'Why's he sending *you* flowers?' I asked. 'Doesn't he live with you?'

'I moved out. He's in my flat still, but we're done. I'm not prepared to be second best.'

I had to think about that. 'So … he sends us both flowers, hoping one option or the other will work out for him.'

Julia's voice was subdued. 'He doesn't even care which one of us responds.' She sighed. 'I don't even know why I am surprised.'

'Me neither.'

We were both silent for a few moments.

'How's the pregnancy going?' I eventually asked.

'Okay,' said Julia. 'Better now that Daniel isn't around telling me how perfectly you handled every moment of your pregnancy.'

I laughed. 'My pregnancy was revolting. I got so swollen they had to cut my rings off my fingers. I vomited three times every day.'

'Really?' Julia sounded so vulnerable.

'Really,' I said. 'And Daniel kept making remarks about how it couldn't really be that bad if millions of women do it every day, and that I needed to man up.'

'Man up?' Julia laughed. 'He told you to *man up* in the middle of a pregnancy?'

'Yes. And I hadn't realised how absolutely ridiculous that is until this very minute.'

'It's seriously ridiculous,' said Julia. 'Seriously.'

We both laughed, and then felt awkward at the same moment and stopped.

'Anyhow,' I said. 'Good luck and all that.'

'You too,' she said.

I thought that would be the end of it, but then we started exchanging messages about the flowers. Sometimes we even sent pictures. And then, out of the blue, Nina wanted to see her, and I took her over to visit Julia at her mom's place. I just dropped her – I didn't stay. But when I fetched her two hours later, Julia thanked me and hugged me. And we started talking sometimes. Never a lot. Mostly by WhatsApp. But yes, we're friends again.

I smile. Without Daniel in my life, I have more time for my friends. And I like that. So today, like every day, my first task after the school run is to check for birthdays and send my wishes. Then I send a few warm messages to people like Janice, catching up, checking in, making time to value them. After that, because it's Monday, I check my diary to make sure the week makes sense – that I know where Nina has to be, where I have to be, what goals I have to achieve. I love Mondays. I love the feeling of a clean page in front of me.

I hear the sound of Laurel arriving and putting on the kettle. I gather my diary and pen, and go to join her. We'll have our daily strategy session before we get down to work.

My phone beeps. I look at it expecting Julia again, but it's Daniel.

'Why don't you join me and Nina for dinner tonight?'

I think of the sweet peas. Identical bunches winging their way to both Julia and me this morning. Six months ago I would have said something rude, or made up a date. Instead, I just say no.

One day it will stick.

TUESDAY

Julia

My first day of maternity leave, and I sleep late.

Thank goodness for maternity leave, really, because an unforeseen side effect of both being pregnant and moving in with my mother has been a busy social life. In the first place, I now have things in common with my old friends again. Heleen is happy to issue dire warnings and give too much advice. Mary-Anne is pregnant too, and we've spent hours talking about how we are feeling and what friends our babies will be. And things didn't work out for Agnes in Jamaica, so she came back last month – so suddenly I have lots of friends again, not just Claire and the pottery widows.

As for my mother! When I arrived, she seemed to be avoiding her friends – those strange people who had crowded into the hospital room with my dad, and some new ones. It brought back hazy childhood memories of my mother giving any overture of friendship a gentle but assured brush off – she never stayed for tea when she fetched me, never invited people in, refused invitations and never returned calls.

She was doing these things to her friends, but now it was making her angry and itchy, and her friends were having none of it. Ewan and Okkie phoned to chat, whether or not she was listening. And they turned up at the house, and scolded her for hiding. And that Eddie, the ageing rock-star one, turns out to have a wife in the home with Daddy. He cornered her when they were both there visiting, crying about his wife and seemingly totally oblivious to the fact that my mother was brushing him off, until she gave in and said, 'Come, Eddie, let's go have some coffee.'

And then there's a chap called Larry. He's ancient, obviously, but kind of sexy in an ancient way. And he turns up and ignores her ignoring him, and talks and talks until she starts laughing. He's even persuaded her to go to dinner with him twice, and a movie. 'It's not a date, Catherine,' he says, although it's clear to anyone with eyes that it is. 'Think of it as your charity work. Comforting a lonely old divorcé.' And he'll wink at me, and my mother laughs and agrees.

'But it's not a date,' she keeps saying, and I just nod because I'm having a baby with a married man so what do I know.

But the weirdest of the lot is this couple Stan and Lizette. Stan is Eddie's brother – they even look alike, only Stan never cries and Eddie cries most of the time. But Stan and Lizette *love* my mother. I don't really know why, because she seems to actively dislike Lizette, and anyway, my mother isn't very warm. But they love her. They're constantly inviting her places, sometimes with that Larry and Eddie, sometimes not. She accepts about one in four invitations, and it doesn't deter them.

'I'm not the sort of person to takes no for an answer,' Lizette told me the first time I met her. 'Your mother's the sort of person who understands that.' She dropped her voice like she was telling me a secret. 'Your mother's the sort of person who needs to get out more.'

I chuckled. 'I would have said my mother was the sort of person who doesn't need to go out *at all*,' I told her. 'But what do I know.'

According to my mother, Lizette apparently interpreted this as a plea for help and now we *both* get invited. Which is what happened last night.

Last night was particularly mad because Lizette was trying to set me up with someone. I'm actually nine months pregnant, and this woman is trying to set me up. I didn't even realise. When we arrived, she sat me down next to an awkward young man and said, 'This is Greg. He's a doctor,' and then walked away, which is very unlike Lizette.

'This is so awkward,' I said to Dr Greg.

'Yes,' he said, a blush engulfing his entire face. Like the whole thing. Even his nose. Even his eyebrows.

'She's put me next to you in case I go into labour,' I said. 'The ultimate in hostessing: a doctor for your pregnant guest. Will you be taking my blood pressure between courses? And shouting at me if I drink wine?' I laughed. 'Not that I will,' I added hastily, because I didn't want even a stranger thinking I was irresponsible.

'I don't think that's why she's put us together,' said Greg. 'And there is lots of evidence that an occasional glass of wine does no harm to a baby, and may in fact be of benefit to the mother.'

'Then why has she put us together?' I asked. 'And I've read all the stuff, but I'm taking the better-safe-than-sorry route. I mean, it's not like I'm an alcoholic or something, so I might as well just not drink. Definitely.'

We seemed to be having two conversations at once.

'She's trying to set us up,' said Greg, the blush happening again. He had very pale blond hair and I expected to actually see blood rushing up the hairs. 'And yes, not drinking is probably the safest route at the end of the day.'

'Set us up?' I said, now distracted from the second conversation. 'But I'm nine months pregnant! Is she insane?'

My mother, who was sitting nearby talking to Eddie, looked over at me, smiled and gave a wink. A wink? My mother?

'Well, I admit it was a surprise when you walked in,' said Greg. 'She somehow forgot to tell me about that when she was telling me about you.'

Something about pregnancy, and the whole ridiculous situation I have found myself in, has made me outspoken. So I called across the room to Lizette: 'Lizette, how the hell do you set someone up with someone and not tell the someone that the other someone is heavily pregnant? How is that even a thing?'

Most people would be embarrassed or apologise, but not our Lizette. 'Well, I'm not the sort of person who wants people to pre-judge each other,' she said calmly. 'So I didn't tell him you were pregnant, and I didn't tell you he's a recovering alcoholic.'

'Lizette, you didn't tell me *anything* about him. Because I would've told you that I. Am. About. To. Have. A. *Baby!*' Then I turned to Greg. 'Not that the alcohol thing would have been a problem, okay? It's the fact that there's another man's child in my uterus that's the problem.' I directed this last part at Lizette, who was unflinching. Then I remembered what I'd said about not being an alcoholic and wanted the floor to just open up and my whole enormous self to disappear into it.

At that point, Lizette's mild husband Stan stepped in. 'You meant well, love,' he said, 'but I did tell you she might find it inappropriate.'

'You *did*,' confirmed Lizette with amazement, not at all upset. 'And you were right. Isn't it extraordinary? People are so strange!' This was all directed at Stan.

'Extraordinary,' he echoed, and smiled at me. Life with Lizette has turned the man into the world's most skilled diplomat – his talent is wasted in suburban Johannesburg.

So then I had to speak to Greg the rest of the night to prove that I wasn't judging him for being an alcoholic, and he had to speak to me to prove he wasn't upset that he'd been set up with a pregnant woman, and at the end of the night Lizette took our hands and said, 'You see, I knew you'd get on. Inseparable.' And we both smiled weakly and my mother started giggling.

Giggling. My mother.

All in all, it was an extraordinary night. And today I'm exhausted.

Claire

Last night while Nina was out having supper with Daniel, I made a few cottage pies. This morning I drop one off at Lynette next door, because she has pneumonia and I suspect she isn't eating. One is for Liandri's family, because Liandri has got such bad post-partum depression that she's been hospitalised for a few days. And one is for Nina and me tonight.

When I drop Nina at school, Mrs Wood is waiting for me.

'Is everything okay at home?' she says, taking me aside.

'It's very well,' I say. 'Thank you for asking.' I'm wracking my brain for what might have triggered this. Homework done. Lunch packed. Nina happy. Tick, tick, tick.

'It's just that Nina's told everyone she's bringing a baby to show-and-tell. A baby *brother*.'

'Well,' I say, 'probably not soon. But his due date is round the corner, so she might bring him when he's old enough.'

Mrs Wood looks down at my stomach, and I laugh.

'Oh, it's not mine. It's her father's ex-girlfriend.' I hold Mrs Wood's eyes, keeping a smile on my face. I'm actually quite enjoying this.

'Ah,' says Mrs Wood. 'Yes. And you're okay with Nina bringing him here?'

I draw myself up slightly. 'Mrs Wood,' I say, 'the baby will be Nina's *brother*. I expect him to be greeted and talked about and celebrated as you would the birth of any other sibling in this school.' I pause. 'Now I know I can totally depend on you.'

'Yes, completely. How totally sensible,' says Mrs Wood, nodding enthusiastically, like what I've just said is the point she wanted to make all along.

As I turn to leave, I remember that when Liandri had her baby, the school sent an enormous bunch of flowers. So I turn back, and scrabble in my bag for my notebook and pen.

'Here is Julia's name,' I say, scribbling it on a piece of paper. 'She'll be having the baby at the Park Lane. I'm sure the school would like to send flowers when Nina's brother is born.'

Mrs Wood looks mystified. 'Of course,' she eventually says. 'I'll tell the PA.'

'You're an absolute blessing,' I say. 'I don't know how any of us will cope with a different teacher next year.'

'Ah, well,' says Mrs Wood. 'I do my best.'

'And we all *appreciate* it,' I say, walking away as quickly as I can.

In the car park I see Janice, who rushes across to me, ponytail bouncing and gym clothes sparkling, a stranger to sweat.

We hug each other. 'You haven't been to gym, you faker,' I say to her. 'You smell of Chanel, not sweaty socks and chlorine.'

Janice laughs and indicates a car park full of women in exercise gear. 'Do any of them really go?' she says. 'And anyway, I actually *am* going after this.'

'Why don't you join that lot?' I indicate the group of moms who use the school as the starting point for their morning run. 'They seem very social. In fact, I think *I* might join them.'

'Okay, that sounds great. We can both do that. But first can we talk about the rhinos ...?'

I've been ambushed by a Janice charity appeal, and I didn't even see it coming. I'm getting soft in my old age.

'The rhinos?' I say. 'Terrible.'

'I know how you feel about them,' says Janice. 'So I thought you and Laurel would like to handle the celebrity golf day we're setting up.' She pauses. 'We'll pay you.'

I see by the laugh in her eyes that she knew I was going to say no. But paid work is different.

I smile. 'And we will obviously give you a hugely discounted rate.' Laurel and I have been looking for a high-profile showcase – and this could be it. 'Give me a call later and let's set up an appointment.'

'Fab. Somebody just has to do something about this scourge.'

'Exactly,' I say, making a mental note to read up on rhino-poaching statistics before the meeting. 'And you are always so selfless, Janice. An inspiration to us all.'

'Lovely,' Janice preens. 'I'll give you a shout later this morning ... *after* I go to gym.'

I actually quite like the idea of joining the running mothers, so I walk over to speak to them. I know a few, and they quickly introduce me to the others – and it turns out they are happy for me to join them. 'The more the merrier,' says a large woman who seems to be the incongruous unofficial leader of the runners. 'Just be warned that we often reward ourselves with chocolate at the end.'

'Even better,' I say. 'Can't wait.' And we agree that I'll join them tomorrow.

As I walk back to the car, mentally running through a checklist of the morning's work, my phone beeps.

Daniel.

'I know you're only pretending to be happy without me. We were meant to be together. We need each other.'

I actually laugh out loud. I want to type, 'The only thing you need is klap upside your head,' but Daniel's never been good with slang for some reason, so instead I just say, 'Nope. Genuinely happy.'

And I am.

Catherine

I wake up with a slight hangover from Lizette's dinner and I have to down two painkillers before I can even think of going to work.

But before I do that, I have a mental word with Jack. I've been doing this every few days since that terrible nightmare four months ago, when Julia arrived on my doorstep and put an end to my suicide plans.

'Mommy remembers you every day, baby,' I say. I wish I could take out a photo and keep it next to my bed. But it is too late to explain it to Julia. I pause, remembering how happy Jack was when Julia was born. It was only a two-year age gap – but Jack was completely delighted by the baby. He wanted to hold her the whole time and touch her and kiss her. When she cried at night and I went to her, Jack would sometimes wake up too.

'Mommy, baby cry,' he would call.

'I'm going, sweetie,' I would answer, and he'd go back to sleep.

People warned me that they would fight when they got older. But it never happened. Jack doted on Julia until the day he died. When we dropped her off at my parents that day, he'd said, 'Is Julia okay here, Mommy? Won't Julia be lonely?' But we'd explained that she was too young, and that we'd take her on other holidays.

'We have hundreds of holidays with Julia ahead of us, Jackie,' Mike had said. 'This one is for Jackie and Mom and Dad.'

I feel my eyes filling up with tears thinking about it. I never used to cry about Jack. I used to hold it all in. But now I cry the whole time. It should make me more depressed, but somehow, it doesn't.

I wipe away my tears, and get ready for work. It's strange not having to wake Julia. I glance into the room, and her head is back and she's gently snoring. Her child will be born any day now. Julia will be okay when the baby is born, I tell myself.

When I get to work, Ewan is already there.

'Have we had the baby yet?' he says as I walk in.

I laugh. 'We've been through this, you dummy. I will message you as soon as the baby is born. And there's a good chance I won't come into work the next day if the baby is born in the night.'

Because Julia has asked me to be at the birth. She has reluctantly agreed that Daniel can also be in the room. But she wants *me* there. I was blown away by her asking me that. I'd never have imagined it. In her teens, Julia spent a lot of time casually mentioning how cold and distant I was, and she was right. So I never thought of myself as the sort of mother who would see her grandchild being born. And be excited about it.

But now here I am, the sort of mother who gets invited to the birth of her grandchild. Julia and I have even been to classes together, where she learns to breathe and I learn to give her ice chips and hold her hand. I feel a bit sorry for Daniel, actually. He's been more than happy to come to the classes to support Julia. She lets him come, but she makes him sit in a corner, and he's not allowed to touch her or really speak to her. Sometimes he speaks to me in the tea breaks. He seems sad and confused. But when I tell Julia that, she gets very cross.

'Sad and confused is his thing,' she said to me last week. 'He's so sad and confused that he doesn't even care who he gets back, me or Claire. And he's so delusional that he doesn't even realise we know.'

When she put it like that, it was hard to argue. And I am angry at how he hurt her – I wanted to kill him when it happened. It's just hard to maintain the anger when he looks up at me with those sad eyes of his, like I might have the answers.

'Be careful of those eyes, Mom,' Julia said when I told her this. 'Look where those goddamn eyes got me.'

And then we both started giggling until Julia almost wet herself, and she looked at me and said, 'That was the best. It was worth having an affair with a married man and getting pregnant with a half-wanted baby just to laugh with you like that.'

And my eyes filled with tears, and I turned away, because nobody has ever said anything that wonderful to me before.

It's halfway through the morning that I get a call from Edward.

'Hey, you,' I answer. 'How's the hangover? Mine's a shocker. Never thought I would feel like this again.'

'Catherine,' says Eddie, and his voice is serious. 'Catherine, something's happened.'

'Is it Julia?' I say, panicked. Although almost immediately I know that would make no sense. Why would Eddie know if something had happened to Julia?

'No,' he says, not particularly confused by the question. 'It's Miriam. She's woken up.'

The words hang between us. I must have misheard.

In the end, with everything that happened, I never told Edward about the time Miriam moved when I visited her. And she never moved again. I was glad I hadn't got his hopes up.

'You mean she moved?' I ask now.

'No,' he says. And I realise his voice isn't serious. It's something else. Flustered and excited and scared and happy. 'She's woken up. She woke up at six this morning, pulled the ventilator tube out of her nose and asked for a cup of tea.'

'Tea,' I echo, unable to believe what I'm hearing. 'She woke up and asked for tea.'

'Isn't it amazing, Catherine? Isn't this the best thing that has ever happened?'

'The best thing,' I echo.

'I knew you'd be happy for me. I knew you'd be the only one who understood.'

'Yes,' I say, because I don't know what else to say, and we are silent for a moment. 'Did they call you right away?'

I have always wondered about this: would they call me right away if Mike woke up?

'Well, it seems they first examined her,' he says. 'And when they asked her what she thought had happened, she said that she'd been in a coma but now she was ready to wake up. Can you believe it? It's just like you said – they know exactly what's going on.'

'Wow,' I say, because I don't know what else to say. 'And you've seen her?'

'Yes,' said Eddie. 'Oh, Catherine, it's amazing. She's exactly like she was. It's like nothing happened.'

'Oh.'

'And they say they just want to observe her for a week, but if she stays like this, she can go home.' He laughs. 'My Miri will be home in a week.'

I realise I have tears running down my cheeks, and I'm not really sure why. But I give myself the benefit of the doubt. 'Edward,' I say, 'I am so happy for you that I'm crying.'

'I can't wait for you to meet her properly,' he says. 'You two are going to be the best of friends, I just know it.'

'Well, I can't wait.' I think of all the things I want to ask Miriam – finally someone will be able to tell me what it has been like for Mike. 'Did she say what it felt like?' I ask.

'She says it was like she was in a deep sleep, and sometimes she knew what was happening,' he says. 'But it's like you said, she didn't really know how much time had passed. She thought it was about three weeks.'

'Three weeks?' I echo.

Edward laughs. 'Mad, huh? I've been alone for almost two years, and she thinks it's three weeks.'

I wonder what twenty-six years has felt like to Mike. I wonder if he thinks it's been three weeks. Maybe he's not feeling trapped at all ... He's just thinking he'll rest for a few more days, and has lost track of time. Maybe while I've lived a lifetime in hell, he's been resting for three weeks. Maybe he just doesn't want to wake up to a reality where Jack is dead. Maybe he's the lucky one.

Edward is talking and I have no idea what he is saying, so I tune back in.

'... maybe this afternoon?' he is saying.

'Sorry, I spaced out for a moment there. Maybe what this afternoon?'

'You can come and meet Miri.'

'Tomorrow's Wednesday,' I say. 'That's my visiting day. I'll come meet her then.'

'Oh,' says Edward. 'Okay.' I can hear how disappointed he is. He wanted me to rush to the hospital right now.

'Edward,' I say, and I decide to be honest, because I know Edward is a kind man and he will get it. 'I am so happy for you, but I am also desperately, agonisingly jealous. I just need time to digest this.'

Edward is silent for a moment. 'Oh, Catherine,' he says. 'I hadn't thought. How selfish of me. Me of all people. Of course this is weird for you.'

I feel my eyes fill up again. 'It really is,' I say. 'But I look forward to meeting Miri properly tomorrow. I really do.'

'Okay,' says Edward. I can tell that I have spoilt his joy a bit, but I can't help it.

'And I'll bring some champagne,' I say, trying to make it better. 'This deserves celebration.'

'Thanks, Catherine – you're the best.'

We say our goodbyes. And then I cry for real.

WEDNESDAY

Julia

My mother *was* invited to the strange baby shower lunch on Monday, but she didn't come. 'I didn't think it would be appropriate,' she said. Instead, she organised to go for lunch with Steve and me yesterday.

I had questioned the whole arrangement.

'Well,' said Steve, 'you really like lunch, and you'll be bored on your first day, and I, well, I don't mind.' And he'd blushed.

'You also really like lunch, right?' I said.

'I really do,' he answered.

My mom and I got to lunch before Steve. At first, she was all jumpy and prickly – snapping answers at me like I had no right to ask her simple things like how she was. But then, after she'd had a sip of wine and I'd had a glass of water, she said, 'Sorry I'm so jumpy' – which was already a huge shock because normally she has no insight into how peculiar her behaviour can be. But then she said the next part: that the reason she was so jumpy was because Edward's wife had woken up. And I couldn't get my head around that.

'From her coma?' I said. 'But she's only been in it for a few years.' Like there's some sort of time that has to be served in a coma.

'I know,' said my mother. 'I guess that's how it was for her.'

'But Dad's been in a coma far longer,' I said. 'It's not fair. It's like she's skipped the queue.'

'I know what you mean, Julia,' said my mother. 'I feel like that too. But we're not being rational. It doesn't work like that.'

'I know.' I paused. 'But it's unfair, right?'

Mom sighed. 'No, it's not fair. But you and I know life's not fair.'

I felt sad and angry, but I also felt kind of happy – my mother recognised that it was her and me against the world. She's never made me feel like that before.

'Maybe Dad will wake up soon too?' I said.

'I don't think it works like that,' she said. 'Like it's catchy, and they all wake up together. As much as I wish it did.'

'Mom,' I ventured, 'he's going to wake up one day, right?'

'I don't know any more,' said my mom. 'I don't actually know.'

'But he hears us, right?'

'Of course,' said my mother. 'I mean, Miriam was on a ventilator. Mike breathes on his own. So he must be at least as conscious as she was.'

'Right,' I said.

'Right,' she said.

But neither of us are actually sure, I don't think. And then Steve arrived and we had to act normal – well, what passes for normal in our family. But I think we were both only thinking about that one thing.

But when we both came home in the evening, we didn't talk about Miriam waking up. We didn't talk about anything much, and Mom just pushed the pasta I'd made around her plate, although she carefully thanked me for it.

'It's nice coming home to a hot meal,' she said, even though she didn't eat it.

'Don't get to used to it,' I said, laughing. 'When this baby comes, you're going to do *all* the cooking.'

That perked her up slightly. 'Maybe I'll take some time off work.'

'Like maternity leave for Grannies,' I said. 'Graternity leave.'

She smiled. 'I'll put in for Graternity leave first thing tomorrow.'

This morning when I wake up, I think about what my mom said about the hot meal, and realise that I haven't been helping much. I've noticed that the towel cupboard is a mess, so I start there. My lower back is a bit sore, but I really want to get the towels sorted, so I keep going. I want to organise the towels in piles of different colours and with the most worn-out ones at the bottom.

This, I tell myself, will make my mother's life much easier.

Catherine

I phone Julia mid-morning to tell her that I've actually successfully arranged two weeks' 'graternity' leave, starting as soon as the baby is born. And to remind her that I will be with Mike this afternoon and stupid-bloody-wide-awake Miriam.

'I've sorted out the towel cupboard,' says Julia. 'And alphabetised the spices and cleaned the fridge.'

'Are you feeling okay?' I ask.

'A few Braxton Hicks,' says Julia. 'Also, I changed all the linen. It smelt funny.'

'Okay,' I say, even though the linen was changed two days ago. Everyone knows pregnant women are strange. And I'm thinking about meeting Miriam, so I don't really have the energy to ask about sheets.

'Mom,' says Julia, 'I have to go. The scones might burn.'

'Scones?' But the line is already dead.

I look at my phone for a few seconds, feeling like I'm missing something. There's a thought at the tip of my tongue, but it's slippery and I lose it. I know I'm nervous about meeting Miriam. Edward and Larry have become so much a part of my life, and Miriam might not like that. And if she doesn't like me, they won't stay friends with me either. I'm trying to tell myself that I'm worried about my friendship with Eddie, but it's Larry I'm picturing. If Miriam doesn't like me, her brother won't want to stay friends with me.

'Friends,' I mutter, loud enough that the people in the waiting room look up, startled. I smile vaguely and pretend to write a note in the appointment book. I can hear Julia's voice in my head, teasing me about Larry, even though she doesn't in real life. All Julia says about anything these days is, 'What do I know?'

Before I can think more about Julia, Ewan comes through.

'Okkie wants to go and see his family in Uganda,' he announces to me and the waiting room. I feel the energy in the room shift. This is interesting. Mrs Beaumont has high blood pressure; I hope the excitement won't kill her.

'That's lovely,' I say, unsure why Ewan looks so angry. 'I believe Uganda is beautiful. Will you go too?'

Ewan looks at me. 'Do you know what happens to gay albinos in Uganda?'

Mrs Beaumont isn't even pretending to read her magazine any more.

'People with albinism,' I correct, almost without thinking. Since becoming friends with Okkie and Ewan, I've become very sensitive to language and feel quite disturbed hearing Ewan say 'albino'. 'And anyway, is that a known sub-group? Gay albinos? Is it like a thing? Like a club?'

Ewan looks at me. 'You're not taking this very seriously.'

'I'm sorry,' I say. 'I'm not myself today.'

'You mustn't let him go,' pipes up Mrs Beaumont from the waiting-room chair. 'The Ugandans are very odd about homosexuality. This Okkie character must stay right here. No good will come of being gay with albinism in Uganda, mark my words.' She says the last part in a dark voice, as if she personally has experience in this field.

Ewan glares at me. 'Mrs Beaumont gets it.' And he goes back into his office.

I suspect Okkie is about to get a phone call telling him that even old Mrs Beaumont in the waiting room doesn't want him to go.

'Dr Marigold is such a nice young man,' says Mrs Beaumont, reopening her magazine. 'I hope his friend doesn't do anything stupid.'

The whole incident is so strange that I feel completely wrong-footed. I send Ewan an email: 'Sorry I wasn't sympathetic. I'm distracted. Miriam woke up.'

A minute later, Ewan bursts out of his room again. 'Miriam *woke up?*' he yells across the floor. 'What the hell?'

'I know,' I mutter, aware of Mrs Beaumont's eyes on me again. 'I'm going to see her this afternoon. Meet her.'

'Bloody hell,' says Ewan. 'That's something for the books. Come through, Mrs Beaumont.'

Mrs Beaumont looks perkier than I have ever seen her, and I can hear her asking whether Miriam is also from Uganda before the door has even closed.

I sigh, and wonder if Ewan expects me to say something to Okkie. This is one of the things about being out of the habit of friends – I'm not at all sure what is expected.

I phone Julia and tell her the story. 'I'm not really sure what to do,' I say. 'Should I say something to Okkie?'

'What do I know?' says Julia.

'Well, you have lots of friends,' I say. 'You know what people expect.'

'Ja, I'm a superstar with friendships, Mom,' says Julia. 'Pregnant with the baby of the husband of the nicest friend I ever had. You should totally follow my advice.'

'Well, I'm not going to get pregnant with Okkie's baby,' I say, and suddenly we're both laughing. I love that, even though the patients in the waiting room are looking at me like I've grown two heads.

'Anyway, Mom,' says Julia. 'Have to go – I'm painting the baby's room.'

'Why? It's already painted.'

'It is completely and utterly the wrong colour. I don't know what we were thinking.'

The room is slightly off-white – 'Battered Stone' I think was the name. Julia spent hours choosing it.

'Oh,' I say. 'What colour are you painting it now?' I've wanted a nice light green all along, and I feel quite hopeful that she is finally taking my advice.

'Distressed Cream,' answers Julia, without any apparent irony.

'Be careful, darling,' I say. 'You're very pregnant. Maybe you shouldn't be painting.'

'Honestly, Mom. I can't possibly leave this like it is.' And she hangs up before I can answer.

She really has been very strange today.

Claire

My morning run with the car-park mothers proves unexpectedly wonderful. Not so much because of the run – I am hopelessly unfit and can barely keep up as we pound the suburban blocks. But my body feels good, and I remember how much I loved running when I was at school. By the end of the route, despite a sharp pain in my calf and me breathing like I'm in the final stages of emphysema, I'm secretly wondering if I should sign up for some glamorous marathon. When we all stop for coffee and chocolate croissants, it turns out that everyone's on the same page, because they tell me they're planning on running the New York Marathon next year. And they say they would love me to join, even though they've just met me. And nobody suggests I come up with a theme, or plan an event, or even research something – they just want me to come along, and I feel a little bit of what I felt when I first met Julia.

Almost as though summoned, my phone starts pinging. I look down, and there are a series of messages from her.

'How do I work the camper cot you gave me? Xx'

'Never mind, figured it out. Xx'

'Do I need a bottle steriliser if I'm breastfeeding? Xx'

'What if I can't breastfeed?'

'Ignore last message. Inappropriate. My therapist can deal with that.'

'Which colour is better?' Accompanied by a photograph of two almost identical shades of off-white.

'Do you need me to fetch Nina today? Xx'

'Ignore last offer. Cannot possibly. Have to rewash all baby's clothes.'

'Everything okay?' asks Evelyn, one of the runners.

'Fine.' I smile. 'My ex-best friend is having a baby with my ex-husband, and she seems to be in a bit of a state.'

The other mothers all gawp at me.

'Gosh,' Evelyn eventually says. 'That sounds very modern.'

'And you seem very calm about it,' says Mpho. 'No offence' – she looks around the table – 'but usually you whites freak out about this kind of thing.'

I try to shrug and look enigmatic and Zen, like the whole thing has been easy from the word go. 'Oh,' I say, 'these things happen.' I pause. 'Okay, not to everyone. And not often. And it *was* pretty shit. But here I am.'

'Well,' says Evelyn, and for a moment I think she's going to throw me out of the group, so serious is the look on her face, 'the immensely good thing about it is that they can look after your daughter when you come with us to New York.'

I decide now is not the time to mention that Daniel and Julia are no longer together – that's just going to make us sound more debauched.

'They certainly can.' I hope this doesn't count as a lie – I mean, I'm sure one of them will. Just not together.

When the others are distracted, I quickly tap out a reply to Julia: 'You'll be great at breastfeeding. Stop worrying.'

'Thank you,' she replies almost immediately. And I feel good.

Catherine

It feels like the morning takes forever. I am so jittery over meeting Miriam that I can't sit still, and I find myself rearranging the filing system – which makes me think of Julia and the spices. But finally it is lunch time, and I hand over to the two afternoon receptionists. At the last minute I try to delay things. I find myself explaining the filing and trying to finish up some random chores.

'Leave us something to do, Catherine,' says Liwa, the older afternoon receptionist. 'Go. Enjoy your afternoon.'

I don't think I can enjoy the afternoon, but I can't put it off any more.

As I drive to the home, I start thinking about Mike. I have been trying hard not to see Miriam waking up as a sign that Mike might too – but now I can't help it. What would it actually be like if Mike woke up? What if he started asking about Jack, and doesn't understand why nobody even knows who Jack is? How would I explain that to him, when I barely understand how it happened myself?

And worrying about this gives me a new, terrible insight: do I not really want Mike to wake up any more? Am I worried about the complications it would cause? Does Mike somehow know that? When he was conscious, he always knew exactly how I was feeling – why should that have changed?

Is Mike staying in a coma because he knows that is easier for me?

And how would he feel about how old we are, if he woke up thinking it had just been three weeks?

What would he think about my wrinkles?

And our pregnant daughter, stuck in our house like a large balloon, who he last saw as a toddler? Would he love her? Would he understand? Would he be excited about the baby?

Would he even know who Julia was if I didn't tell him?

By the time I arrive, I am beside myself. My hands are shaking and tears are running down my cheeks. I can't let Eddie and Miriam see me like this – so I stay in the car, breathing deeply, trying to find my calm. I close my eyes, and take a deep breath in, and then slowly release it. The yoga lessons I started last month are paying off.

I'm starting to feel slightly better when a sharp rap against the window startles me, jettisoning all the calm.

It's Larry, peering in through the glass, his face worried. I roll down the window.

'I saw you park,' he says, 'and then you didn't get out. I got worried.'

'I just needed a moment,' I say. 'Want to be at my best to meet Miriam.' I try to laugh, but it comes out like a bray.

Larry looks at me for a moment. 'This is complicated for you.'

'Yes.'

'Because of Mike?' He's stooping to talk to me through the car window, and there is something so endearing about that.

'Yes. Because of Mike. But also because of you.'

'Me?'

'If Miriam doesn't like me, you and Eddie won't want to be friends with me any more.'

Larry reaches awkwardly through the window to touch my shoulder. His hand is so warm I can feel it through the fabric of my shirt.

'Besides the fact that Miriam is a very nice person, and she *will* like you,' he says, 'even if she didn't, that makes no difference to me. I'm a big boy. My sister doesn't get to choose my friends.' There is an infinitesimal pause before the word 'friends'. I think I've imagined it, but he blushes when I look at him.

That somehow gives me the wherewithal to pull myself together.

'Come on,' I say. 'Let's not stand here chatting all day. Let's go meet your sister.'

Larry smiles and steps away from the car. 'You're going to like her, Catherine,' he says as I get out. 'And she's going to like you.'

I take his arm as if it is the most natural thing in the world. As we walk in, I realise Larry hasn't broached the issue of Mike again.

'I need to pop in and say hi to Mike first,' I say. I feel Larry's arm tense very slightly beneath my hand.

'Sure thing.' He changes direction. 'I'll wait for you outside.'

'You can come in. It's not like you haven't before.'

'I know,' says Larry. 'But I think you need to be alone with him today.'

He's right, and I am so grateful. I want to say something, but instead I just squeeze his arm. I think he understands, because for a moment he puts his arm around my shoulder and pulls me close.

'It's all going to be okay,' he whispers into the top of my head. 'We just don't know what okay means.'

Julia

My belly feels tight around the baby, but I have too much to do to let a bit of discomfort stop me. As well as painting the walls – I mean, what was I thinking with that colour? – I really need to unpack my childhood books, and I don't know how I haven't realised this before. I know they're somewhere in the spare-room cupboard – the room that's now mine. I called it the spare room in my head for a long time, convinced that living with my mother was a temporary measure, but now that the baby is about to be born, I realise I'm going to need her for the foreseeable future. Maybe that's why I got the room colour wrong. Maybe it was a subconscious rebellion against staying.

I think about phoning Jane to ask what she thinks, but then I realise this might not qualify as a therapeutic emergency. When I phoned earlier to tell her the colour was wrong, she reminded me that I'm only supposed to phone for emergencies, otherwise I must save it for therapy. And then, when I told her the names of the colours, she paused and said we would definitely talk about it next time she sees me. And who knows when that will be because I could have this baby any minute.

I go into the bedroom and start digging through the cupboards. There isn't an awful lot – my mother's not the type for sentimental keepsakes, so the stuff I do find is mostly mine. There's a box I've marked 'Do NOT throw this away, Mom', but inside are old school books, and I can't think why I would have thought it was so important to keep them.

I put them back in the cupboard. The only other box has my matric dance dress and my mother's wedding dress in it. When I was little, my biggest treat in the world was to take out the wedding dress and touch it. My mother wasn't mad about me doing this, and she only let me do it very occasionally – which meant that it kept its magic and always felt like a treat. When I was a teenager I once tried it on when she was out. It didn't fit me well, and looked a bit frumpy. The disappointment was huge, and I never asked to look at the dress again.

I touch it gently now. As an adult, I can imagine how painful my mother would have found my obsession with her dress. Not that she showed it. In fact, she might not have even realised herself that it was painful. But it must have been.

Anyway, my books are not in this cupboard. I think of phoning my mother, but I send a message instead. She doesn't reply, so I start wondering where else they could be. Perhaps in her room.

Going into her room feels naughty. I am determined my child will never feel like this – that my bedroom is a forbidden space. My child will always feel welcome and safe in my bedroom.

Opening the cupboards feels even sneakier. First, I just look at her clothes, hanging neatly, sparse enough that they don't even touch each other. My cupboard is always jam-packed with clothes – most of which I never wear – but my mother throws away anything she hasn't worn for a year. Once I asked if she doesn't feel attached to her clothes and sad to see them go, and she looked at me like I was speaking another language. Maybe I was.

Her neat cupboard is an unlikely home for a stash of ill-sorted children's books. But I don't want to give up. I feel a pull across my belly and I absent-mindedly rub it.

'Don't worry,' I tell my baby. 'We'll find your books.'

So I get the stool from my mother's dressing table and stand on it. I have a moment of hope as I see that the top shelf is uncharacteristically messy – a tangle of old jerseys and scarves – none of which I can remember my mother wearing. I reach in and feel, but there's no box and no books. Just a mess. I feel a stab in my stomach.

'Braxton Hicks,' I tell no one. I like the word 'Braxton Hicks'. I will get the baby a puppy called Braxton. I'd think about calling the baby Braxton, given the number of Hicks I've been having, but I already know what I'm naming the baby. I've always known.

I keep expecting my mother to ask about the name, or suggest a name, or anything. But she doesn't. And for some reason I feel awkward initiating a conversation about it. You'd think it would be the most natural conversation in the world, but I guess by now I should be used to the fact that nothing between my mother and me will ever be natural – no matter how different she's been lately. I consider sending her a text saying that I'm naming the baby 'Braxton', just to see how she'll react. That'd be hilarious.

I carefully climb off the stool – I will not be the statistic who falls off a chair and goes into labour – and I take my phone from my pocket.

'I'm naming the baby Braxton,' I text my mother. And then, to be clear, I send another message: 'After the Hicks.'

As I push send, I feel another sharp pain – this one gives me such a fright that I drop my phone, which falls under the bed.

'Dammit!' I yell. 'Enough with the Hicks, baby!' Bending down is the biggest mission with my huge tummy, but I need my phone. After all, I could go into labour any minute. I manoeuvre myself onto my knees with my face flat on the floor to see where the phone has gone. I lift the bed frill and spot it quite far under the bed. Peeping out from behind a box.

A box.

'Eureka,' I whisper.

I reach under the bed, my belly pushed against the floor, and catch hold of the box. I expected it to be dusty, but it's not. My mother's housekeeping is clearly of a very high standard if an old forgotten box of books under a bed is dust-free.

I'm expecting the box to be taped shut, but it's not. Its flaps are loose, and I open it.

It's not books. It's a photo album and some other things.

And lying on the top is a photograph of a very little boy carefully holding a baby.

Catherine

I don't spend long with Mike. I'm jumpy and restless, and I can't seem to sit still. I need to get meeting Miriam over with. There's something else nagging at my mind. I thought it was Mike, but now that I'm with him, that doesn't feel like the answer.

But I do lean down next to his ear and whisper, 'Julia's baby is due any day now. And then we can decide what to do.'

I desperately want to convince myself that he has reacted – that there is a change in his position or his impassive face. But I can't. Mike is still far away from me. Close to Mike's ear, so Larry won't hear me, I say, 'Miriam's woken up. Stupid cow. It should have been you.'

I look at him again. Nothing.

I sigh. I can't feel him today. This happens sometimes, but it seems to be happening more and more. Since the nightmare about Jack.

I pat his hand and leave.

Down the passage from Mike's room, Lizette is standing with Larry. When she sees me, she flings her arms around me.

'Isn't it exciting?' she says. And then before I can answer, she peers around me, at the door to Mike's room. 'Is your husband in there? In a coma?'

'Yes,' I say.

'Should I come and speak to him. I'm the sort of person a person would come out a coma for.'

I try very hard not to catch Larry's eye as I pat Lizette's arm. 'I am quite sure that if I was in a coma, a visit from you would be just the thing,' I say. 'But let's leave Mike for another day. One person recovering is quite enough.'

Lizette beams at me. 'You are so right,' she says. 'And also so thoughtful. I am not one to repeat myself, but I've said it before and I'll say it again, you're the sort of person who puts other people first. You know,' she says, slipping her arms through Larry's and mine – quite a feat given how tall Larry is and how short she is – 'I was just telling Miriam how wonderful Catherine is, and how she's not the sort of person to blow her own horn. I'm always one to give credit where credit is due, you know.'

Larry extricates himself gently. 'Well, let's take Catherine to meet Miri, shall we, and she can judge for herself.'

'Oh, yes,' says Lizette, walking purposefully down the passage I have known intimately for more than two decades. 'Follow me, I know the way.'

Larry and I look at each other. 'Do you think she is actually taking the mickey and laughing at us all?' I whisper.

Larry looks serious. 'Oh no,' he says. 'She's not the type of person to do that at all.'

We are both giggling like naughty children as we follow Lizette.

When we get to the room, Eddie is standing at the door. He hugs me. 'Come in and meet Miri,' he says. And then to Lizette, 'The doctors have asked that she not have too many people at once, and I know you'll understand.'

Lizette nods emphatically, her blonde bun falling loose from its clips and hovering near her ear.

Eddie and I open the door and step in, and Eddie quickly closes it behind him.

'Did you manage?' whispers a voice, and I look over and see Miriam sitting up in bed, a pair of glasses perched on her nose. 'Did you keep her out?'

Eddie laughs. 'Yes, my love. Your wish is my command.'

Miriam turns to me. 'I'm sorry, Catherine,' she says like we are old friends. 'But I couldn't take another minute of Lizette. I sent her to find you to get rid of her. So I already owe you an apology, and we've barely met.'

I don't know what I expected – that Miriam would be weak and hoarse and lying in bed sipping water, perhaps. Being in a coma for so long should leave you feeling a bit done in. But Miriam looks like she's just popped into the hospital to have an ingrown toenail removed and is very likely to leap out of bed at any moment. Indeed, her next words confirm this.

'I'm so annoyed with those doctors because they say I mustn't stand up at all. Because my muscles are apparently too weak, and I could have unforeseen complications or some such codswallop. And I would just love to give you a hug.' She beams at me. 'Eddie has told me so much about you that I feel I owe you a thank you. And as for Larry ...' She gives an exaggerated wink and then a loud laugh that turns into a cough.

'Oh, God Almighty,' she says when she recovers from a coughing fit. 'My body seems to be catching up on all the things it hasn't done. You should hear me farting.' She starts to laugh again.

'You look fabulous,' I say, quite overwhelmed.

Eddie is just standing looking at her like she's the cleverest child in the class. Which I suppose she is because she woke up, which is more than some people have managed despite a generous head start.

'Do you know,' she says, 'I've lost twenty kilograms. Twenty! With no effort at all. I'm thinner than I've been since my twenties.' She starts laughing again. 'Not eating will do that to a person. I'm sure I'm going to have the most wonderful time putting it all back on!'

I smile. 'Eddie told me what a cheerful, positive person you are – but I thought he was idealising you. It's very easy to do in our situation. But I see he was actually spot on.'

'Do you idealise Mike?' she asks, leaning slightly forward and wincing at some discomfort. This should feel like an intrusive question from someone I have just met properly, but it doesn't.

'I must,' I say. 'I remember the time before Mike's accident as idyllic. And part of me knows that can't be true. But it's been a long time and it's all I really have.'

'You have Julia.'

The woman has just come out of an eighteen-month coma, and she's made time to study up on my family. I am awed, and I say as much.

'No,' she says matter-of-factly. 'You visited me that time. You told me about everyone. You were so funny about Ed cooking.' She smiles.

I gape at her. 'You heard everything?'

'Well, of course I did.'

'Did you hear everything *everyone* said?' I'm thinking about Mike. I'm thinking about twenty-six years of talking to him. I'm feeling so vindicated, like I want to run down the passage and hug him because he *has* been hearing me. I always knew it, but it's different hearing it for sure.

'I don't think I heard everything,' Miriam is saying. 'I remember bits.' She pushes her glasses up her nose. 'And I think I heard more and more recently. I think that time you talked about the cooking was the first time I was actively aware that I could hear but not speak or move. I wasn't very bothered, but I was aware. I tried hard to laugh, and then I kind of slipped back to sleep.' Miriam smiles widely. 'Oh well,' she says, and then lies down and falls asleep. Just like that – no pause in-between, no warning.

Eddie takes my arm, where I'm standing frozen, looking at Miriam, who is now snoring gently.

'The doctor says that's normal,' he says, steering me out the room. 'Well, so far as any of this is normal. Apparently waking up after eighteen months is almost unheard of, and waking up completely compos mentis is even more unusual. They're now saying that she might not have had a stroke like we thought, but actually entered into some sort of psychological fugue state, because people don't actually wake up from comas. But then they don't know why she couldn't breathe alone. They're awfully interested in her and keep doing tests.' Eddie sounds almost proud of Miriam, like a certain sort of mother I remember from school days – pretending to lament their bad fortune but actually bragging about their unusual child. 'Of course,' says Eddie, sounding a bit more like the man I know, 'they say she might still die.'

'What?'

'The chances of her waking up were almost nil. The chances of her waking up okay are even less. You read these stories on the Internet, but the doctors say they're never entirely true – like they leave out that the person was completely incapable of normal functioning after they woke up. But Miriam is completely okay. That shouldn't be possible. So they don't know what's going on. The best-case scenario is that it was this fugue thing, but then we have to wonder why.'

'What do you mean?'

'Something like that only happens if there's some huge emotional trauma. Something bad must've happened to make her shut down.'

'But she's awake for now. And quite jolly,' I say. I'm not really trying to cheer him up. I'm just saying it like it is.

'And I am so lucky,' says Eddie. 'I always thought she might wake up. But now that she's awake, it's like I can finally hear what the doctors were saying all along – that people in comas don't usually recover. That, mostly, whatever trauma put them there is permanent. They always said it, but I never heard it. The longer she was out, the worse her chances were. And eighteen months is pretty long. Even the best stories on the net are about months, not years.'

I think Eddie's forgotten who he's talking to. But it's not like I haven't been told – I too know the statistics. Mike's been in a coma for so long, and information has shifted around over the years. But it's always been a grim prognosis. And every time Mike gets a new doctor – seven at the last count – they sit me down and explain it all over again. And I nod and I smile and I go back to Mike and tell him that his doctors are cretins because obviously he is not brain dead like they say, and obviously he might wake up. Jack is dead, but Mike isn't.

But standing outside Miriam's room – having witnessed the miracle that should prove to me that all my hope has been based on fact; that people do make inexplicable and complete recoveries – somehow, for the first time, I'm understanding the exact reverse. Maybe it is hearing it from the voice of the one person who had hoped, like me, who had dreamt, like me, who was determined to keep the faith, like me. Maybe hearing it from Eddie makes me take in the words like I never have before. But suddenly I think of Mike – unresponsive, unmoving – and I know. People in comas almost never wake up. And when they do, it's not pretty.

Mike is not going to wake up. There's nobody in there.

I've spent twenty-six years talking to a living corpse.

I don't know what to do. My whole life seems meaningless in the face of this truth.

I don't know how I say goodbye to Eddie, but I'm alone and I'm walking as fast as I can towards the exit. For the first time, I can't be bothered to say goodbye to Mike as I leave. What would the point be?

What *is* the point?

I can feel a sob building up in my chest, like an animal waiting to be released. I don't want to release it. I don't know what to do.

And then my phone rings.

Claire

When I pick up Nina from school, I'm still in a good mood. It's been one of those days when nothing's going to get me down – the sort of day that seems to be becoming more and more the norm.

As Nina gets into the car, she's talking about the baby. Not that there's anything unusual about that – she's pretty much obsessed with the baby, so it's lucky I've made my peace.

'How will Julia know when it's time for the baby to come out?' she asks.

'Well,' I say, 'she'll feel really sore, and she'll know.'

'What if she thinks she needs a poo? That can be *really* sore.'

'When I started to have you, I was pretty sure you weren't a poo.'

'Of course I'm not a poo, Mommy!' says Nina. 'I'm nothing like a poo.'

'True.'

'What if Julia's alone and she's sore?' says Nina after a while – I presume spent thinking how un-poo-like she is.

'She'll phone someone.'

'Daddy?'

'I guess. Or her mom. She has a really helpful mom.'

'I know,' says Nina. 'I know her mom. She's a bit weird. But really helpful.'

'And then Daddy or Catherine will take Julia to hospital to have the baby,' I explain.

Nina thinks a bit more. 'She should choose her mom.'

I smile. 'Daddy will want to be there. He loved it when you were born.'

For a moment I feel the loss. I think I will always feel the loss.

'Anyway,' I say to distract myself, 'you can usually tell when a lady is going to have the baby. She gets a bit nutty sometimes, and cleans everything, and pretends she can't feel any pain and...' I stop mid-sentence, thinking about the messages I got from Julia this morning.

We're nearly home, but I don't want to wait. I grab my phone from the console and throw it to Nina at the back.

'Phone Julia,' I say. 'Ask her if she's okay.'

Nina is thrilled with the responsibility.

I wait.

'She's not answering,' says Nina. 'It goes to mailvoice.'

'Voicemail,' I say reflexively. But I'm worried. I pull over. 'Give me the phone.'

'No, but I can—'

'Give it!'

I dial Julia's number but it goes to voicemail again.

We're two minutes from home, so I decide to drop Nina there and go straight to Julia to reassure myself.

'Phone Daddy,' I tell Nina as I drive.

'Mailvoice,' says Nina with a sigh, as if she never expected anything different from her father. Then again, why did I?

Once Nina is safely at home with Thandi, who looks faintly disapproving when I tell her where I'm going, I decide to take the risk of driving and phoning. I try Daniel again, and leave a message. I don't know what else I can do. I don't have Julia's mom's number – why would I? – so all I can do is wait until I get there. There's probably nothing to worry about; Julia's probably distracted herself repainting the walls or something.

At Julia's mother's house, I ring the bell at the gate. Nothing happens. I ring again.

I can't get in any other way. The house has high walls and electric fencing – this is Joburg after all, and I am not a professional house-breaker.

'Julia!' I scream. Peering through the gate, I can see Julia's car. She is home. I pick up my phone and try Daniel again.

Now I'm worried for real.

Daniel

The first time I saw Claire's number, I ignored it. Claire never phones me with nice things any more, like she used to. She used to be such a fun, spontaneous person – supper dates and weekends away and calls just to tell me she misses me. Now it's all boring stuff, like I must pay her money or pick Nina up or have Nina for the weekend. It's like she's had a personality change. Inexplicable.

Then I start thinking how little I understand her. Or Julia, for that matter. And how I never know which way the wind will blow with those two, and what will happen next. And it occurs to me that maybe Claire is finally coming around, and that she has in fact phoned to tell me we can get back together. Which would be great – the best thing for everyone. We would all be so happy.

I pick up my phone and I'm about to phone Claire back when it rings again, and it's her. My instinct was right. She must want me back – badly.

'Babe?' I answer.

Recently she's shouted at me when I call her 'babe', but this time she doesn't, which I take as a good sign.

'I'm outside the house and nobody's answering the bell—' she starts.

'Babe, I'm at the office. Not the house. Actually, I don't live in a house at all.' Poor woman, driven mad by her need to be with me.

'Not your fucking house, you fuckwit,' she says. '*Julia's* house. Well, her mom's house. Catherine's house.'

This is not going the way I expected. I'm not entirely sure, but Claire sounds quite hostile.

'You sound quite hostile,' I say.

'Now listen carefully, Daniel. I think Julia might be in labour. I need you to phone her mom and tell her to get home as soon as possible, so we can get in.'

'Shouldn't she go to the hospital?' I ask, reasonably I think. Claire had Nina in a hospital and Julia hasn't said anything about wanting a home birth. Although nobody tells me anything these days. 'Or does she want a home birth?' I ask, to show I'm thinking about her needs. Claire likes that sort of thing.

'Daniel,' says Claire, 'for once in your life, just once, listen. I think Julia is in the house, in labour. I can't get in. Phone Catherine and tell her. Or send me her number. Can you do that?'

'Why don't I just come and help?'

'Do you have the keys?'

'No. Why would I have the keys?'

'Then phone Catherine first, and then come. Can you do that?' She sounds very patronising, to be honest.

I sigh. 'Sure. There's no need to be so rude about it.'

'Just. Fucking. Do. It,' says Claire, and rings off.

Honestly, I'm sure she didn't have such a foul mouth when we lived together. It's not very attractive, to tell the truth.

With a sigh, I dial Catherine's number.

Catherine

At first, I have no idea what Daniel wants. He seems to be complaining about women being incomprehensible – but I know that I'm very distressed and it might be that I'm not understanding properly. Eventually, I manage to understand one sentence.

'… So I said I would tell you,' he says.

'Tell me what exactly, Daniel?'

'To go to your house to let Claire in because she has this idea that Julia's in labour.'

'Claire thinks that …' I think about all the manic messages I received this morning, and the nagging feeling I've had all day. Bloody hell – *of course* Julia's in labour. How could I have missed that?

'Of course she's in labour!' I yell. 'I'll meet you at the house. And call the hospital to tell them to expect her.'

'What hospital?' says Daniel.

For a moment I wonder if perhaps Daniel is slightly stupid.

'The same bloody hospital you went to for the scans.' Then I reconsider. 'Never mind, I'll call them. You just come to the house, okay?'

Daniel is still speaking when I hang up – but I have better things to do, more important things. Part of me wants to run in and tell Mike that the baby is being born. Another part thinks, *What's the point; he can't hear me.*

But I've been telling Mike stuff for almost my whole life. Who cares if he can't hear me? I run back into the home, into his room.

'The baby's coming!' I say, and then I leave.

Julia needs me.

Julia

The cramps are so bad, and suddenly I feel wetness seeping down my leg. I drop the photograph of the little boy on the floor, and climb onto my mother's bed. I know I should phone someone for help, but my phone is still under the bed where I dropped it, and every time I summon the energy to stand up and get it, there's another cramp. My mother has a landline next to her bed, but I don't know anyone's phone number, not even Daniel's, which is ridiculous when you think about it.

Finally, I summon a number from my memory – my mom's work number that I used as a child. I'm pretty sure it hasn't changed.

I dial, and someone who isn't my mother answers.

'I need to speak to Catherine,' I say. 'It's her daughter, Julia.'

'Julia, sweetie,' says this strange woman, like she knows me. 'It's your mom's afternoon off.'

Fuck it. She's gone to meet that coma woman, I remember now.

'D'you have her cell number?' I ask. I can feel another contraction coming.

'Her cell number, sweetie?' The woman sounds like I've asked for a kidney. Before I can yell at her, she says, 'Wait, Dr Marigold wants to speak to you.'

My whole belly is tight and sore, and I grip the phone.

'Julia, it's Ewan.'

'I'm in labour,' I squeak. 'I want my mommy.'

'Where are you?'

'At the house. No one's here. I want my mommy.'

'I'm coming, Julia. And I'll find her.'

I drop the phone as the contraction fully kicks in.

It could be five minutes later, it could be an hour – I don't know – when Claire and my mother and Ewan suddenly all run through the door at once, all pushing each other out the way, all yelling.

'Don't push yet!' is what Ewan is saying.

Strangely, 'Mike's never going to wake up,' seems to be my mother's rallying cry.

'Daniel's a fucking idiot,' Claire adds to the mix.

I focus on Ewan, who appears to be the only sane one.

'I have to push,' I say through gritted teeth.

He rushes past me into my mother's en suite, and I hear the sound of handwashing. I presume this because my mother suddenly yells, 'Clean hands,' and runs in after him.

When he comes out, he says, 'Julia, you know I'm a doctor, right?'

'Is this really time for small talk?' I ask.

'I thought I'd just mention it before I put my hand inside you,' he says.

'*Go for it!*' I shout, but only because a contraction's just hit.

Ewan examines me, and then turns to my mother. 'We're not getting her to a hospital. You're going to have to help.'

Something happens to my mother. She smiles, and then – I swear I am not making this up – her eyes fill with tears, and then she suddenly becomes a nurse. You can see it happen. She hasn't been a nurse for years; she's been a receptionist. But now I can see it. I can see the super-efficient nurse she must've been. Before I can tell her how glad I am that she's my mom, there's a towel on the bed and a basin of steaming water next to it, and Claire is sitting next to me feeding me ice chips. (Where the hell did she get ice chips? Being Claire, she probably has a little ice-chip maker in her car for when she finds people in labour.) Really, I'm pretty sure this is how it would have been in a hospital.

And then I'm pushing and pushing, and Ewan is saying, 'He's crowning,' and my mother is standing with a towel ready for the baby, and Daniel arrives.

'Fucking hell,' he says, and vomits on the carpet. Nobody even turns to look at him, because the baby is here.

Catherine

I don't know at what point in the drama of Julia's delivery I noticed the photo of Jack sticking out from under the bed. Jack holding Julia.

For a moment I wondered, *How on earth did it get out of the box? And how did Julia end up in my room anyway?* But then she let out a piercing shriek, and I quickly pushed the photo under the bed with my toe, and carried on helping deliver my grandson.

In movies when there's a highly dramatic home delivery, once the baby is delivered, everyone steps back and smiles and all is well. Well, I don't know what that's all about, because once this baby was delivered, we got even more busy. We put him straight onto Julia's chest, and admittedly she did get all cross-eyed with hormones and start crying – but Ewan and I had a placenta to deliver, a cord to cut and a mess to clean up. We also had a baby to check for birth defects.

We offered Daniel the chance to cut the cord, but he started heaving again, and Claire laughed and said, 'Not a chance,' and so I got to do it – cut the cord between my daughter and grandbaby. And it would have been strangely moving except that Daniel vomited again, and all I could think of was how much vomit I was going to have to clean out of the carpet, not to mention how much blood was in my bed.

But finally, it was calm. Ewan declared himself happy with the baby, and he and Claire took themselves off to the kitchen to make tea for everyone. Daniel had managed to rally, now that the baby was wiped down and Julia's nether regions were safely under the blankets, and he held the baby and declared him a fine chap, and kissed Julia on the head and said, 'Everything's going to be okay,' and beamed like he had done something awfully clever.

Julia wiped away his kiss and said it was my turn to hold the baby.

And suddenly, my grandson is in my arms.

I don't know if it's because I've just seen the photo, but he looks exactly like Jack. I feel like I've been hurled back through time, and my own son is in my arms. My son who had such a short time with me. And now, here is this boy. This boy who is tied to me by blood. And I can't even process the waves of love I feel. I don't know who they are for – this boy now or that boy then. And I don't know if it matters.

'So,' booms Daniel's voice, as if from another galaxy, 'what are we going to call this little chap, Julia?'

I turn to look at her.

'I've always known what I would call a little boy,' says Julia. 'My whole life, it's been like I've been waiting for a baby boy. His name is Jack.'

I look up at her and she's looking at me, not Daniel.

'Mommy,' she says, 'who's in the photo I found under the bed?'

I hug Baby Jack to my body, and I go and sit right next to Julia on the bed.

'Daniel,' I say, 'could you leave us for a few minutes? There's something I need to tell Julia.'

And, thank goodness, Daniel leaves, planting a kiss on the baby's head. And I am alone with Julia.

PART 4

March

Dear Mike

Our grandson is six months old today – but I feel like it's really my own anniversary. My anniversary of being me again.

It feels strange to write to you – knowing you'll never read this. Accepting, finally, that you're never coming back to me. That in all the ways that matter, you died with Jack.

It's a strange thing – I never used to remember anything bad about our years together before the accident. When I was depressed and suicidal and believed that my only peace lay in both our deaths, I painted the past rose-coloured. But since I've accepted the truth, I'm remembering the bad things too. The way you slurped your tea; the way you drank milk from the bottle; the way you left the toilet seat up; the way you never, ever put a towel in the wash basket; the way you always blamed me when we got lost. And you had a temper sometimes, and you were grumpy for whole days when we lost the rugby. These memories make me miss you more, not less. They make you feel more whole in my memory. But yes, they also allow me to let go of you. To love another imperfect man.

I should tell you about the baby first, though. Oh, Mike – the baby is magnificent. He is funny and cuddly and warm and giggly and perfect. When I look after him, I can lie for hours just watching him. And when I make him laugh, it's like all the angels in heaven are laughing. I bury my face in his stomach and blow raspberries, like you used to do for our Jack – and he

276

chuckles and laughs his baby laugh and time flows together and I am you and this baby is that baby and it all suddenly makes sense. Because life goes on, Mike. For too long, I didn't get that. But it really does. And I have so many years to make up for, and so many mistakes to make up to Julia.

Julia.

When I told Julia about Jack's death, about the brother she had forgotten, she was angry and sad and incredulous. But mostly she was relieved. I don't know how I thought she would have forgotten him in her bones. I don't know *what* I was thinking, to be honest. But for Julia, the story of Jack made everything fall into place. Sometimes she looks at me, and then at Baby Jack, and her eyes fill with tears and she says, 'How did you bear it, Mom?' And I explain that, of course, I didn't. And because I didn't, I failed her. I failed her completely. But she has her own Jack now, and I think she understands. She can't imagine losing him, and neither can I.

Julia's still living with me. She makes half-hearted noises about moving back to her flat, but we both pretend it would be very cruel to throw Daniel out. We don't let the fact that Daniel's worth more than the GDP of a small country bother us with this pretence. Or even the fact that Daniel now has a girlfriend. 'Where would Daniel go?' we ask ourselves, shaking our heads at the impossibility of it. If Claire is here, as she often is, she snorts and says, 'Anywhere, actually,' and we all laugh. But Julia stays put. I know one day she'll take Jack and move on with her life, but I'm not going to push her. And maybe she needs to be looked after for a while – because I didn't really do that before.

But I'm being careful not to make her my whole world. I have all these friends. God, Mike, I don't know where they all came from, or how I went so many years without them. I belong to a yoga group that I joined with Claire and a group of widows she and Julia know, and a book club, and a gardening club. And I go to dinner parties and lunch parties. And I've started nursing again. Proper nursing. I've decided to train as a midwife. It seems right.

And then there is Larry. My *boyfriend*, Larry (Julia rolls her eyes when I say that).

'You don't have to sound so proud of it, Mom,' she says. Not that Julia can talk – I can see where things are heading with her 'friend' Steve. But still, I *am* proud of it. I have a boyfriend. We even have sex. How did I go without sex for so long, Mike? You never would have wanted that for me. Never.

In fact, you wouldn't have wanted any of it for me. But the thing I know now is that you aren't lying there thinking about it, or me, or anything really. Whatever was 'Mike' disappeared in the accident. Miriam's recovery somehow made me see that. Nobody understands why, but that doesn't matter. I do.

I miss you, Mike. And I miss Jack. But finally – finally – I'm ready to be whole again. And I know that is what you would want for me. And my life has a purpose: Julia and Baby Jack. Because in Baby Jack I have rediscovered the joy of unconditional love.

And that's what it's all about, really.

Love, always,

Cathy

ACKNOWLEDGEMENTS

Writing acknowledgements for a book is always a challenge. No matter how many people you remember to thank for their input on various ideas and facts, you will always forget a few. It doesn't help that I have written this book during a particularly busy time in my life, and I can barely remember when I found time to do it – let alone who helped me along the way!

I know that I consulted my lovely GP, Dr Jacquie Yutar, early in the writing to find out if Mike's condition was medically feasible. If it isn't, don't blame her! I know that Ian Rijsdijk entered into a lively debate about Julia's music choice, making it the second time he has helped this tone-deaf writer bring some music to her characters. I have a vivid memory of telling my PA, Phumzile Mhlongo, that I would include her in the acknowledgements for something specific … but I can't remember what it was, over and above the general service of keeping me sane and supplied with tea. And at home, Queen Morapama and Joyce Netshivhale perform a similar service and much more for my family.

One of my day jobs involves sub-editing *without prejudice*, a legal magazine. A few years ago I read about the case of *Fourie and Another v Road Accident Fund* (2014 (2) SA 88 (GNP) C) and was badly traumatised by the facts, which haunted me for a long time. As is the way with writing, the basic facts re-emerged in this book. I feel a bit like a vulture – although I only realised afterwards that this had happened. Having now gone back to find the case reference, I am re-traumatised. The facts of the real case are worse than anything that happened in this book, and my deepest sympathies go out to that family.

The character of Claire was inspired by the many amazing mothers who I know at my children's schools. Women who always seem to have it all together, who always know what's going on and can tell the less organised (me) what to do. I think every mother knows a Claire – but my fictional Claire has the benefit of drawing from the best of a whole group of lovely women.

This is my fourth published novel, and my fourth time working with Nicola Rijsdijk as my editor. I don't know what I would do without Nicola, who instinctively understands what I am trying to say. It's got to a point where I find it hard to write without an ongoing conversation with Nicola in my head. Thank you, Nicola.

Thanks also to the wonderful team at Pan Macmillan. A particular thanks to Andrea Nattrass, who is kind enough to give me deadlines, knowing how I need them; and to Eileen Bezemer, who makes sure that more than only my immediate family have heard of me.

As always, my husband, Paul van Onselen, and our children, Thomas and Megan, are my support and inspiration to keep reaching deeper.